Lucy Dawson has been a journalist and magazine editor. Her first novel, *His Other Lover*, is also published by Sphere.

Praise for *His Other Lover*

'Lucy Dawson's debut novel puts every woman's nightmare into words . . . You'll identify with the character, regardless of the choices she ends up making. You'll feel her distress, you'll turn pages in anticipation . . . *His Other Lover* is dark, compelling and will leave you with an uneasy feeling in the pit of your stomach' ★★★★★   *Heat*

'Funny, dark and very surprising – a compulsive new breed of chick lit'
                                                              Louise Candlish

'If you like your chick lit with a bit of a twist, then *His Other Lover* by Lucy Dawson is for you . . . most definitely a cut above, [this] reaches dark places which other novels in the genre would steer well clear of, on the way to a thought-provoking ending'   *Peterborough Evening Telegraph*

Amazon reader reviews for *His Other Lover*

'This is the only book I have ever read in one sitting. I started it at six p.m. and did not stop reading until its completion at 12.45 that night/morning. I could not put the book down; I loved it right from the very first paragraph'

'I couldn't get over how good this book was. It pulls you in right from the first page . . . This one will really stick in my mind. I've passed it round to all my friends and they all loved it'

'I started this book at seven p.m. and finished it in one sitting! I was addicted and totally engrossed in Mia's story. I have not read a book for years that I could not put down'

'Very, very good, very different and a welcome change from the chick lit that has saturated the market without leaving much of an impression. This was extremely memorable'

Also by Lucy Dawson

His Other Lover

WHAT MY BEST FRIEND DID

Lucy Dawson

SPHERE

First published in Great Britain as a paperback original in 2009 by Sphere

A CIP catalogue record for this book
is available from the British Library.

ISBN 978-0-7515-4051-2

Typeset in Bembo by Palimpsest Book Production Limited,
Grangemouth, Stirlingshire
Printed and bound in Great Britain by
Clays Ltd, St Ives plc

Papers used by Sphere are natural, renewable and recyclable
products made from wood grown in sustainable forests and certified
in accordance with the rules of the Forest Stewardship Council.

Mixed Sources
Product group from well-managed
forests and other controlled sources
www.fsc.org Cert no. SGS-COC-004081
© 1996 Forest Stewardship Council
FSC

Sphere
An imprint of
Little, Brown Book Group
100 Victoria Embankment
London EC4Y 0DY

An Hachette Livre UK Company
www.hachettelivre.co.uk

www.littlebrown.co.uk

For Jay, Luke and Guy

Acknowledgements

I am very grateful to Sarah Ballard and Joanne Dickinson for their advice, support and faith. The teams at both United Agents and Little, Brown have worked tirelessly and enthusiastically on this project, but in particular I would like to thank Jessica Craig and Lettie Ransley at UA, and Emma Stonex and Jennifer Richards at Little, Brown.

The help Lee Tomlinson, Sally Dawson and Camilla Dawson gave me proved invaluable, but as anyone with a medical background will realise, I only took their advice as far as it suited the plot. Thanks to the rest of my family, my friends and James for being there when I needed them too.

Finally, to Ruth Easton, for your encouragement and kindness, thank you.

Chapter One

'Can you tell me what's happened Alice?' says the calm voice on the end of the phone. My heart is thudding, squishing around in my chest, making it hard for me to breathe. I can feel the *thump, thump* of it in my ears.

'It's my best friend,' I gasp, my voice rising involuntarily, shrill with fear. 'I think she's tried to kill herself.' I look at the smashed whisky bottle at Gretchen's feet, shards of glass mixed in with the scattered pills. 'Please, someone needs to help her!'

I manage to stay coherent enough to give them the address and then with my useless, rubbery tubes of fingers that seemed to bend off the buttons seconds ago when I dialled 999, I hang up, slip-sliding the phone back into the holder. Then it's just me and Gretchen, in the quiet of her sitting room. Despite the fact that it's early evening and people in flats and houses all around us are probably getting home from work, tiredly kicking off shoes and putting on kettles, there isn't a sound in here – everything has gone eerily quiet. No TV, no radio, no sign of life.

I back up, not taking my eyes off her, and when I feel the wall behind me I sink to the floor. All I can hear is my own ragged breath as I try to get it under control.

Gretchen is seated, not with her usual sassy poise, but slumped in the corner where two walls meet. One knee is hitched up, her head is lolling forward and one arm is stuck out rigid. She looks as though she's had too much to drink and, from standing, has now just slid down the wall gracefully, to a stop.

There is a sticky, sickly smell of alcohol in the air and a dark pool of it by her feet, dotted with confetti-like small white pills. I can't see her face; her long, wavy blonde hair is covering it. She is silent and still. I don't know if she is unconscious or – *oh God* – dead. I can taste vomit in my mouth and my teeth are starting to chatter. I know I ought to be doing something, trying to put her in a recovery position, but I can't for the life of me remember what that is and I'm scared of touching her. She looks like a heroin awareness poster I was shown in sixth form – only that girl had been dead for three days before anyone found her.

I pull my knees in tightly to my chest, bury my head, close my eyes really, really tight and picture the ambulance, forcing mopeds and four-wheel drives alike off into bus lanes as they come to rescue us. I am aware that I am rocking slightly on the spot and whimpering, but I can't seem to stop.

After what feels like for ever, I hear distant wailing sirens becoming louder and louder. Then blue lights flash on the wall above Gretchen's head.

The buzz of the door makes me jump violently, even though I am waiting for it. I clamber stiffly to my feet and rush across the room. A male voice says my name through the intercom and I press the release for downstairs, saying urgently, 'Third floor – we're up here!' Then I hang up and

2

open the front door to the flat. Immediately I can hear feet clattering up the iron stairwell and then they're here. A man and a woman, both older than me – dressed in green uniforms, moving across to her quickly, taking over. The relief is immense but then everything becomes a blur of questions: 'Do you know if she took all of these pills Alice? Has she ever done anything like this before Alice?'

I can see what they are doing, using my name, trying to keep me connected to reality, and I try to be helpful. I tell them everything I can.

Then we're in the back of the ambulance. The woman is driving, which surprises me, although I'm not sure why it should, and the man is quietly sat behind Gretchen's head, adjusting a tube as I grip the side with one hand and try not to slide off my seat. I'm also trying not to look at her body, bound to the stretcher, rocking from side to side with the motion as we slam through traffic, all sirens screaming.

My fingers are starting to shake and it's suddenly getting very hot in this small space full of unfamiliar machines and wires. I let out an involuntary gasp and the paramedic looks at me sharply. I think he said his name was Joe – I can't remember.

'It's OK, Alice,' he says reassuringly. 'We're nearly there now.'

I think this must be what shock is.

'So Gretchen's your best friend then?' he asks above the noise of the sirens, like we're having a conversation over a drink in a bar. 'From school? University?'

'Er,' I try to drag my mind back. 'No, I met her through work.' I think of LA; us giggling like crazy as we walked through the Sky Bar, arms linked as Gretchen whispered to me delightedly, 'You've got to see this!'

'What is it you do?' he says.

3

'I'm a photographer.'

'So does Gretchen work with you too?'

What the hell does it matter? 'No, but I met her through work,' I say in an effort to be polite, and instinctively glance at Gretchen, lying there on the stretcher, strapped in. The ambulance seems to slow and weaves jerkily from side to side – I guess we must be cutting through heavier traffic – but then suddenly it slams into fast forward again. My head snaps to the left. Gretchen stays completely motionless, although the trolley holding her slips slightly and slides an inch towards me. If it came loose at this speed it would crush me against the side of the ambulance. The paramedic puts out a hand to steady it. 'Whoops!' he says.

We slow to a stop. The doors swing open, the cold January air blasts in like a slap round the face, but I feel a little better for it. I can see the gaping hole of the double doors to A&E, and nurses waiting, looking up at us from their lower vantage point down on the ground. I sit still as Gretchen is taken out first, then stumble out after her.

She is wheeled straight past the staring eyes of bored, zombie people who have minor twisted ankles, light bangs to the head and have been there for hours, condemned to read ancient copies of women's magazines bursting with reader letters about their grandchildren's 'hilarious' antics, tips on how to get oil stains off a silk blouse, knitting patterns and a fat-free cheesecake recipe. I follow the stretcher uncertainly, then I feel a light, firm hand on my arm guiding me to one side as Gretchen is taken into another room and the doors flap shut behind her. I can see through the porthole; heads of medical staff are moving urgently round the room.

'Alice?' The nurse is speaking. 'Can you come with me? We need some information.'

She takes me to a small room which contains a chair, table and a sink, above which is a PLEASE WASH YOUR HANDS sign. She asks me who Gretchen's next of kin is and if there is anyone I would like them to call.

'Er, her brother, Bailey . . . my boyfriend . . . Tom,' I say, dazed and automatically. Then I remember actually that's not true any more and I should say ex, but the moment has passed. 'Bailey is in Madrid – at the airport, or at least he was. He rang me from there earlier to ask me to go over to Gretchen's. Tom is at a work do in Bath . . .'

'Do you have a contact number for Bailey?' she asks.

I start to shift through numbers in my head. 'He has a work mobile. It's not often switched on though. It's 079 . . . no, hang on . . . 0787 . . . Sorry, I can't think straight, I can't . . .'

'Take your time,' the nurse says kindly.

I get there eventually and, having written it down, she looks up from her pad and says, 'What about Tom's?'

'07 . . .' I begin, then hesitate. 'Actually, can I phone him myself please? If that's OK?'

'Of course,' she says. 'Now, do you know how we can contact Gretchen's parents?'

I shake my head. 'She has a difficult relationship with them. Bailey is the one who—'

The nurse cuts across me. 'Her parents really should be called,' she insists gently, and that's when I realise what she is saying . . . without actually saying it.

'I don't know their number,' I reply hopelessly. 'I've never even met them! Where's Gretchen now? What's happening to her?'

'She's in Resuscitation,' she says soothingly. 'I'm going to give this information to someone then I'll be right back. I'll just be a second.'

5

Once I am alone, I reach for my handbag and pull out my phone, but in this small room I have no signal and anyway, I'm not sure if I'm allowed to use it inside the hospital. I slide it back into my bag – I will have to wait until the nurse returns. I stare very hard at the PLEASE WASH YOUR HANDS sign and try not to panic.

She isn't long. They have found Bailey at the airport on standby for a flight back to London; his phone was on but, typically, he had barely any battery left and apparently it cut out just seconds after the nurse told him I was here with Gretchen and what hospital to come to. I imagine him waiting, alone and terrified on those rows of airport seats it's impossible to get comfy on, powerless to make his wait go faster – or maybe by now he's boarding the plane.

I ask if it is possible to use my mobile to call Tom and she shakes her head regretfully. 'Only outside, I'm afraid.'

I tell her I'll be right back and make my way purposefully through A&E, into the car park. It's a typically cold and dark January night. I shiver involuntarily in my thin tracksuit bottoms, finding his number and waiting as it connects, my breath clouding in front of me, one arm wrapped round my body, my hand in my sleeve for warmth.

It goes straight to voicemail. Either it's switched off or he busy-toned me.

'Hi, it's me,' I say after the bleep, my voice shaking. 'Tom, I'm at the hospital with Gretchen. You need to get here. We're at A&E. I have to go back in a minute and I'm not allowed to have my phone on, so you can't call me – but please just come straight away . . .'

I give him the address, more or less, and hang up. Was that the right thing to say? Should I have told him what's happened? Or is the less he knows until he gets here the better? I don't want him driving in a blind panic, feeling like he's having to race death and crashing. Suddenly I see why practised hospital staff make these calls. I wait for a moment or two – just long enough that he could check his voicemail – but he doesn't immediately call back, so very reluctantly I switch my phone off and go back in.

Forty minutes later I'm given a message that Tom has called the hospital to say he is on his way and by nine p.m., Gretchen has been moved to intensive care, or ICU as they call it. She is still unconscious but I'm told Bailey asked for me to sit with her. There are three nurses buzzing around her efficiently, murmuring to each other in a technical language that makes no sense to me and includes words like pumps, drips, sats and pressure drops.

I'm sitting as far away from the hospital bed as I can, letting Gretchen's name trip across my tongue soundlessly, like a mantra to focus my very chaotic mind. It is a name that suggests a little doll with a porcelain face, plaits weaving round her head and eyes that do not close when she lies down. She certainly looks breakable now, lying in this hospital bed, all hooked up to machines and tubes, silent apart from mechanical bleeping.

Her skin is a little waxy and where she would normally have a faint flush to her cheeks, she is pale. She is closer to Coppélia than a little girl's plaything, just waiting in the workshop to come to life. A real life-sized, creamy-skinned girl who might sit up in the bed and pull the covers back; but her eyelids don't lift, she doesn't flinch and her mouth stays forced wide by the tube that is keeping her burnt throat open, making me think in turn of a blow-up plastic doll being forced to perform an obscene act.

I look at her hands. Thumbs, fingers. With their small, neat, square nails. They don't and have not moved – not even a flicker. Her long, loose hair has been combed back

7

by someone and tucked out of the way, which I know would piss her off. Gretchen'd want it to be spread about her on the pillow; she'd appreciate the theatrical potential of her situation. She still looks ethereal though. Gretchen has the kind of beauty that can't be diminished by dull hair or a lack of make-up.

There's a painting I've seen, I think maybe in the National Gallery. A girl is being floated down a river to her grave, clutching pale pink flowers to her chest in a locked grasp of icy fingers. Her wavy blonde hair streams out behind her like seaweed and her limpid green dress trails over the edge of the funeral pyre and drags lightly through the surface, causing ripples. That's what Gretchen looks like now.

I am horrified to find myself wondering if she will look that beautiful dead, or if at the crucial moment, something will wisp away from her, unseen, up towards the ceiling on its way to Gretchen's version of heaven. Tears flood to my eyes and I start to shake slightly again. One of the nurses glances at me curiously and I manage a frightened, watery smile. She smiles sympathetically back and I wonder if she can see everything written all over my face. I don't think she can, because she turns away and then writes something down – there is just the rhythmical bleeping of machines helping Gretchen breathe. Outwardly, it looks like a scene under control.

Except in my head, even though I am trying to ignore it, to push the thought underwater and hold it there until it stops breathing, I can't stop thinking:

Please don't wake up, please don't wake up, please don't wake up.

Chapter Two

I jump as one of the nurses cuts across this hideous thought and says kindly, 'You can hold her hand if you want – it's OK. And you can talk to her, too.'

I shake my head vehemently, watching the other two nurses slip out of the room.

'I won't listen,' the remaining one says with an honest smile. She looks about our age, twenty-nine or so.

'I'm OK, thanks,' I manage and she nods understandingly.

'Well, if you change your mind feel free. I know it'll seem a little bit weird, but lots of people do talk – we're very used to it. I'm sorry we've been so rushed tonight and haven't had much time to explain to you what we're doing, what's happening.' She sits down next to me. 'There isn't very much I'm able to tell you, Alice, because you're not Gretchen's next of kin, so I can't give you specific details right now, but quite obviously, Gretchen is still unconscious.'

'Is she going to come round soon, do you think?' I ask anxiously.

'Gretchen's in a very deep state of unconsciousness,' she says gently. 'She's not able to respond to her environment. It's not like being asleep, so we can't just wake her up. One of the symptoms of a severe overdose of the drugs you found near Gretchen is coma.'

'She's in a coma?' I echo, shocked, and twist to look at Gretchen. A coma to me means days and days of the patient lying there, suspended between life and death, or cheap hospital TV dramas where someone has an agonising decision: switch off a life support machine or wait indefinitely for ever? That's not what could happen here, is it?

'How long will she be in a coma for?'

'I don't know,' the nurse says. 'It's too early to tell.'

'Is that why you said I should talk to her?' I ask, looking at the nurse directly as a thought occurs to me. 'Can she hear me? Could she be aware I'm here?'

The nurse hesitates, and I can see she's picking her words carefully so she doesn't give me any false hope. 'Some studies have documented coma sufferers recovering and reporting conversations they heard, yes.'

Oh, shit.

I turn back to Gretchen and look at her. On one long school trip in primary school I pretended to be asleep on the coach so I could hear what other people said about me. Actually no one said anything apart from, 'I'm going to eat her crisps.' Obviously I don't think that is what Gretchen is doing now, pretending, but the thought that underneath those eyelids is a whirring brain aware of everything that is going on in this small room chills and stills my blood. She will know if I betray her confidence and tell her secrets.

10

'I'll be right over here if you want to ask me anything else,' the nurse says. She stands up and moves to the back of the room.

'There is something actually,' I blurt, turning to her. 'When – if – she starts to regain consciousness, will she just open her eyes?'

The nurse pauses before speaking. 'People in comas,' she says, cleverly making it general and not specific to Gretchen, 'don't do that, except on TV. They start to make little movements, like trying to lift their head or fluttering their fingers when they begin to come round.'

'Can they talk? Straight away?'

The nurse shakes her head. 'You see that tube in her mouth?'

I nod.

'That's helping her breathe and she can't talk with that in.'

'But she could write?' I ask. 'If she came round.'

'She'd find a way to communicate with us.'

The nurse looks at me steadily.

'I'm scared that she's conscious but paralysed,' I say, which isn't true and if Gretchen *can* hear me, she'll be doing an inward sardonic snort right now. Actually she won't, she'll have other things on her mind, like why and how her carefully laid plans have gone so awry – thanks to me. '*You promised*,' I can hear her saying. '*Some best friend you turned out to be!*'

'I read a book recently about a French man that happened to, it was called locked-in syndrome,' I say, trying to focus on the real sound of my own voice.

'That's not what this is,' the nurse assures me, and then pauses before saying, 'Gretchen won't be able to communicate with us until she regains consciousness and

11

she's very ill, she's not going to just wake up like you see in the films. I'm sorry.'

We fall silent and I look at Gretchen again, feeling more tears well up. Oh, Gretch. How the hell did we wind up here? How can this be happening to us? I just want to go back to us laughing together, laughing so much we could barely stand, I can even hear the sound of it! Please, I want *those* moments back.

I can't do this – I can't just sit in this room pretending. Not when I know, I *know* what we both did . . .

'I have to go and check my messages,' I say, unable to bear it a moment longer, standing up so quickly I surprise my legs and they almost give way beneath me. 'In case Tom has called me.'

'OK,' the nurse says and smiles encouragingly, but I've already turned and I'm bursting back out into the corridor and practically running out of the ICU, shoving determinedly out through the double doors back into the main hospital. I see an exit. Having pushed through the door with a sickening relief, I find myself in what looks like a small, spill-over staff car park. I've no idea where I am in relation to A&E now – I've completely lost my bearings. I just scrabble in my bag for my phone and switch it on. I have three new messages.

The first one is Tom, left twenty minutes after I called him. 'Alice? What the hell has happened?' He sounds cross but I can tell it's because he's very frightened. 'What do you mean you're both at the hospital? Why? Look, if you get this in the next five minutes call me back, OK?'

The next one is him, six minutes later. 'It's me again. I'm going to call the hospital.'

And then, eighteen minutes after that, him shouting above a roaring car engine, obviously on the road, saying, 'I'm on my way, don't panic, Alice. It'll be all right. I'll be there just as soon as possible, I promise. I've left Bath – I don't know how long it'll take me – but luckily I'm going against the traffic, I'll be as quick as I can.'

I picture him gripping the steering wheel firmly with one hand, mobile to his ear with the other, hurtling down the motorway in his work suit, and it makes me want to cry with relief that he is on his way. My bottom lip trembles and tears spring to the corners of my eyes. Thank God. I feel better just having heard his voice.

Tom is a fixer, someone to rely on. He's the sort of person friends ring when they need advice on selling a car, filling out a tax return or have some heavy furniture that needs moving. My dad wanted me to marry Tom the second he found out he owned a fully stocked tool kit – with no bits missing – *and* knew what to do with it. He sorted a leaking tap for me the first day I met him, for God's sake.

'That should do it,' he said, climbing out of the bath – fully suited sadly – and turning the tap on and off experimentally, still clutching the pair of pliers I'd given him, the only tool-type thing I'd been able to find in the whole flat. My flatmate Vic and I stared at the tap, waiting for the inevitable drip to begin – but it didn't. We were totally delighted.

'So Tom,' Vic said quickly. 'You're a management consultant – which sounds well paid and stable . . .'

Tom nodded modestly.

'You're a friend of a friend so you're unlikely to be a lunatic,' Vic continued. 'You can mend things . . .'

And you're fit, I thought, staring as his light blue eyes crinkled behind his glasses because he'd smiled.

'The room's yours if you want it,' Vic said, having looked at me for the OK first.

13

'That's it?' he laughed. 'Don't you want to see any references? You should, you know,' he said, suddenly serious. 'I could be anyone. I'm not – but I could be.'

But he was of course the model flatmate and, it turned out ten months later, boyfriend.

The phone rings in my already cold, numb hand. It's him. 'Tom?' I answer quickly. 'Where are you?'

'. . . fen . . . M4 . . . like a wanker . . . but flyover . . . passed Olympia . . . twenty min . .' It's cutting in and out so badly I can barely hear him, but it sounds like he's still in the car. '. . . happened? . . . hospital reception and I'll . . .' Then it goes completely dead. I call him back but it goes straight to voicemail. He said twenty minutes though – I heard that. Gripping my phone like a talisman, I try to go back in through the door I just came out of, but discover I can't because it requires a code.

I spend the next ten minutes walking faster and faster around the outside of the hospital, following signs that say they are taking me to the main reception but in fact lead me down unlit, narrow passageways between very dark, old red-brick clinic buildings which have open curtains on eerily empty rooms. I try not to look in through the windows as I speed past them, scared of glimpsing ghostly figures moving silently around inside – past patients who died there and are now bound to the austere Victorian building for ever. I'm almost sick with the fear I've worked myself into and have to, need to, hear someone's familiar, no-nonsense voice. So I call Frances.

'Hello?' My elder sister answers the phone with a hushed tone.

'It's me.' My voice is wavering around all over the place, not just because of my hurried footsteps.

'Oh hi, Al. Look I'm really sorry, but now's not a great

14

time – I've just put Freddie down. He's really unsettled tonight.'

I try to picture Frances sitting in her neat little semi-detached, curtains regimentally pulled, tea washed up, TV on – calm and normal.

'It's a dreadful line anyway,' she says. 'It sounds like you're in a wind tunnel.'

I turn a corner sharply, look to my left and nearly collapse with relief. Oh thank God – I can see the front of A&E. I slow down, trying to catch my breath as I walk past several stationary ambulances, but then leap out of my skin as one suddenly blasts out a brief siren, begins to flash its lights and then swiftly pulls away to go and rescue somebody else. I hadn't even noticed a driver was sitting in the dark front seat.

'Where *are* you?' Frances says immediately.

I take a breath. 'I'm—'

'Oh no!' she interrupts. 'I think Freddie heard that. Oh please God, don't let him wake up! Just don't say anything Alice!' she whispers urgently and obediently I fall silent, although I can't help but wonder how Freddie could possibly have heard an ambulance down a phone that he's probably nowhere near. He's a baby, not a bat.

'It's OK,' she breathes. 'He's fine. Actually I'm glad you rang, I can't get hold of Mum. Do you know where she is? I've tried at home, but there's no answer. They can't *all* be out – it's a Thursday night!'

I pause, knowing full well that, on my advice, Mum and Dad have taken to unplugging the phone during meal times for half an hour of peace from the incessant baby-related calls. They've probably forgotten to plug it back in again.

'Freddie feels a little flushed,' Frances says. 'And he's only just recovered from that cough last week. I think it might be the start of pneumonia and Adam's still at work.'

'I have no idea where Mum is,' I say and then I burst into tears.

'Alice? Are you *crying*? What on earth is the matter?'

'I'm at the hospital and—'

'Why? Are you hurt?' Frances says sharply, automatically swinging into big sister mode.

'No,' I begin. 'I'm fine but—'

But she bulldozes over me, 'You're not ill? Nothing's broken?'

This is typical Frances. Back in secondary school, there was a group of 'cool' girls in my class who bullied everyone from time to time. They used to cluster round their victim in the corridors between classes, always one of the worst times, or at lunch when the teachers would be shut away in the staffroom reading the paper, having a fag and angrily watching the clock hands which had dragged all morning suddenly whizzing round.

It was my turn on the day I was the only person to get an A in art and the teacher warmly and stupidly praised me in front of the whole class. The cool girls' eyes all swivelled on to me – and I just *knew* what was going to happen at break.

Sure enough, six of them circled round me on the top corridor and began jostling and pushing me. I kept quiet and looked at the floor, because saying *anything* only made it worse. I'd seen what they'd done to poor Catherine Gibbons, who'd bravely chanted 'Sticks and stones may break my bones.'

One of the girls had just given me a rather half-hearted push that made me stumble and clutch my bag a little tighter when, amid their increasingly bored jeers, there was a sudden bellow of 'HEY!' We all turned to see Frances

16

steamrollering towards us, red in the face with rage. Within seconds she grabbed the ringleader round the neck and growled, 'You touch my little sister again and I'll break your face, understand?'

She dumped the girl down, at which point they all scarpered. I remember she looked at me and sighed. 'Pull your shirt out, Al, no one tucks it in like that . . .'

'Alice,' she says, waiting for me to answer her. 'You're frightening me. Are you sure nothing's wrong with you?'

I take a deep breath and try to calm down. 'It's not me. I've brought Gretchen in.'

'Oh God,' Frances snorts. 'You poor thing! Your friends are such drama queens. You're too nice for your own good Alice, you really are. I take it this is some sort of alcohol-related injury you're having to surpervise?'

'Kind of. I went round to her flat earlier this evening and—' I suddenly really want to tell her. I am, however, interrupted by a thin wail in the background.

'Oh I don't believe it!' Frances says. 'He's awake. Fuck, fuck, fuck. You promise me *you're* all right, Al?'

The crying in the background becomes louder with renewed vigour – it's a lusty, determined demand for attention and I can't help but feel a moment of respect for my tiny, no doubt scarlet-faced nephew.

'How the hell can you be awake *already*?' Frances says in disbelief. 'I only fed you fifteen minutes ago.' She lets out a heavy, slightly desperate sigh.

I close my eyes and take a deep breath. 'Fran,' I insist, 'I'm fine. I can deal with this. You go.'

'If you're sure?' I can hear the relief in her voice. 'What's happened to Gretchen anyway?'

Freddie cranks up the volume to a level that could break glass.

17

'Nothing, nothing major. I'll call you later if I need to.'

'Just try Mum, OK?' she says guiltily. 'She'll know what to do. They might be back by now. If you get her, tell her to call me when you're done, all right?'

'OK,' I say dully, a fresh tear trickling down my cheek, and then she hangs up without even saying goodbye. I want to dial her back straight away and say, 'Actually I do need you. I'm frightened, Fran!' Instead, I dial my parents and begin to walk slowly down to the main doors. But just as Frances said, it just rings and rings before eventually going to answerphone.

So I dial my younger brother Phil's number. If he's at home, he can go downstairs and tell them to plug the phone back in, that *I* want to speak to them. I suddenly very urgently need to talk to Mum or Dad – have someone tell me this is going to be all right because—

'This is Phil. I can't come to the phone right now, I'm probably busy. And by busy, I mean out. And by out I mean having a smoke. You can leave a message, but no promises, alriiittttteeee?'

For a moment I can see exactly how Phil can drive my dad into a rage in under five seconds flat. What kind of recorded message is *that* given prospective graduate employers might be calling him? He won't even get an interview, never mind a job. I just hang up and drop my phone into my bag in defeat.

I glance desperately up at the black sky and try to calm myself down. There are no stars, and no navigation lights of planes visible either. I can hear one, distantly buried in the thick cloud above my head. I can't see it, but I wish I were on it, going somewhere, anywhere away from here.

I bring my head down and look at my watch. Has it been twenty minutes yet? Tom must be nearly here by now.

He could have parked and slipped in another door? Perhaps he's up there already? I don't want him walking into Gretchen's room on his own.

I hurriedly clatter up the disabled ramp leading to A&E, arms tightly wrapped round myself. The persistent wind is managing to bite at my very bones, but before I can plunge back into the stifling warmth of the hospital, the mechanism of the automatic double doors yanks into action and a mother and daughter begin to slowly hobble through. I have to stand to one side to let them pass. The daughter supports the mum as she leans heavily on her and a crutch. She's perspiring with the effort, even though it's freezing, and is clutching furiously at her daughter's hand. I glance at her heavily bandaged foot and notice two unattractive purple toes peeking out at the top, adorned with fat blobs of coral polish. 'Well done, Mum,' the daughter says kindly. 'Dad's just bringing the car round. Nearly there.'

The mother glances up to thank me for waiting and her eyes widen briefly as she takes me in. I catch sight of my reflection in the glass and raise a hand self-consciously to my jaw, twisting my face slightly so I can get a better look. There is nothing obviously untoward, just my pale, make-up-smudged face; red eyes and nose attractively set off by my long, unstyled dark hair, but she's right – I'm a state. My baggy tracksuit bottoms and old hoodie top complete the look, but then, I thought I had a night in front of the TV ahead of me, not this.

I drop my head and dart past them as soon as I'm able to. Scanning the waiting room, I can see no sign of Tom, only a drunk verbally abusing the receptionist, so I step away hurriedly, moving towards the corridor that I think will lead me to the ICU.

But once I'm back up there, I pause outside the heavy

19

doors leading on to the unit. He *will* be here by now, won't he? I don't want him in there without me, but I don't want to sit waiting alone either.

The doors unexpectedly swing open, nearly hitting me as a doctor marches through with energy. 'Sorry!' he says automatically, though he also frowns slightly as if he's thinking, 'bloody stupid place to stand', so I walk through. I can't just stand here like a weirdo doing nothing.

The nurse looks up expectantly and then smiles with recognition as I enter the room. Tom is not there. I don't look at Gretchen, just put my bag back under the chair and sink down on to it uncomfortably. As I wipe my nose, which is streaming from the cold outside, I wonder for a moment if the nurse can tell I've been crying. But she'd expect me to have been, wouldn't she?

Eventually, after staring at the floor for what feels like for ever, I shoot a glance at Gretchen. I can't help it, I don't want to, but she looks just the same as when I left. Calm and, ironically, untroubled – but equally she looks sick, colourless. Once, I would have wanted her to be sitting up in bed, excited and shrieking, a wide smile across her face as I push her down the corridors, making doctors and nurses leap to safety as we hurtle past them. That couldn't happen. Not now.

Oh, if I could go back and change it all I would! I really, really would. I would give anything to be us just starting out again. I should have done what she asked, I know I should have. She needed me and I didn't do it . . .

I can feel myself creasing and crumpling up inside. I'm scared and the chair suddenly feels like it's shrinking under me – the whole room feels too small. Gretchen looks scarily fragile, vulnerable, and yet I am too terrified to touch her. My own friend.

I start to cry, and that is unfortunately how Tom finds me as he bursts into the room in a creased work suit, tie askew, shaken and breathless from having run in to find us.

Chapter Three

He visibly blanches at the sight of Gretchen hooked up to all manner of machines and a drip. Literally stops in his tracks in the doorway, like Road Runner screeching to a halt.

The nurse opens her mouth to say something, but I'm too quick for her. The reassuring sight of someone so familiar to me is totally overwhelming, and through my tears I say, 'Oh Tom! You're here!' as I'm mid-way up and out of my chair. It scrapes back underneath me and the noise goes through all of our teeth, but I don't care – I just fling myself into his arms so hard I almost knock him off his feet.

He automatically wraps his arms round me, hugs me. It's tight and reassuring and he presses me very tight to his chest. I can feel the shape of his pec muscles under his clothes and even though I want to stay there, because he's hugging me so close, all I can breathe in is shirt, so reluctantly I pull back and, as I do, his arms loosen around me and drop to his side. I look up at him and he's just staring at Gretchen, shocked rigid.

'What the hell has happened?' he whispers. All of his usual poise and calm seems to have drained away. 'No one would tell me anything – I was terrified.'

I gulp and try to get myself under control as tears slip off my nose.

'What's wrong?' he says, stunned, unable to take his eyes off her. And then he repeats himself. 'What's happened?'

I hesitate. I have to be really careful. 'I got a call, I went round to the flat . . . there were pills everywhere and . . .' My voice dissolves into a mess of tears.

He pales and opens his mouth to speak, but the nurse gets there first.

'Can we take this outside?' she says firmly. 'We don't want to upset Gretchen.' And that freaks me out even more; Gretchen just lying there, listening to everything we've just said. I very willingly move quickly into the corridor and the nurse pushes the door to behind us.

Tom waits and I try to explain again. 'There were pills lying on the floor and—'

'What sort of pills?' he asks, like he's already afraid of the answer.

I swallow and then clear my throat. 'I don't know. There was a bottle of whisky, mostly gone. I've no idea how many she took, she was unconscious.'

'Oh shit!' he says, stepping back and raking his fingers up through his hair. He takes another pointless step right and then back again. 'Oh shit, Gretchen!'

'I called an ambulance,' I say quickly. 'They arrived and said she was breathing. We went to A&E first and then they moved her here. She's in a coma!'

Tom shakes his head lightly, as if he can't quite absorb what I'm saying, as if it doesn't make any sense at all.

'They won't tell me any more until Bailey arrives.'

At the very sound of his name, a flash of intense dislike and anger flashes across Tom's face.

'Do they know where he is?' he asks tightly. 'Have they tried to call him?'

I nod. 'Madrid – I'm pretty sure he's on his way back though. He must be by now.'

'How did they know he was there?' Tom frowns.

'I told them,' I confess. 'He called me earlier this evening. He was supposed to be going over to see Gretchen but he missed his flight or something. Or it got delayed, I don't know. He called her to say he wasn't going to make it and she was drunk, really drunk. He asked me if I'd go over and check on her after work. So I did . . .' I peter out. I'm feeling really hot again, I can feel sweat collecting and pooling on my spine and my top starting to stick to my back.

'And . . . ?' he says, waiting.

I take a deep breath. 'She was unconscious in the living room. It was pretty obvious what she'd done.'

'Shit!' Tom looks at me. 'And they won't tell us anything until he gets here?'

I shake my head. 'Only stuff like "she's stable", that kind of thing. No detail.'

Tom looks furious. 'But that's absurd! Have you said that to them? What did they say?'

I feel sick. 'I didn't know what to say, Tom, I just came with her and . . .' I falter under his demanding gaze and raise a shaking hand up to my head. 'I can't think straight. It's all happened very quickly and—'

'OK, OK – Alice, I'm sorry,' he cuts across me, stepping forward, taking my hand. 'I didn't mean to sound so fierce.' He takes a deep breath. 'I'm just very fucking angry with *him*.'

He waits and I try to steady my breathing.

'Still,' he sighs eventually. 'At least she *is* stable.' Then he falls silent for a moment while he obviously toys with the unimaginable, horrific alternative, because seconds later he says, 'We should be in there, with her,' and makes for the door.

'Just a minute,' I call, utterly desperate not to go back into that room now I'm out of it. 'I need a moment to get myself together.' I lean on the wall – well, it props me up actually – and Tom waits heavily next to me, looking suddenly devastated and very confused.

'I can't believe she did this,' he says. 'I mean there were no signs, nothing at all. In fact she seemed,' he glances at me and picks his words carefully, 'pretty happy. I'm sorry – is this too hard for you?'

Yes it is, it's practically impossible. The most horrendous situation I've ever found myself in in my entire life.

I shake my head again. 'I'm OK,' I say, but the words are more of a whisper. I find that my head is starting to hang, my eyes fill again and I am weeping, tears splashing on the squeaky hospital floor. He moves to hug me, but a nurse turning into the corridor and approaching us distracts him. 'Come on, Al,' he says as the nurse opens the door to Gretchen's room and goes in. He leads and reluctantly I follow.

We are just starting slowly to pull up chairs, Tom staring at Gretchen, when the nurse who came in ahead of us, who is obviously quite senior and busily checking charts, remarks to her more junior colleague, 'She keeps getting ectopics. Is she normally having that many?'

I lift my head and start to pay attention.

'I saw a few earlier but they're becoming more frequent,' the junior says.

'Hmm. Keep an eye on that. What's her potassium?'

'3.1.'

Is that good or bad?

The senior nurse's eyebrows flicker. 'We need to top it up immediately. It's on the chart, isn't it?'

The junior nods and says, 'I'll go and get it.'

As she leaves the room, Tom shoots me a curious look and I shrug.

'Excuse me,' Tom begins to ask out loud, but he is cut short by an alarm starting to sound shrilly.

The senior nurse ignores him and moves quickly round to Gretchen, pushing past Tom, making him yank his chair back. She reaches for Gretchen's neck and I realise she is checking her pulse. My own responds by increasing rapidly.

I look up urgently and see a green line going manic on a monitor, it's spiking about crazily – but about three screens down, a red line is going flat. Oh my God.

'Can I have some help in here?' the nurse suddenly shouts very loudly and then things start to happen very quickly.

Tom stands up and looks wildly at me, my mouth has fallen open in horror and I find I'm rooted to the spot with fear. Another nurse appears immediately in the doorway.

'Can you put the arrest call out? She's in VT,' someone shouts.

There's a slamming noise that makes both Tom and me jump violently as the head of the bed cracks down and Gretchen is suddenly totally flat.

'Oh shit, she's in VF now!' the first nurse calls.

'What's VF?' Tom says desperately. 'What's happening?'

A third nurse dashes in and I hear someone, I'm not sure who, say firmly, 'Can you get the friends out?'

Then there is a hand on my arm and Tom is yelling,

'No! We need to stay. What's going on? What's happening to her?' I'm being pulled insistently to my feet as I look at Gretchen – they are yanking blankets down, reaching for her gown and . . .

We are suddenly back out in the corridor, being ushered quickly down it, away from the noise of the alarm, still going. A doctor bursts through a set of double doors and hurtles past us. I look back over my shoulder to see that a stream of medical staff are now pouring like ants into the small room.

'They just need some space to work in,' the nurse with us says insistently. 'That's all. Come on, we'll wait down here in the relatives' area.' It's a command, not an option. She tries to hurry me away, but I can't take my eyes off what's happening behind us. Another doctor has appeared from the other end of the passage and is running. All these people fighting for Gretchen, her life – her actual, real *life* in their hands. A picture of her slumped up against the wall back in her flat slams into my head. A nurse runs past me, almost banging into me in her haste and disappears into the room. Again I see Gretchen, pills at her feet . . . Oh my God. Everything seems to start moving in slow motion and I'm barely aware of my own voice suddenly shrieking, 'No!' And then I'm collapsing to the floor, Tom is bending and trying to scoop me up, pulling me to him and I'm crying, crying, crying . . . as if it's *my* heart that is breaking.

Chapter Four

'Her name is Gretchen Bartholomew, for God's sake,' I sighed, sitting on the small suitcase and trying to ignore the resulting ominous crunch that was probably every bottle in my toiletries bag breaking. 'I've never even met the girl, but I can tell you that with a name that pretentious she can't be anything *but* a massive twat. Why, why, *why* did I say yes to this?'

'It's an all expenses paid trip to LA and if you do a good job, this magazine might use you for travel features,' Tom said sensibly, slipping his shoes on. 'And she can't help her name. She might be really nice.'

'The whole thing just sounds really tacky!' A pair of my knickers that seemed determined to ping free were caught in the teeth of the suitcase zip. I shoved them back in and started to tug it closed. 'And she's a kids TV presenter, which means she'll be thick as two short planks. Oh *come on*, you . . .' My fingers were going white with the effort of trying to do the bloody thing up.

'Why are they shooting her?' Tom asked absently.

'She's moving to Hollywood to make it big over there or something,' I said, puffing slightly, 'like anyone cares. This case is going to literally explode when I open it at the other end.' I looked at the straining seams worriedly. Maybe four pairs of shoes was a bit excessive. I very gingerly got off it and waited. Thankfully, it held – but bulged like a swollen water balloon ready to burst.

'On the subject of coming and going,' Tom picked up the ends of his tie, which was looped around his neck, 'while you're away, shall I ring that Spanish bloke and let him know he can have Vic's old room?'

My face fell. Tom smiled sympathetically as he tightened the tie and came over to give me a hug. 'I know you miss her, Al, but we can't keep her room empty for ever, we can't afford to.'

'Paris,' I growled, muffled by his shirt, 'is a really stupid place for her to live. I hate that gitbag French doctor with all his smooth, "Come and live in my chateau, cherie."'

'No you don't,' Tom laughed, 'we like Luc. You were the one who spent hours on the phone reassuring her she'd done the right thing! And now, she's very happy.'

'Fine, we'll phone the Spanish bloke then,' I said rather crossly, thinking about Vic, who I missed badly. 'He did seem the least clinically insane of all of the applicants.'

'But on the other hand,' Tom pulled back, a considered expression spreading across his face, 'are we sure we don't want to live somewhere just us, rather than with some over-pumped-up Spanish beefcake we got out of the back of the paper?'

'We can't afford to, we've been over this,' I said through a mouthful of toast that I'd grabbed from my plate, before looking around for my handbag. I couldn't remember where I'd last seen it.

29

'Unless, of course, we start looking for something smaller, maybe to buy. Together.'

I immediately stopped looking for my bag and turned to him instead. That was the first time either of us had openly and *formally* suggested anything of the kind. I waited for my heart to leap joyfully. To my surprise it didn't, but then my taxi was due to arrive in minutes. How typically male of Tom to pick absolutely the worst time in the world to debate a major life changing issue and randomly chuck a statement like *that* into the pot.

'Renting long term is just dead money,' Tom continued, taking a quick sip of his tea. 'It's great when you're younger and you need flexibility, but we could save so much by paying into a mortgage now . . . and the market conditions are *great* for people like us.'

'People like us?' I said, confused.

'Settled people, couples . . . most of our friends have bought somewhere,' he said pointedly. 'I've saved a really reasonable deposit and—'

'But shouldn't we do it because we want to, rather than as a practical solution to Vic moving out?' I asked.

Tom looked at me blankly and said, 'Well we do want to – don't we?'

I paused.

'Ahh!' he continued, looking at me carefully. 'I'm so stupid! You mean this isn't a very *romantic* way of doing things. Shit Al – I'm sorry. I take your point. You're right. Although getting a mortgage *is* just as much a commitment as getting married . . .'

My eyes widened. *What?*

'. . . Or at least legally it is, should anything go wrong – which it won't.' He held my gaze significantly and then smiled at me.

Wow. I just stood there, feeling slightly stunned, realising that my boyfriend of two years had just calmly told me he fully intended to marry me.

I waited to feel thrilled, like I was 'coming home', as if all the pieces in the jigsaw were slotting into place . . . but it was a bit of an anticlimax. I didn't feel anything really, but given that I'd been eating, sleeping and drinking Frances' wedding preparations until very recently, that was hardly surprising. I pretty much wouldn't have cared if I'd never seen another seating plan, or order of service, for the rest of my life. And Tom had, after all, told me this over breakfast like he was announcing he'd paid the electricity bill. At the age of twelve or so, when I had dreamily imagined I would be married with several children by the age of twenty-three, I'd never pictured the moment someone would drop down on one knee and say, 'Alice, will you get a mortgage with me?' He hadn't even really asked me to do that.

'Actually,' Tom rolled his eyes, appearing not to notice I'd apparently gone mute, 'what we should do is get this flat-mate in now and start looking to buy in a couple of months – best of both worlds! That would give us,' he glanced up at the ceiling briefly, 'just under an extra three grand, which should cover the legal fees and some of the stamp duty on whatever we find.' He smiled happily at me. 'You're right, that's by far the best plan.'

I hadn't actually said anything, had I?

'I'll ring him later today and get him to move in asap. Time is money!' He rubbed his hands gleefully. 'Mortgage-wise, what do you think realistically you could say was your annual income now? Net, not gross?'

'Tom,' I said slowly, finally recovering the power of speech, 'I'm about to get on a plane to the other side of the world, I don't even know where my handbag is and my taxi will be here any minute. Do we have to do this now? Can't we just wait until I get back?'

'OK.' He seemed rather disappointed that I didn't appear to have a relevant spreadsheet of figures in my back pocket. 'I'll just tell the Spanish bloke he can move in then.'

'Good idea,' I said through slightly gritted teeth as we came full circle. 'You do that.' Now, where the arse was my handbag?

A car horn honked outside. I dashed to the window and looked out. A silver Ford, its driver pretending he was itching and not picking his nose, sat just below the window, presumably waiting for me. 'Shit!' I said in dismay, 'He's here!' I rapped on the window and the driver glanced up to see me frantically holding up one hand, fingers spread, silently mouthing 'five minutes'.

I whirled round quickly to see my handbag swinging lightly in Tom's outstretched hand. 'Your passport is already in there,' he said. 'I checked. Just calm down, you've got plenty of time.'

The taxi honked again.

'All right!' Tom said, frowning at the noise. 'He's keen. I'll get the case.' He walked over and picked it up. 'Jesus, Al! You *are* only going for two nights, right?' He puffed as he lifted it up and walked quickly to the top of the stairs. 'You're not secretly leaving me?'

I laughed, rather more loudly than I meant to, which seem to disconcert me more than it did him.

'So what's the theme behind this shoot?' he asked as we went down.

Men were *weird*. How could they one minute be talking about something so serious and then the next switch to complete trivia like nothing had happened? 'Hooray for Hollywood,' I said in answer to his question. 'So much for my

plan to start doing more creative, less commercial stuff . . .
I'm just a big fat superficial sell-out.'

Tom laughed as I pushed past him and opened the front
door. 'It's not that bad! OK, it's not exactly *National
Geographic* and it does sound a bit daft, but it's all cash in
the bank.' He waited as the taxi driver got out. 'Just think
of the greater good,' he added as the driver took the case,
shoved it in the boot and got back in the car. 'I know it's
not what you really want to be doing, Al, but it's only
two nights. You'll be back before you know it. Hey, don't
forget on Saturday it's Bunkers' and George's engagement/
Christmas do.'

'It's a bit early for a Christmas party, isn't it? It's barely
the end of November!'

Tom shrugged. 'That's George for you. Super organised.
And you know Bunkers – he'd never miss a chance like
this to get as many women as possible under the mistletoe
before the wedding ring gets slipped on his finger.'

My heart sank even further. Edward Bunksby, known as
Bunkers (a 'witty' play on his name and the fact that he was
an enormous solid rugby prop), was a raging lech from Tom's
office who liked to squeeze women's bottoms in lieu of a
handshake. His aggressive fiancée Georgina had the sharp eyes
of a shrew, spike heels and an engaging line of chat which
usually went along the lines of, 'Hi, I'm George. I'm the
youngest female partner in my firm. So how much do *you*
earn?' Rumour had it she kept Bunkers' balls in her brief-
case and only let him have them back on special occasions.

'I know he's a bit of a prat and George is pretty full on,
but I ought to show my face really. It's at their house –
he's invited everyone from work. I'll get them a present
though, so you don't need to worry about that.'

I sighed.

'Sorry, did you want us to see some of your friends this weekend?' he said.

'Like who? I've not seen anyone for weeks, I've been working so hard – I'm practically a social recluse.'

'Which is why you should try and have fun while you're away,' Tom said soothingly and pulled me into a hug, planting a kiss on my mouth.

'I'll try,' I promised, suddenly feeling completely over-whelmed. Engagement parties, mortgages, weddings. It wasn't even eight a.m. yet. 'Do I look all right?' I asked anxiously, glancing down at my nude-coloured coat over my black tunic dress and thick black tights. 'I thought I could take the tights off when I get there, if it's hot. I've got flip flops in my bag. That'll be OK, won't it?'

'You look great. Text me when you land.' He opened the car door. I got in and wound down the window.

'Love you, Al,' he said. 'Safe journey.'

'Love you too,' I replied automatically. 'So just phone that bloke then, tell him he can have the room. Don't do anything else though, will you? Oh and don't forget to call your mum – tell her we'll come to them on Boxing Day and do my mum and dad on Christmas Day.'

'Sir, yes sir!' He pretended to salute me and I shot him a ha ha look as the car began to pull away. I turned at the end of the road to see him still standing there, waving cheerfully. I waved back, but as we rounded the corner, sank back into the seat heavily and was discomfited to find myself thinking that perhaps three days' escape in LA might have some advantages after all.

Later, strapped into my seat on the plane and reading the safety card, I still couldn't settle, which was daft, because it wasn't like Tom'd said 'Will you marry me?' All we'd actually agreed to do was rent our spare room out, which was hardly dramatic. But he was *thinking* about mortgages and marriage . . . and thinking seriously too by the sound of it.

That was a good thing, surely? It wasn't like I hadn't imagined myself walking down the aisle on my father's arm and Tom, beaming, turning slowly to face me. I had. Why was I feeling stressed out?

To be fair, I'd been stressed about everything recently. It'd been tough going self-employed, particularly money-wise. I hadn't been able to ask Mum and Dad to help me out either because they'd been totally rinsed by Frances' wedding. I thought Dad was actually going to explode when he'd received the quote for the flowers. But then, why should Mum and Dad have bailed me out anyway? It'd been really hard work but everything I'd achieved, I'd done myself – which I was quietly proud of, although it had meant doing a lot more of the sort of jobs I didn't much enjoy, like the one ahead of me.

I found having to make myself do the whole 'That's *brilliant*, look at me like the camera *loves* you!' excruciating – it felt so fake having to force myself to be someone I wasn't and didn't especially want to be either. That was the beauty of travel photography: I didn't impose myself on anything or anyone, just recorded everything as it would have been, even if I hadn't been there, and then quietly left. This gig, however, was completely different. Whatever very small satisfaction I would squeeze out of taking a picture of a pretty girl against a city backdrop wouldn't outweigh the sheer embarrassment of being in public and taking pictures of someone dressed as – I checked my brief – a British office worker/naughty schoolgirl astride a star on the Walk of Fame. Oh God. I felt myself cringe inwardly, my stomach squirming. It was so cheesy.

35

A plate of plastic plane food, which managed to taste curiously of nothing and yet had a uniquely gross texture and scent, didn't do much to help matters, but once I'd watched a couple of movies and had a little nap (although I got three electric shocks from the tartan blanket and discovered in the tiny toilet cubicle festooned with bog roll that my hair resembled Doc Brown's from *Back to the Future*), I began to calm down a bit.

I was just going to have to get with the programme. I was going to LA. It was a new experience, which was a good thing, another stamp in my passport and an opportunity to do a good job that would lead to a *better* job. One I really would enjoy. Glass half full, Alice, I told myself firmly, looking in the mirror and deciding that the two spots on my cheek that had appeared from nowhere, as if they'd been forced through my skin by the pressure of being several thousand feet in the air, were *not* going to bother me. I was going to make the best of this.

After all, most people would give various parts of their body to be flying to LA, staying in a posh hotel and meeting a famous presenter, and all I had to do was point a camera at her. It wasn't like I got to do this sort of thing all the time, for goodness' sake. Last week I'd taken pictures of twenty different lip glosses from various angles, which had hardly been bloody exciting. 'Hooray for Hollywood,' I sung lightly under my breath, peering at myself more closely in the mirror, psyching myself up. 'Where you're a star if you're only good . . . or something.' I could do this! I was *going* to do it.

'Nice hotel we're in, isn't it?' said Gretchen Bartholomew chattily to me as the make-up artist dabbed her skin and then commanded, 'Look up for me, lovie.'

'Very,' I agreed sincerely, wondering what it must be like to be her, having her make-up done by strangers, having people she didn't know reading all about her in magazines, looking at her picture, ripping apart what she was wearing. Urgh.

'Apparently the Dalai Lama is staying there too,' Gretchen said, unfazed, 'so we're in good company.' I was just about to ask her how she knew that when a tour bus drove past us for the umpteenth time, full of gawking, slack-jawed tourists clutching digital cameras, noses pressed eagerly to the window at the sight of a *real life camera crew!*

I glanced away as the tour guide shouted, 'How you folks doin'?' Gretchen, however, without moving a single muscle in her face, somehow managed to give him an enthusiastic thumbs up. I had to hand it to her, she'd been a tireless and enthusiastic worker from the moment I'd met her at our first location of the day – a Rodeo Drive jewellers'.

'You must be Alice,' she'd said, standing up immediately and offering me a hand so small and delicate it was like a child's, but with a surprisingly energetic grip. 'I'm Gretchen, pleased to meet you.' She gave me a bright and engaging smile, and I saw immediately how she came across so well to the millions of children whose homes she was beamed into. She looked exactly the sort of girl any six-year-old would long to be when she grew up.

The stylist had already dressed her as the archetypal kids presenter, pulling Gretchen's blonde, bouncy hair off her heart-shaped face and into two bunches. Each one was secured with a bit of pink sparkly fluff that could have been yanked off the underside of an indignant flamingo. Her T-shirt, obscenely tight and yellow over two perky breasts, read 'Lollipop us up'. To ensure the readers got the message that LA was the town where all grown up girls' dreams came true, the stylist wanted her draped in as much ostentatious bling as the shop was prepared to provide.

We eventually wound up with a shot of Gretchen flanked by two enormous unsmiling security guards, as she looked delightedly into a mirror. Her eyes were wide with glee as she inspected Liquorice Allsorts-sized yellow diamond earrings dangling at her jaw, and fat rings like sucked and spat-out gobstoppers on her fingers. It was a perfectly respectable image, if a little predictable. What the client wanted, the client got. To be fair to Gretchen though, she'd done exactly what I asked without complaint and given it her all.

'You must have been doing this sort of thing for ages,' she said to me as we packed up to move locations. 'You're very calm and organised. I think this is the least hysterical shoot I've been on for a long while.'

I looked up and smiled gratefully at her. 'That's kind of you to say so. I don't do a lot of this type of work actually, maybe that's why. Am I not being exciting enough?'

She held up her hands. 'No, no, it's a good thing, believe me. I feel much more relaxed than normal, despite her.' She nodded in the direction of the coke-honed magazine stylist who had been taking VERY URGENT CALLS on her mobile all morning. 'I can't believe anyone can be that indispensable. Silly cow. It's been like having the bloody Batphone go off every five seconds. What exactly *is* a celebrity editor anyway?'

I had shrugged in a non-committal 'your guess is as good as mine but also I can't really comment seeing as she's technically my boss' sort of way.

Things were much better creatively once we set up outside on the Walk of Fame, but worse from the perspective of traffic slowing and random people becoming interested in what we were doing. I felt pretty self-conscious as I peered through the lens at Gretchen with people watching me interestedly, arms crossed, like they were at a magic show. It didn't seem to bother Gretchen though, and she was the one dressed in a tight black jacket, suit shirt slightly unbuttoned from the bottom up, and black shorts that barely covered the crease of her bottom. She stayed focused and obeyed every instruction instinctively, lean legs either side of a Hollywood star as she leant on a terribly British black umbrella and peered up at me from under long lashes and a tilted bowler hat.

I twisted to the right slightly to cut out a pneumatic blonde who had appeared from nowhere and seemed determined to ease her tits into the frame. As I moved, a male passer-by in trainers and baggy jeans whistled appreciatively, walking past to Gretchen's left, looking back over his shoulder at her. '*Damn*, girl!' he called, as her long, blonde curls lifted lightly on the warm breeze. She glanced at him coquettishly, and good naturedly laughed.

It turned out to be just what was needed. We all inspected the shot of him looking at her in rapt admiration, the bright LA sun illuminating the edges of the black bowler hat and the stark, crisp lines of the umbrella. I couldn't help feeling that all I'd done was take the photo at the right time – it wasn't exactly styled, more luck than anything – but at least it had some movement, and Gretchen had a genuinely happy expression on her flawless face.

She looked as if she was poised to take over the world . . . and absolutely knew it.

Chapter Five

'It's always so good to kick back after a long day's shoot,' Gretchen sighed happily. 'Do you want some more wine?' She passed a bottle to me and sat back for a moment, peering at my plate. 'Your fish looks amazing – I've got food envy.' She was still making a real effort to be friendly, which was a pleasant surprise and not at all typical of most people like her. My somewhat limited experience had taught me that the more middle of the road a star was, the more self-obsessed they were likely to be; and the more tired they were, the more precious they became. But she didn't seem to fit that mould at all.

She shook her head and laughed. 'I'm so stuffed, and yet I seem to be keeping on eating.' We were all sitting about a large table in a lively open air restaurant. The edges of the terrace were lined with giant terracotta flowerpots that were dripping with brightly coloured bougainvillea. It was a warm night; a lot of laughter and excited chatter was going on around us.

'OK, second wind,' Gretchen said determinedly, picking

up her chopsticks and attacking her food with renewed relish. She popped a prawn in her mouth and rolled her eyes. 'To be fair, this *does* taste amazing! Here, try this.' She passed the bowl to me and waited eagerly. I tentatively speared a piece of what looked like tuna with a chopstick and put it in my mouth – she was right, it was incredible, just melted away like it had never even been there, leaving me wanting more.

'You know, I can't believe you've been a photographer for so long and we've never worked together before.' She shook her head.

'Umm,' I agreed, through a mouthful of my food, 'but I've not been freelance for very long, I've only just branched out on my own.'

'Good for you,' she said. 'You seem very good at it – I'm sure you'll do brilliantly. So,' she grinned, 'were you saying to the make-up girl that it was your first trip here? What do you think of LA?'

Honestly? Bits of it had totally sucked. I'd had low expectations, but I hadn't even realised we were driving down Hollywood Boulevard until someone told me – it was full of crappy fast food outlets and looked really shabby. But then equally, in spite of myself, I'd enjoyed the swanky restaurants, the ridiculously fluffy hotel dressing gown, the staff warmly saying 'You have a great day, Alice.'

'I think it's probably a good thing we're going home tomorrow,' I smiled, and picked up my glass of wine as I watched a rather glamorous couple take their seats two tables away from us. 'I ordered room service for breakfast this morning and this amazing plate of fresh fruit arrived; the sun is always shining; the people are really friendly, and this is so lovely, sitting outside to eat – it's November, for God's sake!'

Gretchen nodded enthusiastically.

'I think I could get worryingly addicted to such an exclusive lifestyle, which is funny because,' I paused carefully, I didn't want to appear rude, 'I really wasn't expecting it to be my kind of place.'

'I know what you mean,' Gretchen agreed. 'I like visiting once in a while to have my fix of fun and easy living, but then it's good to get back to reality. You're wise to be wary – it's really easy to get sucked in. Everyone seems friendly, but they're actually so ruthless, they would literally sell their own grandmother with a smile to get the part they want or the movie deal they're after. LA likes people to think it wears its heart on its sleeve but actually it prefers naked ambition. Quite an unhealthy little bubble.'

I was totally taken aback by such an unexpected and sharp comment. I remembered my rather bitchy remark to Tom about expecting her to be thick. She wasn't at all.

'I prefer New York,' she grinned. 'What you see is what you get. You been there?'

I nodded. 'A couple of times.'

She glanced at me. 'You look very Greenwich Village actually, sort of arty, understated but confident.'

I looked down at my slightly dishevelled black shift dress in disbelief, the only thing I'd managed to salvage from my suitcase that hadn't been plastered in Pantene. 'Thanks,' I said, feeling secretly flattered. 'I went there last year with my—' I was about to say boyfriend but then stopped and added instead, 'friend.'

It was a split second thing. My mouth said it before my brain connected. I slipped into the shoes of the savvy free spirit photographer she appeared to think I was, just for fun. I was only trying them on for size, to see what it felt like to be a fascinating creative type who flitted from country to country, carelessly. I knew I was flying home to Tom and a sinfully boring engagement party, but no one else knew that.

'So what other places have you been to?' she asked, reaching for her drink.

I tried to think. 'Fair bit of Europe, parts of Africa.' Which actually was true. 'I'm really trying to break out into more . . .' I struggled for a way of phrasing it that wouldn't offend her, 'reportage photography, travel stuff – but it's hard, this is where the money is and all my contacts are.'

Gretchen nodded understandingly. 'My older brother is a travel writer, I could introduce you if you like, he's bound to know some people you could network.'

'That would be really great!' I said in genuine amazement. '*Thank you!*'

Then a thought occurred to me.

'Oh God,' I said in dismay and put down my napkin. 'This is what you mean, isn't it? I've already gone all LA – I've just contact-pimped you. I'm so sorry.'

She laughed. 'Don't be silly! *I* suggested it to *you*!'

'Well, thank you. It's really kind of you,' I said, feeling embarrassed nonetheless. 'So do you have just one brother?'

She chuckled, appreciating my attempt at recovery. 'Yeah, just Bailey. How about you?'

'One incredibly lazy younger brother called Phil and an older sister called Frances.'

'Oh?' she said, her eyes lighting up. 'I always wanted a sister.'

'You can have mine if you like,' I said quickly.

'Ah,' said Gretchen. 'Not that close?'

I pictured Fran standing looking at me with her arms crossed, unimpressed eyebrow raised. Feeling horribly disloyal, I started to back pedal. 'It's not that,' I explained.

43

'We are, it's just she very recently got married, which was great, but the lead up to the wedding was pretty . . . full on. Frances can be . . .' I paused for the right words.

Gretchen sipped her drink, listening intently.

'A bit domineering. We've all spent the last few months organising and stressing. Phil's got away with murder, Mum's lost about a stone without even trying and I don't think Dad can retire for another five years now.' I smiled. 'I'm just a bit all wedding-ed out.'

'Were you her bridesmaid then?' Gretchen asked.

I shook my head. 'I was taking the photos.'

Gretchen looked confused. 'At your own sister's wedding?'

'I didn't mind. She really wanted me to and it's pointless arguing when Fran has her heart set on something. I just kept my head down and got on with it. She was five when I was born – she had a long time to wrap my parents round her little finger. When we were little,' I wriggled more comfortably into my seat, 'her best game was to tie a lead to my wrist and drag me around telling everyone I was her puppy; that gives you a good idea of what she's like. Sometimes the attention wasn't always a good thing.' I tucked an escaping bit of hair back behind my ear. 'She cut my fringe off once, which was nice of her. Mum left the back long because she wanted everyone to know I was a girl so, thanks to Frances, in the pictures of my third birthday party I look like Rod Stewart circa "Do You Think I'm Sexy?"'

Gretchen laughed.

'It's not funny,' I smiled. 'She could be really mean. I had a hamster I really loved called Verbal James Gerbal and—'

'I'm sorry,' Gretchen interrupted, holding up a hand. 'He was called *what*?'

'Yeah, we had really weird names for our toys and pets,'

I said, trying to remember why on earth I'd called him that.

'If it makes you feel any better, I had a toy elephant I called Mr Price. I have no idea why either,' she laughed. 'God, I'd forgotten about him! So what happened to Verbal James Gerbal?' She ate another mouthful of food and looked at me. 'I have a feeling you're about to tell me events took a tragic turn?'

'I'm afraid so. Frances set Verbal James Gerbal free in the night. On purpose.'

Gretchen shook her head. 'That was a low blow. Did he come back?'

'Unfortunately, no.' I shook my head, suddenly wondering why on earth I was telling her this, and why she was humouring me. It was nice of her. 'We heard him scrabbling around under the bathroom floorboards, but Dad didn't want to take the new carpet up.'

'He probably just escaped to a better life of freedom . . . To Verbal James Gerbal,' she said and raised her glass.

'I think, given the stink from under the floorboards that made everyone spontaneously gag every time they went in there, it's unlikely. But thanks anyway.' I grinned.

'OK – Verbal James Gerbal, RIP.' She raised her glass again, without missing a beat.

I laughed, and then after a pause said, 'I have no idea why I just told you all of that, I think I'm a little bit drunk. And it's the heat.'

Gretchen shook her head emphatically. 'Not at all. It's refreshing to meet someone on one of these things who's normal.'

Normal? Oh fuck. I felt crestfallen. I clearly hadn't fooled her for one second. Mind you, what enigmatic creative would talk about their childhood pets? She must have seen the look on my face because she raised her glass again and said, 'I mean that as a compliment. Cheers!'

We chinked glasses and Gretchen drained hers in one.

An hour later, we moved en masse upstairs to the Sky Bar, which centred round a decadent roof-top pool of enticingly still water. Around the edge were huge squashy cushions and tables lit by flickering candles, all set off by the dramatic backdrop of downtown LA, twinkling like fairy lights. I was starting to feel pretty pissed and had said just about all I could to the make-up girl on the subject of skin firming creams when Gretchen excitedly appeared by my side, arm in arm with the stylist – who was completely sloshed – and said, 'Alice! Come and see! You'll never guess who's here!'

She reached out her hand and I allowed her to lead me into a more formal seating area where, when I refocused slightly, I became aware of a rather small man, looking very bored, surrounded by a lot of fawning blonde women.

'It's only Rod bloody Stewart!' she whispered and then cracked up as my jaw fell open. 'Go and tell him you had his hair aged five or whatever it was.'

'You didn't go and say anything to him, did you?' Tom chuckled, the phone line crackling slightly. I could imagine him sitting at his desk, absently checking work emails as we chatted.

'No,' I laughed and leant back on my vast hotel bed. 'Of course not. What time is it?'

'Ten a.m. So that's what, two a.m. with you?'

I groaned. 'I'm going to be wrecked tomorrow, but you know what? I'm actually having fun. I can't believe I've only just got back from a club. Tom – *I* went clubbing! And I thought those days were over!'

46

'What are you talking about?' Tom said. 'We went clubbing three weeks ago when we went home for Sean's birthday!'

'Tom,' I said good naturedly, 'your old school friend's birthday in a small sweaty room on your local high street that smelt like an armpit was *not* clubbing.'

'Hey! There's nothing wrong with Images,' Tom laughed. 'God, you have one trip to LA . . .'

'Yeah, yeah.' I smiled and lifted a foot up and looked at it. Both of them were still throbbing. It had been a long time since I'd danced properly like that. 'The other girls are really nice,' I said enthusiastically. 'Especially Gretchen Bartholomew. We chatted quite a lot over dinner. The stylist is a bit of a pain though, one of those aggressive pissed types.'

'Sounds good,' said Tom, not really listening. 'I can't be too long, I've got a meeting in a minute, but I phoned that bloke about the room. It's all sorted. He's going to call me tomorrow to confirm when he's actually moving in.'

I closed my eyes. 'Well done,' I said.

'I think I'm going to draw up a contract though, just to protect us. Also, if we sublet, I'm not sure how we stand on an insurance front.'

'We'll sort it out later, don't worry about it.'

'I know it's boring, Al,' he said straight away, 'but what if we came back and he'd cleared the place out while we were at Sainsbury's or something?'

Oh God. 'Tom,' I yawned, twisting on to my tummy, 'can we do this when I get home?'

'Sure,' he said, slightly huffily.

'I'm just tired, Tom,' I appeased him. 'That's all. It's not that I don't appreciate,' I took a deep breath, 'the *importance* of what you've just said.'

47

There was a slight pause. I could tell he was frowning, five thousand miles away. 'You're so patronising sometimes,' he said eventually.

I closed my eyes again briefly and managed to suppress a heavy sigh. I'd been having such a fun evening and now he'd totally ruined it, but in my disappointment and irritation as I felt the moment slip away from me, I realised I couldn't be bothered to start a row. 'Sorry,' I said, in the sort of voice that meant I wasn't at all and thought he was being an arse.

'That's quite all right,' he said loftily, also being deliberately annoying. 'Apology accepted. You'd better get some sleep. Have a safe trip. Night.'

'Night,' I said shortly and flicked a V sign at the phone as I hung up crossly. I knew he was right – we probably *did* have to sort out the insurance or whatever, but bloody hell, I was in LA. Didn't I just deserve one night off?

There was a knock at my door. 'Alice? It's me, Gretchen!'

I opened the door to see her standing there clutching a champagne bottle and a few glasses. 'Nightcap,' she grinned as she held them up. 'Come on!'

'I shouldn't,' I said uncertainly. 'Long flight tomorrow and all that.'

She looked puzzled. 'But won't you just sleep on the plane?'

I hesitated. And then I heard Tom's voice in my head saying, 'You'd better get some sleep.'

'Go on!' Gretchen smiled mischievously. 'You know you want to!'

And actually, yes – I did.

'I think she was just a little surprised,' I laughed at eight the following morning in the hotel's outdoor hot tub. I sat

48

back in the water and tried not to get champagne or water bubbles from the jets up my nose. 'As put-downs go it was pretty left-field. You're right, I do feel better for this.' I took a sip of my bucks fizz.

'Told you,' Gretchen said. 'Hair of the very hairy dog. Cheers.' We chinked glasses and Gretchen sighed as she leant her head back. 'Well, I had to say something. She was really rude. I mean OK, that poor little make-up girl truly had nothing else to talk about, but you can't just round on people like that. She was the stylist on another shoot I did yonks ago. She was just as bad then, a nasty piss-head bully.' She closed her eyes for a moment. 'I don't want to go home. We've been so lucky with this hot weather! How nice would it be if we could just laze here by the pool all day? Just think, in England we'd be having to drag around in thick jumpers and tights, and here we are *sitting outside*.'

'Don't,' I said, thinking of the brain-freezingly boring Fulham engagement party that lay ahead of me at home. I didn't want to leave LA. I wanted to stay after all.

Gretchen reached for her glass and I noticed, for the first time, a faded squiggly mark on the inside of her left wrist. 'Is that a tattoo?' I said curiously.

She glanced at it. 'Yeah. I got it when I was a dickhead seventeen-year-old.'

'Teenage rebellion?' I asked.

She looked at it thoughtfully. 'Boredom actually. Or maybe I thought I was being anarchic, I can't remember. Nowadays everyone's got one – they're about as anarchic as big pants.'

'Can I see?'

She held her wrist aloft and I spelled out 'T.T.W.P.' then looked at her enquiringly.

'This Too Will Pass,' she said, looking embarrassed. 'It was supposed to remind me to make the most of good times and not let the bad times drag me down.'

'That's impressively profound for a seventeen-year-old, isn't it?' I said. If I'd have come home with a tattoo at seventeen my parents would have spontaneously combusted on the spot – that was much more the sort of stunt Fran would have pulled.

She pulled a face, and then smiled. 'Not really. I didn't know my arse from my elbow . . . or my wrist it seems,' she began, leaning her head back again, but then she frowned and tried to focus. 'Oh my God! Look!' She nudged me.

A hush descended as I looked up to see a tiny, bespectacled gentleman in long orange robes, head down, walking quietly over the wooden footbridge that arched above our heads. He was accompanied by ten other similarly clad, serenely quiet men. It was the Dalai Lama and his entourage.

'Ha!' said Gretchen delightedly. 'It's true! He *is* here. I heard someone at reception say he was staying here but I thought it was bull . . . I mean rubbish,' she said, awestruck. 'Look! He wears Hush Puppies!' she exclaimed. 'How completely random!'

We watched in amazement as the procession silently trotted back to their rooms and finally disappeared out of sight.

'I have a toast,' Gretchen said finally. 'To good times and surreal moments.' She raised her glass again. 'Long may they continue.'

Chapter Six

'She was just really, really nice,' I said enthusiastically to Tom. 'Last night, after I got off the phone to you, we all had a drink in her room and the stylist, who was a complete wack job, suddenly turned on the poor little make-up girl for no apparent reason and had an absolute rant, but Gretchen completely stood up to her.'

'What a warm festive tale,' Tom said drily. 'Celebrity looks after the little people – it's practically a modern day nativity story.'

I gave him a look.

'Oh come on, Al!' he laughed. 'The stylist was hardly going to tell *her* off, was she? It's pretty easy to stand up to people when they're beneath you in the first place.'

I slung my bag down and flopped on to the sofa. 'You're a very cynical man sometimes. All I'm saying is I was wrong about Gretchen, that's all. She was very friendly and extremely professional. She's going to go down a storm in America and she's a genuinely nice person. I felt really bad for being so dismissive of her before I'd even met her.'

'Well good,' said Tom, dropping his car keys on the table and sitting down next to me, facing me side on. 'Seriously, I think it's great you had a good time.'

'Thanks for coming to get me.' I leant towards him to give him a brief kiss.

'You're welcome,' he smiled and kissed me back. 'Want a cup of tea?' he said, our unspoken apologies for the night before over with. 'I thought you'd be totally exhausted but you seem to be buzzing.' He patted my leg, stood up and made his way over to the kettle.

'I think I passed through tired about three hours ago,' I said, 'and no thanks.'

'Vic rang for you last night by the way.'

'Oh great!' I said quickly. 'I'll call her back in a bit – she'll *love* the story about the Dalai Lama. I told you about that, right?'

'You might have mentioned it,' Tom said, shooting me an amused look. 'Oh, and your mum rang too.'

'What? Why? I told her *and* Dad I was going away. They never bloody listen.'

'She wants you to have a chat with Phil about the import-ance of working hard in your last year. Apparently he's not really getting down to studying for his finals as he should be. I told her to ring you on the mobile but she said it'd be too expensive and could you call when you got back. Now, at the risk of *me* pissing you off again by talking about house stuff,' he held up his hands defensively, 'all I need to tell you is that the bloke is moving in on Friday and his name's Paulo. At least I think it is. We had a couple of language problems on the phone.'

'Maybe I'll teach him better English and he can teach me Spanish once he moves in,' I said brightly. 'I've always wanted to learn.'

Tom raised an eyebrow and said, 'How much coffee did you have on this flight back?'

'I'm just happy,' I said. Surely it wasn't that hard for him to believe? I felt slightly irked that he assumed my good mood was in fact hysteria-induced tiredness or a caffeine overload. 'LA rejuvenated me!' I exclaimed. 'That's a good thing, don't you think?'

'I think,' Tom said, coming over and pulling me off the sofa, then wrapping me in a bear hug and planting a kiss on the top of my head, 'that you're very cute and it's nice to see you smiling again. You've had a lot on your plate with the business and Vic going to Paris and everything. It's about time some positive things started to happen for you. Trust me, Al.' He paused. 'There are good times ahead.'

'I hope so.' I leant my head on his chest and closed my eyes.

'I know so.' He began to twirl me lightly on the spot.

'You really enjoyed this trip to America, didn't you?' he said after we'd been standing there companionably for a moment or two in silence, just hugging.

'Yeah, I did,' I said. 'It was fun. Why?'

'No reason.' He hugged me a little tighter. 'No reason at all.'

Vic, however, was a little confused when I recounted the LA jaunt to her on the phone later: 'But I thought you were trying to knock that sort of fluffy stuff on the head?'

'I was,' I said, folding my legs under me and sipping a tea, shivering a little. England was *cold*. I thought longingly of the hot tub.

'So how come you said yes?'

'Money, honey,' I shrugged.

'Ah, the evil lure of the dollar,' Vic conceded. 'Fair enough. So was LA full of fakes, flakes and freaks?'

'Actually no,' I said. 'I had a really good time! The weather was great – I'm so effing freezing back here – and we had a *really* good laugh, although mostly because of Gretchen. Everyone stared at her so blatantly during the shoot, Vic, you wouldn't believe. She took it all in her stride, though. God, I felt hungover on the plane back.'

'Sounds like you had fun. How's Tom?'

'Fine,' I said dismissively. 'Well, I say that, but just before I left he started blathering on about getting a mortgage, saying they were just as much of a commitment as getting married – but since I got back he's not said a word more about it, the big weirdo. Talking of which, can you even believe I saw the Dalai Lama?'

'I know,' Vic agreed. 'Who'd have thought His Holiness would be hanging out in Beverly Hills?'

'Pasadena actually,' I corrected. 'It was at the hotel while we—'

'—were in the hot tub and Gretchen made a toast to surrealism,' finished Vic before I could say anything. 'You said. So backtrack a bit. What do you mean Tom said about getting married? That's huge! What did you say?'

'Nothing really. It's not huge at all, I promise. It felt like it was at first, but it's not. He didn't ask me to marry him, he said he intended to ask me – there's a big difference. You know what he's like, Vic, he was just getting his knickers in a bit of a financial knot. All he actually said was we ought to think about getting a place together because it would be a good time for us to try and buy, and that I shouldn't worry about anything going wrong, because it wasn't going to.' I yawned. 'I think the jet lag is starting to catch up with me.'

'Still, he said the actual M word?'

'Yes,' I admitted. 'But in a forecasting sort of way.'

'Oh. Well I won't buy my hat just yet then. Dear old Tom – always doing things by the book. So. What have you got coming up in the next few days? Any other interesting jobs?'

'Not really,' I considered. 'Gretchen's got a brother who is a travel writer and apparently might know some people who could put some stuff my way. She said she'd call me. She probably won't though – I think it was one of those things you say on a trip like that and don't actually mean.'

There was a silence.

'Hello?' I said. 'Vic? You still there?'

'Yup,' she said eventually.

'There's a hell of a time delay on this line,' I said. 'Do you think I should call her? Or would that look like I was hustling?'

'I don't know.'

'You'd really like her you know, Vic – she's very funny.'

'She sounds a hoot.'

Right on cue my mobile, which was lying on the sofa next to me, began to ring.

'Oh my God!' I said in surprise, catching sight of the name on the phone. 'You're not going to believe this but that's actually her calling me now! I'd better take it. Can I call you back?'

I quickly hung up and grabbed my mobile.

'Alice?' said a bright voice. 'It's Gretchen Bartholomew.'

'Hello!' I exclaimed happily. 'How was your flight back?'

'Oh great, thanks,' she said. 'Couple of movies, nice glass of champagne and the most fantastic foot massage I think I've ever had. I'd marry Richard Branson if he weren't already taken . . . and didn't have hair like Aslan.

Not that it was actually him who did the foot massage, of course.'

'I kind of got that,' I smiled.

'So how was *your* journey? It's such a shame we were on different flights.'

I thought of the stinky bloke who'd sat next to me, exuding such potent curry fumes from every pore on his body, I'd subtly asked to move, and then had to suffer the embarrassment of the hostess coming back and saying, 'There are no free seats, I'm afraid. I can get you a blanket to wrap round your head though if the smell,' she nodded at the man, 'gets much worse?'

Horrified, I'd looked at the man, who had stared, deeply insulted, back at me. It had been an uncomfortably long eleven hours in every sense.

'It was OK,' I said to Gretchen.

'Good! Now, I spoke to my brother and he told me about some luxury travel magazine launch party he's been invited to. He's away though so he can't go, but I thought it might be right up your street . . . I've got my agent to wangle us two invites. It's next Friday night at the Dorchester. You free?'

It turned out I was. Very. I called Vic back excitedly to tell her, but she didn't pick up – probably Doctor Luc had just got home from work. A luxury travel magazine! Tom had been right: good things *were* waiting just around the corner!

'Well, I'm just so sorry,' Gretchen said in the back of the taxi, smoothing out her skirt as she crossed her legs and flicked an invisible spot from her very high heels. 'What a bunch of leathery, mahogany, Hooray Henrys. It was like Eton does *Saga* magazine. Who the bloody hell goes on cruises these days anyway?'

I laughed. 'Please don't feel bad. It was very kind of you to fix it up for me in the first place.'

'Well, I tried,' she shrugged. 'Still, we had a laugh anyway, didn't we? And unlike the readership of that magazine, the night is still young. I need to make this up to you. Let's go and grab a proper drink. I'm a member of a club not far from here.'

I hesitated. I'd never actually been to a private members' club and, much as I didn't want to be, was quite curious to see inside one. Then equally, our new Spanish flatmate was moving in later. But Tom was also a bit on edge, marching around talking firmly about getting off on the right foot, not giving an inch or sliding down a slippery slope, which all sounded exhausting. It would probably be better if I just stayed out of the way and let him deal with it. Anyway, a drink would be fun. Gretchen was certainly dressed for it in an artfully cut midnight-blue dress that I'd admired on sight. She was the perfect person to have a glamorous Friday night drink with. It was nice to see her again.

'That,' I smiled, 'sounds very good to me indeed.'

Chapter Seven

At the club, Gretchen found us a table with two deep armchairs and ordered us a couple of cocktails. I looked around discreetly. It didn't really look that much different to a nice bar, except there were more people staring furiously at laptop screens and some *very* good looking and attentive bar staff. There was also a quiet air of excited expectation, but that might just have been me.

'So,' said Gretchen. 'Tell me what's new with you. What interesting jobs have you got coming up? My agent loved the LA shots you did, by the way. She said you did some work for some of the gossip mags – inside Surrey footballers' houses, that kind of thing. That must have been . . . an experience.' She kicked her shoes off easily, curled her legs under her, took a sip of her drink and waited eagerly.

'That's one way of putting it,' I said, remembering the monogrammed carpet and outdoor infinity pool the couple were determined to pose in, although they almost went blue it was so cold. 'That was just a one-off really, as a favour to a friend. I do quite a lot of studio stuff, too.'

'Do you do any of the fashion mags?' She sipped her drink.

'I've done some of them, yeah. Not so much since I've gone out on my own, but one or two. They're all completely mad.' I shook my head and sat back in my seat comfortably.

'I'll bet,' she laughed. 'Quite cliquey too, I'd imagine.'

'I can see how they'd appear that way,' I said, thinking about it, 'but it's mostly because they're—'

Before we could continue, a couple of men wandered over to us, completely ignored me and said excitedly, '*Hiiiiii*, Gretch! You coming to the party in a bit?'

'Oh, who's having one?' she said interestedly, sitting up like a meerkat and peering over my shoulder.

'Not *entirely* sure,' the man wrinkled his nose, 'but Daniel Craig is supposed to be coming, so who gives a fuck? Want me to stick you on the list?'

Feeling a bit like Cinderella, I reached for my drink, annoyed with myself for minding that I wasn't invited to a party that, until three seconds ago, I hadn't even known existed.

'Yeah, why not. Could be good for a giggle,' said Gretchen. 'Alice's surname is Johnston.' She nodded at me pointedly, forcing them to acknowledge me too.

'Cool.' The blokes smiled at me vaguely before drifting off.

'It'll probably be crap,' Gretchen said conspiratorially, 'these things usually are, aren't they? But we could have a couple more here and then go over and see if we can damage Daniel?' She reminded me a bit of Vic when she said that. Was it the glint of mischief in her eye? Or maybe it was because sitting around plotting together was the kind of thing Vic and I usually did. Not in a members' club, obviously.

'I think he's got a girlfriend,' I said, although I was with her on that one, he *was* pretty beautiful.

Gretchen smiled naughtily. 'I'm sure she could lend him out for the night. Tell you what, let's get a bottle.' She looked up for a waiter and then, as he began to approach, said, 'We don't want to be the first ones there. Now, dish the dirt about the fashion mags. You must have had some funny things happen?'

An hour and a half later we were still talking. Eased along by the booze, we had started to open up to each other a bit and were beginning to trade stories about ourselves. I had just burst out laughing so loudly at something she'd said, several people had turned round and looked at us.

'I'm being *serious*!' She grinned delightedly at my reaction and swatted my arm.

'Of course you were,' I chuckled and placed a hand on my stomach. 'Sorry. Carry on with what you were saying.' I wiped an eye and steadied myself.

'My point was, you *did* just know you wanted to be a photographer,' Gretchen said. 'See?'

'But who just falls into presenting on TV? I don't get it.'

'I swear to God it's the truth,' Gretchen said. 'I honestly never really wanted to do all this in the first place. If Mum hadn't *shoved* me into it, I probably would have just quite happily pratted around in a band at a university or something and that would have been as far as it went. That was the bit I really liked, you see. Singing.'

Just as she finished her sentence, my mobile lit up on the table. I saw *Dad mob* flash up on the screen.

'Sorry, Gretchen, would you mind if I just take this very quickly? It's my father – he practically never uses his mobile, so it must be an emergency.'

'Not at all. Go for it.' She sat up straighter in her chair, interested.

'Everything OK, Dad?' I said, picking up.

'No, it's bloody well not. Have you borrowed the car?'

What? '*Your* car?' I asked, completely baffled. 'Why on earth would I have your car? I'm in London! You do know I haven't lived at home for about eight years or so, don't you?'

Gretchen looked amused, which absurdly, for a second, made me feel pleased. Then I remembered at twenty-eight I was a little old to be showing off in front of new friends. Dad didn't laugh either. 'Hmph,' he said. 'Well I didn't really think it would be you, you're the only bloody sensible one, but I've just got back from a walk with the dog and it's gone.'

'The car or the dog?' I said, trying to focus.

'The car!' he said impatiently. 'I'm actually standing in the space where it should be. Your mother took her car to the shops, Frances doesn't even drive, which means either it's been stolen *or* that little toerag brother of yours has come home and swiped it. Have you spoken to him today?'

'No,' I replied, 'Mum did say he might be coming back to you from uni this weekend, though. Dad, can I call you back? It's just I'm—'

'I *knew* it!' he cut across me. 'Bloody boy!'

Then he hung up.

I shook my head in disbelief and slid the phone on to the table. 'Sorry about that. My dad's having a trying day.'

'Don't worry about it,' Gretchen said airily. 'My mum's been having a trying day for the last fifteen-odd years. Parents, eh? Who'd have 'em?' She grinned and took a large slug of her drink.

'So,' I picked up the threads of conversation again, 'where were we? How's your campaign to conquer the States going, by the way?'

'Oh I doubt anything will come of that.' She waved a hand dismissively. 'It was my agent's idea – create a bit of false buzz, make it look like everyone wants me . . . people only chase things they think someone else wants, it's human nature. I don't really want to move to the other side of the planet much anyway. It'd be nice to get some distance from my parents . . .'

'Indeed.' I grinned and nodded at my phone.

'Exactly,' she agreed, 'you know what I mean. But I'd miss my brother loads.'

'One of my friends just moved to Paris,' I said. 'With her boyfriend.'

'Yeah you see, I wouldn't even have a bloke to take with me. I *was* dating this chopper from a boyband – complete twat – it was like going out with a cocktail sausage who thought it could sing.'

'I think I remember reading you were seeing him,' I said carefully, not wanting to feign ignorance, but equally not wanting to make her feel uncomfortable.

'I'm sure.' Gretchen was unfazed. 'But what it wouldn't have said was he was so obsessed with keeping his six-pack he used to do four hours of exercise a *day*. I once found him in the loo jogging on the spot because he hadn't been able to get to the gym to do his last hour. Between that and him only wanting to talk about his music – even though he couldn't strum more than "Smoke on the Water" – *and* him having to wear outfits approved by his management, he wasn't exactly ever going to be husband material. Also he hated that I could sing better than him,' she grinned.

'So if you like singing so much, why don't you pursue your own music career?' I could see she'd make the perfect pop princess.

She shook her head. 'I'd get slated. "Kids' presenter turns

singer." I'd only get offered novelty records, then before you can say "Pantomime", your career is in the toilet. It's a shame though. When I sing, I feel like I'm on top of a wave . . . just totally free. At times like that, you can almost capture the essence of what you are and everything that you can be. It's like a high. Sometimes you *are* a bit high, obviously, but everything is still amplified and brighter somehow. I love that feeling. When everything seems to make sense. You get total clarity about what you can do, what you can achieve. You know?'

She wasn't really asking me though, she was staring into space as she contemplated the compelling state she'd just described. I looked at her curiously; she had suddenly become a quieter and more reflective version of herself.

'Well it's never too late,' I said after a pause. 'I never thought I'd start out on my own, but I did and I don't regret it for one second.'

'Oh I don't regret it,' she said quickly. 'I don't do regrets – waste of time and energy. It's really great that you were so brave though, you should be proud of yourself.' She drained her drink, suddenly cheerful again, like she'd been plugged back in. 'Thanks for letting me bang on about that. Right, we need to go and have some fun. All this bonding is lovely, but Bond himself might actually be in that room over there. Whoever sees him first gets first go, OK?'

Watching Gretchen work a room was a masterclass in how to make an impact, although she didn't even seem to be aware she was doing it. She paused, poised on the threshold just long enough for everyone to notice her, smiled as she saw someone she knew and then cut straight through to the centre of the room, long blonde hair bouncing around like she was in a pop video. People even stepped back slightly to let her pass. I, however, made my way to the side bar and got a drink so I could people-watch in peace. There seemed to be a lot of arm touching, laughing, air kissing and peering over shoulders to see who else was arriving. Sadly there was no sign of Daniel Craig; only Craig David, which wasn't the same thing *at all*.

'This is rubbish,' Gretchen said, appearing by my arm ten minutes later. 'You seen him yet?'

'No,' I shook my head, 'these drinks are nice though.'

'I reckon they must be in some VIP bit somewhere.' Gretchen looked around thoughtfully. 'They have private rooms here.'

'In a private members' club?' I giggled. 'Just how much privacy can anyone need? It's like MI5 in this place.'

But before she could answer me, there was a loud 'Ladies and gentlemen' from the front of the room, and a man I vaguely recognised holding a microphone said, 'Welcome on behalf of The Bengal Tiger Protection Society – keeping these beautiful beasts alive for the next generation to enjoy. We've now reached the auction part of the proceedings.'

'Come on!' Gretchen hissed to me. 'Let's go and take a look about while they're all distracted!'

She grabbed my arm and rather reluctantly I began to follow. It wasn't that I didn't want to explore; when I was little and we were dragged around draughty castles and National Trust houses, what fascinated me more than anything were the doors marked Private, behind which I imagined secret passages stretching away. I used to long to slip through them and see what was going on behind the scenes, but, much like now, I really didn't want to get into trouble either.

As we reached the doorway, however, the compere said, 'Our first lot is a *signed* pair of Christian Louboutins. You may never want to wear these out in the rain, ladies! A slightly early Christmas present for yourself perhaps?'

Gretchen stopped in her tracks, spun round and said, 'Hang on a minute,' putting her arm out to stop me.

'Who will start the bidding at five hundred pounds?' the compere asked warmly.

I shook my head. It was a pair of shoes for crying out loud, and wouldn't it be easier to save the tigers, wherever they were, just by donating directly?

'Thank you, madam, five hundred pounds I am bid,' he said, quick as a flash, pointing in my direction. My mouth fell open – I'd not shaken my head to bloody bid! Then I realised he was talking to Gretchen, who was standing next to me, excitedly biting her lip and jiggling lightly on the spot with one hand in the air. Five hundred quid! Was she mad?

It seemed she wasn't the only one, however. Several women wanted to get their paws on those red soles and the amount quickly rose to fifteen hundred. I had sobered up completely and couldn't believe what I was hearing. Tigers were a worthwhile beneficiary but . . .

Then it all leapt into fast forward. The compere, delighted at such a frenzy on the first lot of the evening, daringly raised the bar to two thousand pounds – and Gretchen nodded. I reached out and put a hand on her arm. 'Do you even know if they're your size?'

'Who cares?' she said. 'I'll just buy new feet.'

Another woman raised the amount to £2100. Gretchen frowned and impulsively called out '*Five* thousand pounds!' A low murmur of appreciation swept round the room as people turned to look at us and I nearly dropped my drink. The camera equipment I could get with that!

The compere beamed at her. 'Wonderful! Do I have £5100?' The room hushed in anticipation. No one spoke. 'Then going once, twice, three times and sold to the enchanting lady at the back of the room!'

Gretchen laughed excitedly. 'Oh what fun!' she said. 'This is even better than Daniel Craig!'

In the taxi home to mine and then Gretchen's – that she'd made wait while she finished a cigarette – she stroked her new shoes and said, 'I just love them.'

I shook my head in the dark. 'I still can't believe you did that.'

She leant her head back on the seat. 'I know – I should have listened to you. Still, it's only money. It ended up being a great night, didn't it?'

'Absolutely!' It actually really had been. I was buzzing – just like LA again.

She suddenly became serious and said, 'Al, I've got a confession to make. Promise you won't hate me?'

'I promise,' I said, intrigued.

'I sort of asked you out tonight because I thought if I made it look like I was helping you, you might get me in with some of your fashion mag contacts. You have no idea how hard it is to get them to even consider you for a feature unless you've married Brad Pitt or won an Oscar or something, and I really need to raise my profile.'

'Oh,' I said. And felt really crap. All of a sudden she didn't remind me of Vic at all.

'Sorry.' She was a little shamefaced. 'It was a bit underhand of me. Oh, don't look like that!' She grabbed my arm. 'I know what you must be thinking, but I've genuinely really had fun. I really *have!*' she sounded almost surprised, 'and we did have a blast in LA. I've got another confession, too: these shoes are about half a size too big for me. What size are you? Do you want them?' She held them out to me.

'Don't be stupid!' I said. 'Put them on eBay or something. I don't think you're going to recoup the five grand you spent on them though, you loony.'

She looked at me intently. 'I haven't pissed you off, have I? Still friends?'

I hesitated. She waited anxiously, hands clasping the Louboutins, framed by the black cab window. She'd merely wanted a leg-up the glossy magazine ladder, in her point-less, ludicrous shoes . . . but then she had been big enough to be honest with me and come clean. She must genuinely mean what she was saying. Otherwise, why bother? I'd enjoyed her company. It was rare to meet someone interesting and funny but good at listening, too. Sparkly new friends like her didn't exactly drop into my lap every day of the week and you could have different friends for different reasons, couldn't you? Not everyone could know me inside out, like Vic did, and be there for every problem. Gretchen'd make a great coffee and cocktail partner in crime.

'Still friends,' I said.

Chapter Eight

I think it's the smell — the smell of hospitals that I can't handle. I close my eyes and try to breathe deeply through my mouth.

Tom cannot sit still next to me; he's twitching and stop-starting with panic, fear and powerlessness. I can feel his every movement run down my arm because we are gripping hands as if our lives depend on it. We are waiting in the mercifully empty relatives' room, the walls of which are a washy, spearmint green and I think it must be cold, despite the big old-fashioned iron radiators, because I am shaking. Helpful leaflets are stuck all over the place, some resting on top of a drinks machine. There are seven chairs and a small table, tucked tight against the wall, which I am next to. Tom is to my left.

We are both so frightened that, for the first time ever, we have nothing that we can say to each other. My teeth start to chatter and when I try to stop them, they won't. Neither of us can bear to think about what might be happening down the corridor in that room. All I can see is that red, flat line on the monitor slicing through the centre of the screen; continuous, unarguable and definite. I'm trying to think of something, anything else – for some bizarre reason I imagine me, Fran and Phil as children playing on a roundabout, Phil is using his foot to push us faster and faster – but then the red line appears at the edge and crashes right through the middle of the picture, cutting us all in half.

The door opens at that point and a very real nurse comes in. The line vanishes immediately and I scan her face desperately, looking for clues – is she smiling? Is her brow creased with empathy, ready to help us through the shock of hearing, 'I'm so sorry, we did everything that we could but . . .'?

She walks straight over to us and sits down. Then it's actually happening before I have time to imagine the rest.

'Gretchen has had a problem with her heart,' she says. 'She's had a cardiac arrest.'

Everything slows right down around me again, this time like I've been plunged into an ice bath. Her words feel unreal; I'm staring at her face but it sounds like she's speaking underwater. I begin to squeeze Tom's hand so fiercely it must hurt him.

'It's beating normally again,' she continues, her voice becoming clearer in my ears, like I'm surfacing, 'but it's a concern that it happened at all. It shows how strong the drugs she took are, that they've had a very real effect on her body.' Her eyebrows knit together in concern and she waits for us to digest what she's saying. 'She wasn't aware of what was happening, though. It won't have caused her any distress.' She pauses again, as if that knowledge is somehow supposed to make a difference. It doesn't.

'Is she all right now?' Tom asks the only thing that really matters.

'We've managed to stabilise her.'

He looks at the nurse bravely. 'Could it happen again?'

'It might, yes. She's young and strong though, that's very much in her favour. I'll come and get you just as soon as they're done in there, take you back through, OK?' She smiles reassuringly, calm with experience and being older than us – all of about thirty-five, I'd say. 'You know, this bit is actually harder for you than it is for her.'

I want to laugh at that, albeit hysterically. I watch her enviously as she leaves the room; smoothing down her subtly highlighted hair, stepping neatly and nonchalantly out of the nightmare.

Tom stands up, reaches into his pocket and pulls out some change. Then he walks over and slots it into the machine, placing a cup under a spout that dispenses not even enough brown liquid to half fill it. Then he empties three sachets of sugar and stirs it lightly with a plastic stick.

'Try and drink this,' he says, coming back and handing it to me, 'it'll help.' The tea is the colour of watered-down tar and is giving off the bitter aroma of burnt tyres, but it's warm, so I huddle over it and even take a small sip. He collapses down next to me, drained by the dissipating adrenalin.

We sit in silence for a moment more, then he says, 'You did tell them everything about Gretchen? Didn't you?' His mind is still circling.

'What, that this isn't the first time she's tried to do this?'

It's like forcing a door marked Private. I feel invasive and voyeuristic discussing such intimate and painful secrets from Gretchen's past like you might say, 'Did you mention she's allergic to aspirin?' I know Tom doesn't want to do it any more than I do.

He nods, with difficulty. 'So they know that . . .'

70

'Tom,' I say, my head swimming. 'I told them everything I could.' Which, strictly speaking, is true.

'I'm not having a go, Al, I'm just trying to think of something, anything we can do that might help her.'

Watching him desperately struggle with trying to make sense of this is breaking me. I put my cup down and reach for a magazine, setting it on my lap, but tears are welling up in my eyes again and the model's smiley face goes all blurry. They threaten to splash over, down on to the ancient cover, which is undulating like sand dunes but is as crisp and brittle as old bone – a thousand different liquids having been spilled and dried on it.

Tom's hand gently appears and removes the magazine, as he reaches an arm round my shoulder and draws me to him. As I release a sob on his shoulder he says, 'Shhhhh' quietly, and, 'It's going to be all right, you'll see.'

But I don't see. I don't see how this can be all right in the slightest and him soothing me is almost more than I can bear. After everything I've put him through . . . as if that wasn't enough, now this. What kind of person am I?

'Her mum and dad,' Tom says, obviously trying to think rationally, 'they really should be here. Did Bailey . . .' He says his name stiffly.

'I expect so. I'm sure he would have done.'

I can feel him tensing up, his arm tightening round me. 'Well you say that, but—'

'Tom!' I exclaim bleakly, which he totally misinterprets.

'Don't "Tom" me!' he bursts angrily. 'If he'd just got to hers when he said he was going to –' He releases me. 'He might have found her earlier! Before she'd done anything – when she was just drunk!'

'That's not fair, Tom,' I begin. 'It's not his fault that—'

'Of course it fucking is!' Tom explodes. 'It's absolutely

71

his fault! He wasn't there when he said he was going to be! He never thinks of anyone but himself, never stops to consider other people and the impact of his actions.' He balls his fist up so tightly his knuckles go white. 'This is fucking typical of him!'

I wait and then I say quietly, 'He just missed a plane, Tom. That's all. You have every right to be angry with him for –' I struggle to find the right words '– other stuff. But he'd never have *let* something like this happen to her. He was worried sick when I spoke to him earlier.'

There is a silence and Tom clenches his jaw. 'Other people manage to be reliable, do what they're supposed to do, so why can't he? What's so fucking special about *him*?'

He almost shouts that last bit, right there in the relatives' room, and I look shamefacedly at the floor, because I'm not sure if that's just a rhetorical question, or he's actually asking me.

Chapter Nine

'Alice Johnston!' Gretchen's voice carried jauntily down the phone. 'It's me. So here's the thing – are you around this morning?'

'I can be.' I turned over in bed, glancing at the space next to me that meant Tom had already left for football training. 'All I had planned was a run. Why?'

'A *run*?' she said. 'What on earth do you want to do something like that for?'

'Because it's March! I can only hide the effects of my mother's annual Christmas force-feeding under baggy jumpers for so long – and next Saturday she's going to stuff a load of Easter eggs down our necks too. Before you know it, it'll be bikini weather and I'll want to kill myself.'

'Al, don't be such a prat,' Gretchen said dismissively. 'Running sucks. Come and have a coffee and some cake instead. I'm meeting my brother in a bit and I want you to come too so you can talk to him about his contacts. It's only taken four months for me to sort it, but your patience, my darling, has paid off.'

'*Finally*,' I said, 'because it's been a real hardship having to be friends with you in the meantime . . .'

She laughed. 'I know, I'm crap. Sorry. Still, better late than never.'

'Gretch,' I yawned, 'I'll happily come and have coffee with you because it'll be fun to finally meet your brother, not for any other reason. D'you want to come into town with me afterwards? I've got something to pick up.'

'A fun something or a boring camera something?' she asked suspiciously.

I laughed. 'A camera something, but we can have a poke around some nice shops too if you like?'

'OK,' she said happily. 'Sounds fun. I'm hooking up with Bailey at about half twelve, does that give you enough time?'

Actually, if it hadn't been for my mother ringing and making me late because she was ranting on about how Frances had taken a family-run dry-cleaners' to the small claims court over a rip on the hem of her wedding dress, which was very embarrassing because the dry-cleaner lady was in her slimming group on a Tuesday night and would I ring Fran to try and talk sense into her?, I'd have been slightly early.

As it was, I emerged bang on time from the tube to make my way to the address Gretchen had given me. Pale sunshine was trying to break through indecisive cloud as the shop fronts I passed started to become smaller but more enticingly expensive. They all had glossy, confidently painted names and weren't selling things you'd need, but things you'd want: handmade chocolates, hats, silky-rich bottles of wine, contemporary jewellery . . . It was one of those pockets of London that inhabitants claim feels cosy and village-like, but everyone reads about in the society pages of newspaper supplement magazines.

I wasn't feeling very cosy in the soggy, cold ballet pumps that had proven far from ideal footwear for the flash of rain I'd got caught in my side of the underground. I'd been aiming for a whole Springtime in Paris look, but was actually freezing in my silly, thin jacket. All in all it was a relief to arrive at the café, although I had to have a brief tussle with the stiff door, which seemed to have swollen in the damp air. I burst in with more energy than I'd intended to.

The intoxicating smell of roasted coffee wrapped warmly round me. Caffeine-fuelled customers were busily peering at papers over piled plates of food, as hot, harassed waitresses tried to seat newcomers while balancing full trays of tipping and slipping cappuccinos. I scanned the room and saw Gretchen waving frantically at the back.

She was wearing worn, artfully faded, stompy leather boots on bare, smooth brown legs and a sort of cotton, cream, ethnic-looking tunic thing under an oversized chunky knit cardigan that looked like it was about to slip off her slim shoulders. A long string of brightly coloured beads dangled round her neck and tangled with her loose hair. She had her hands wrapped tightly round a steaming mug of coffee and looked delighted to see me. As ever, both men and women were trying not to stare at her, but if she was aware, she didn't let on.

She set her coffee down unsteadily as she jumped up and wrapped me in an impulsive, enthusiastic hug. 'Hello!' she said. 'Perfect timing, I was just about to succumb and order one of those incredible-looking almond croissants. Have you even *seen* the cakes over there?' She pointed and I looked over curiously. She was right, they looked amazing. Big sugary wheels of glossed, flaky pastries, fatly snug blobs of cream bursting out of choux buns, delicate cupcakes adorned with cherries and angelica.

I sat down opposite her, facing the door and commented, 'You're very bouncy today. Have you had good news about that American ice dance thing?'

'Nooooo,' she pulled a face. 'Still nothing. I got asked to do a guest spot on *Good Haunting* yesterday though.'

'Oh. Did you say yes?'

'What, so I can stand in some dark, tumbledown shack in the back end of beyond with a crew filming in infrared while their "expert" deliberately throws himself over a table and then claims a ghost attacked him?' She raised an eyebrow. 'It's not come to that yet – although no one told me the switch between kids to adults would be *this* hard. Anyway, what do you want to drink and eat?'

'Shouldn't we wait for your brother?' I said.

She waved a hand dismissively. 'He's already here, he's in the bog. Oh hang on – talk of the devil.' She looked over my shoulder and grinned. 'Bay, this is my friend Alice, the one I've nagged you about. Alice, this is my brother Bailey.'

I turned and saw a tall man standing to my right, smiling a friendly smile. He had scruffy, sandy-coloured hair that was drifting into sleepy, green eyes. In fact he looked as if he'd just woken up and tumbled out of bed. He was wearing a white T-shirt with a very faded image of a wave on it and, when he extended his hand, I saw a pale scar running the length of his tanned forearm, which I imagined he'd got from rock climbing, white-water rafting or something equally as adrenalin junkie-fied – he looked the type. He saw me looking at his scar. 'Gretchen pushed me off a space hopper because I wouldn't let her have a go,' he confided. 'I cut it open on the rockery.' Which wasn't quite what I was expecting. Then he yawned and stretched like a cat.

'Ouch,' I said, embarrassed to have been caught staring. 'It must have been really deep – how old were you?'

'Twenty-six,' he grinned disconcertingly. 'Nice to meet you, Alice, excuse my impolite yawn.' He leant over the table and kissed me briefly, stubble grazing my cheek as I caught a brief tang of expensive-smelling aftershave. 'I'm a bit jet lagged.'

'Just ignore him, Al,' said Gretchen. 'Sit down and stop showing off, Bay.'

Bailey threw his arms open in easy protest as he scooched his chair round and asked, 'So Grot tells me you're a photographer?' He reached across Gretchen and grabbed her coffee. 'Nice of you to wait for me and Alice,' he said pointedly. 'Rude.' He set the cup back down again, his eyes flickering interestedly back on to me for a moment and then moving away just as quickly. 'Ah, is that our waiter?' He looked over my shoulder.

'Can you *not* call me that?' Gretchen sighed. 'What with me not being six any more? You were in the loo for ages, I thought you'd fallen in. I'll get someone to come over now. Hang on.'

She stood up abruptly and walked to the front of the café. A waiter looked up appreciatively as she approached, along with the entire table he was serving. I watched as one of the girls at the table covered her mouth and whispered something to her friend. The friend then stared unabashed at Gretchen, her eyes widening as she recognised her, and whispered delightedly back. I was beginning to get more used to people openly talking about Gretch as if she wasn't there, but hadn't got to the stage where I could completely ignore it – like Gretchen herself.

'Shit, isn't it?' Bailey said, following my gaze. 'Thank God she's not Tom Cruise famous. I don't know how it doesn't bother her, but she claims it doesn't. The first time I read some of the online comments people had made about her, people who have never even met her, I just wanted to track them all down and beat them to a fucking pulp, the bastards. You know it's the women that write the most vitriolic things? Whatever happened to sisterhood?'

I shrugged and smiled in what I hoped was an enigmatic way, because I couldn't think of anything clever or insightful in response to that.

'I think you chose the right side of the camera,' he said lightly. 'So what sort of stuff do you do?'

'At the moment?' I cleared my throat. 'Pretty much everything: products, people, locations. I used to work for a large studio but I've recently gone out on my own.'

'Hats off to you,' he said. 'Is it going well?'

'Pretty well, thank you. Except I keep finding myself saying yes to work I'm not wild about because I'm worried about keeping the cash flow up, but then I don't have as much time to chase the jobs I really want to do.'

'The travel stuff? Yeah, Gretchen said. Well, I'll gladly give you some names of editors I write for. How much use they'll be I couldn't say, but it's a toe in the door, isn't it?'

'Absolutely,' I said gratefully. 'That's very kind of you.'

He shrugged. 'Not at all – I'm happy to help out.'

Gretchen reappeared. 'He's coming over in a sec. I really need a wee. I'll be right back.'

Bailey glanced at her disappearing back. 'So how long have you known my sis?'

'Um, about four months-ish?' I watched his long, slender fingers pick up a paper napkin absently and begin to play with the edges. He had surprisingly elegant hands. 'We met on a shoot in LA . . . towards the end of November.'

'Ahh.' He sat back and draped his arm across the top of Gretchen's empty chair, which made his T-shirt ride up a bit, exposing a strip of flat, brown stomach which he made no effort to hide, and saw me glance at. 'Did you go up into the hills? There's some good hiking up there.'

'It was quite a tight time frame actually,' I said quickly, thinking of us lounging around in the hotel hot tub drinking champagne. 'I'll have to do that next time. I suppose that's one of the great things about being a travel writer, you must know all the best places to go and things to see?'

'Kind of. It's just given me an brilliant excuse to explore really.' He smiled and looked directly at me. 'It's such a big, beautiful world out there. If I lived to be a hundred I'd never see everything I want to. I just came back from Tanzania. Have you been to Africa before?'

I nodded. 'Not Tanzania though. What's it like?'

'Incredible. I was up in the mountains for a couple of nights where it was just crystal clear and cold, sat round this campfire under the stars, and then the day after we were down in the Ngorongoro crater which is about 10k by 10k, it's vast, just stuffed full with the most incredible animals – elephants, hippos, lions, you name it . . . totally wild, just going about their business.'

'Wow,' I said. 'You lucky thing.'

'I know!' He shook his head in disbelief. 'I was in the back of this safari jeep at five in the morning clutching a pair of binoculars as we bombed around thinking, "And I'm getting *paid* for this?" Life is good. I'm a lucky man.' He smiled again and then glanced away from me at an approaching waiter.

I snuck another quick look. I could just see the edges of a tattoo on a very honed arm peeking out from the sleeve of his T-shirt. I wondered if, like Gretchen, he thought his was a mistake – I couldn't really see what the design was. His arms were *really* strong. I lifted my gaze and realised he was watching me looking at him.

'You've got a very nice bicep – I mean tattoo!' I said, horrified.

Bailey laughed, but before he could say anything in response, the waiter arrived at our table. 'Helllllllllooooooo!' he said in a very heavy accent I couldn't place, pen poised. 'And what are we eating today?'

I could feel myself getting hot under Bailey's amused gaze. 'I'll have a coffee and a shovel, please,' I said. 'I'd like to dig myself a hole and this isn't quite up to the job.' I picked up Gretchen's teaspoon and held it up to the puzzled waiter. Bailey smiled.

'OK.' The waiter was clearly confused. 'You want haf a bigger spoon?' He spoke so fast I could barely understand him.

'No, no. I was saying I needed a different . . . spoon.'

'This spoon is *dirty*?' the waiter exclaimed, mortified. He grabbed the offending item from my hand suspiciously, holding it up to the light. 'Madam! I am so sorry!'

'She meant she needed *another* spoon,' Bailey explained and pointed to the one the waiter was still holding. 'That one was not enough.'

'Ahh!' The waiter said, brightening. 'I understand. I will do it now. Coffee for you as well, sir?' Bailey gave a thumbs up and the waiter scribbled on his pad. 'And for food, madam?'

'Just a muffin, thanks.'

He nodded. 'Chuckle a sheep or plan?'

I stared at him blankly. 'I'm sorry?'

'Chuckle a sheep or plan?' he repeated.

Bailey leant in towards me. 'Chocolate-chip or plain?' he whispered helpfully.

'Ah!' I grinned as the penny dropped. 'Sorry! Plain, please!'

Once the waiter had left, we sat there in silence for a

moment. 'It's unfortunate really,' I said eventually, 'that my initial joke wasn't even that funny in the first place – it certainly didn't stand up to that much scrutiny.'

Bailey nodded. 'I know, I felt bad for you. Even the poor spoon was embarrassed.'

'Oh come on!' I laughed. 'It wasn't *that* bad.'

He stared at me again. 'You have a really lovely smile,' he said. 'Ah ha! Here's the coffee already! Wow, that was quick! Thank you!' He moved Gretchen's cup so the waiter could proudly set down our order as I sat there wondering if I'd just heard him right.

My coffee was accompanied by two teaspoons balanced on the saucer and a completely random blueberry muffin. Gretchen returned a second later to find us laughing.

'What's so funny?' she asked.

'Oh, nothing,' Bailey waved a hand dismissively. 'It was some complex cutlery comedy. Too highbrow for the likes of you.'

'Tell me!' she insisted. 'I hate being left out.'

'Honestly Gretch, it really was a crap joke,' I said apologetically.

'Please don't make her repeat it,' Bailey shook his head. 'It *stank*.'

'Oh come on!' I said, pretending to be outraged. 'It was no worse than your "I was twenty-six ah ha ha" remark.'

'You laughed at that!'

'I was being polite!'

Gretchen looked between the two of us, rubbed her nose rather loftily and said, 'Sounds *hilarious*. I guess you had to be there.'

Bailey chuckled. 'Oh don't go getting all huffy, just because it doesn't concern you. If you really want to know, it was about a spoon and—'

'I'm not bothered really,' she interrupted dismissively. 'In fact, you can fork off.'

I groaned and Bailey laughed.

'*Now* we're done with the cutlery jokes,' she finished smugly and took a satisfied sip of her coffee.

We all chatted away for another hour before Bailey eventually checked his watch and said, 'Right, ladies, I have to get back and finish this piece I'm doing on the Marathon Des Sables. It's this crazy race people do across the Sahara; six days and a hundred and fifty-one miles. In that heat? Can you believe it? I was talking to this guy that did it and he said it nearly killed him, but talk about the ultimate endurance test . . . I might do it next year.'

Gretchen snorted. 'Bet you five hundred quid you don't.'

He offered her his hand, but at the last minute before she could shake it, whisked it away and good naturedly flicked her a V sign instead. 'Thank you both for a really nice brunch.' He stooped and kissed Gretchen's cheek, then reached into his back pocket and pulled out a fat roll of notes. He flicked a tenner on to the table and said, 'That should cover me.' Gretchen reached for her bag but Bailey held up a hand. 'Don't worry about the change. Alice, I'll get your number from Gretchen and text you those contact details, OK?'

'Thank you,' I said sincerely. He waved cheerfully and I watched him walk out of the restaurant.

'He's so full of shit.' Gretchen spoke through a mouthful of cold toast. 'A hundred and fifty-one miles over six days. He'd never do that. He's like Tigger – always bouncing into things thinking he likes them and then, oh, discovering he doesn't. Sorry he went on so much about his travelling.'

'Not at all, it was interesting. Good chat, nice cakes and coffee. I'd say it was the perfect Saturday.' And I meant it.

'It is actually, isn't it?' she smiled, reaching out and squeezing my arm happily. 'Aren't you going to eat that last bit of muffin? Oh come on, it's *tiny*.' She leant across me and swapped our plates round.

'I thought your brother was very nice,' I said.

'Yeah?' She looked up. 'Well, he's single at the moment,' she winked at me, 'want me to put in a good word?'

And in the gap where I should have said, 'Well actually, you know I told you that I was very casually seeing one of my flatmates? That was a bit of a fib. He's really my boyfriend of two years, we live together and he wants us to buy a house and get married, so no thank you,' my mouth said nothing. I waited for it to open and to hear myself saying the words but, to my surprise, it didn't happen.

I didn't say anything at all. I just sat there wondering if being evasive with the truth was the same thing as lying.

Gretchen waited. 'You still involved with that Tom bloke? Or is that properly over now?'

'It's properly over,' I said.

Chapter Ten

'What would you say if I told you I'd done a very bad thing?' I asked Vic in a low voice, unable to keep quiet a second longer.

'I'd say "Ooohhh, tell me more, birthday girl,"' Vic said, linking her arm through mine.

We were strolling lazily through the lush gardens of Versailles, bathed in warm April sunshine. Tom and Luc were chatting earnestly some way ahead of us and I'd been trying to broach telling Vic about my whopping and worrying fib for the last fifteen minutes. It was bad enough that I hadn't told Gretchen the truth, but that I'd lied about my relationship with Tom to someone at all had been eating me up inside with confusion since the very moment the words had come out of my mouth.

'So Gretchen . . .' I began, and Vic immediately shot me a sideways look through narrowed eyes.

'Would that be poxy, stupid Gretchen who you're always out with when I call? It's such a crap name. Makes her sound like she's Heidi's little sister. Does she also keep goats?'

'Er no.' I thought of Gretchen. 'That's about as far removed from her as you could possibly get. You know, I get the feeling you don't like her,' I teased.

'I totally hate her,' she shot back instantly, 'for doing such a blatant snatch and grab on my best friend. It's rude, is what it is.'

I smiled. 'You'd actually like her a lot.'

Vic pondered that. 'Nope,' she said, 'I definitely hate her.'

'Sorry,' I said, shielding my face as I turned to look at her, 'I forget, who was it that moved away and abandoned me for some smooth medical git? Oh, that'd be you.'

'Yeah, yeah,' Vic grinned, but then her smile faded. 'I do miss you though, Al,' she said. 'Lots. Just because I'm out here doesn't mean I don't think about you loads and stuff. Don't totally replace me.'

I squinted at her. 'You don't really think that's what I'm doing, do you?'

'Sometimes,' she confessed. 'Well no, not really, but lately you've been all "Gretchen this and Gretchen that . . ." I spoke to Jess the other day and she said you'd blown out her and all of the other uni girls for dinner because you were snowed under with work again, but yet you seem to have plenty of time to spend with *her*.'

That was true, I did, but it was because Gretch was around a lot during the day to chat and meet up with when I had quieter periods, stretches of time when everyone else – like the uni girls – were at work or in meetings. It was just easy for both of us and nice company. There was no conspiracy.

'I don't want you to be lonely without me,' Vic said quickly, 'I just don't want you to have a friend you like more than me.'

'Not possible,' I smiled at her. 'And you know that.' I meant it too – I liked her and Gretch in completely different ways, but I privately resolved to make more of an effort to phone Vic.

'Tell me a secret *she* doesn't know,' Vic said decisively, lightening the tone again.

'Well, that sort of leads me back to the bad thing.' I glanced ahead to make sure the boys were still out of earshot. 'I met Gretchen's brother over coffee and after he left, I told Gretchen I thought he was nice. I meant to talk to and stuff – he's a travel writer and has been *everywhere* – but then Gretchen sort of hinted he was single and got all nudge nudge, wink wink, should she put in a good word?'

'What?' Vic looked puzzled. 'She knows about Tom though, right?'

'Um,' I scratched my neck uneasily. 'Sort of. She thinks I've been casually seeing my flatmate.'

'Why does she think that?'

'Because that's what I told her,' I said and suddenly found I couldn't look Vic in the eye. There was a pause. 'And she asked me if I was still seeing him or if it was over and my mouth said it was over.'

'Alice!' Vic was shocked. 'Why on earth did you say that? That's an out and out lie!'

'I know,' I said in a small voice. 'I don't know why I did it and I've been driving myself nuts with worry about what it all means.'

'I don't understand,' Vic said. 'You didn't just tell Gretchen you had a boyfriend when you first met her?'

I hesitated and realised what I was about to say was not going to make me look good.

'I know this is really sad,' I confessed, 'but when we

were in LA everyone was really cool and I got a bit swept up by all of it. I just wanted to seem a little less predictable and settled, a bit edgier . . . I know, I know, you don't have to tell me how pathetic that is.' I held up a hand defensively as Vic pulled back slightly and wrinkled her nose at me. 'You'd think I'd have grown out of that kind of crap at school, but I actually tried to be one of the cool girls. At age twenty-eight. I'm a complete knob.'

'Twenty-nine now,' Vic pointed out and sighed. 'You don't secretly fancy Gretchen, do you, and that's why you told her you were single? This isn't your way of telling me you've become a lesbian?'

'Oh shut up, I'm being serious. Remember I told you me and Tom had been talking about mortgages and settling down and this horrible smug engagement party we were going to? I felt like the personification of a Boden cardigan.' I sighed. 'I just wanted to play at being someone else, someone exciting, I didn't think I'd wind up being friends with her, and by then it was too bloody embarrassing to come clean.'

'You tit,' laughed Vic. 'I wonder if Madonna has this much trouble every time she reinvents herself? Look, it's no big deal. It's not like I don't understand what you get out of being friends with her, Al – she's fun, lively, glamorous, you don't have a very deep or demanding friendship – and that's great for you. You just get to have fun. It's nothing to worry about.'

'But when she hinted about me and her brother hooking up, I actively said it was over with me and Tom,' I said. 'You can't tell me that's OK. I feel so guilty about it I can't even begin to tell you. What the hell was I playing at? That's not like me – and now, as if that wasn't bad enough, I keep thinking about him and I'm . . . feeling confused.'

'By "him" do you mean your boyfriend of two years, Tom, who brought you out here for this surprise birthday trip because he thinks he needs to be more spontaneous and romantic—'

'He said that to you?' Shocked, I shielded my face from the sun again and squinted at her, feeling even worse.

Vic nodded. 'Or do you mean the coffee bloke you obviously have a thumping crush on?'

'You think that's all it is?' I said hopefully. 'A crush?'

She pulled a face. 'Of course! What does he look like?'

'Tall—'

'If you say dark and handsome next, I'll punch you,' she interrupted.

I ignored her. 'He's got light hair. He's outdoorsy, obviously works out a lot. At the coffee shop he looked like he'd ridden a wave up to the door of the café and hopped off his board at the last moment, you know? I think he's a bit edgy though – he's a travel writer but he had this massive wodge—'

'Oh la la!' grinned Vic.

'Of money,' I gave her a look, 'in his back pocket. He's got these really green eyes, too, and a cute bum, and . . .'

Vic laughed. 'Oh please! You just want to shag him, that's all. Don't beat yourself up about it! Everyone likes a bit of window shopping now and then. I've got this crush on this bloke I see every day on the Metro and I've barely finished unpacking my stuff at Luc's. He's so my fantasy shag – although I'm pretty sure he must be gay, he's that fit.'

'Really?' I said eagerly, relieved, checking again that Tom still couldn't hear us. 'Because I seriously can't get him out of my head. I keep thinking about how nice he was – he's creative, well travelled, *interesting* and,' I blushed, 'he told me I had a lovely smile, but then he could just like flirting

I guess. He's funny too, Vic . . . we had this sort of spark, I'm sure we did.'

'Whoa.' Vic stopped dead in her tracks. 'He's funny?'

I nodded.

'And you had a spark?'

I nodded again and blushed like a fifteen-year-old.

'Oh shit,' she sighed. 'Oh poor Tom. What's this perfect man's name then?'

'Bailey,' I said dreamily, and she went 'Ha!' so loudly the boys turned round and I practically had to push her into a fountain to shut her up. 'Their parents really hate them, don't they?' she said, trying to suppress another snort of laughter. '*Bailey* . . . what kind of a name is that?'

'His,' I replied warningly and, wisely, she let it go.

'So are you saying you want to do something about it?' she asked eventually.

'Of course not!' I exclaimed. 'He probably has a million women drop at his feet all the time. And he's Gretchen's brother! There are rules about that sort of thing.'

'I'd let you hook up with my brother,' she said.

'Vic, your brother is married with three kids.' I looked ahead at Tom and found myself wondering what it would be like to have Bailey walking there instead, talking to Luc. Then I felt awful that the thought had even occurred to me.

'If he were free, I mean. I don't want your brother though.'

I pulled a face. 'Don't blame you,' I agreed. 'My parents are going to have to pay some woman to take Phil on. Either that or move to a country where conscription is still legal. His exams start soon – God knows what we'll do if he fails them. Mum and Dad are wetting themselves with worry, mostly that he'll be living with them for ever.'

'Why do *you* have to do anything about it if Phil fucks

up? Let your mum and dad sort it out, it's not your problem, Al. You need to be a bit more selfish.'

I fell silent. Vic occasionally got this way about my family. I knew she liked them immensely, but she had also made it very clear that she thought I got the rough end of the family deal.

'Anyway, you realise of course you made no mention of Tom in your reasons why you won't pursue Bailey?' Vic said, after a short pause. 'Which, technically, one could argue should be top of your list?' I was absolutely horrified to realise with a jolt that she was right.

We fell silent and walked a little further.

'What's sex like?' she said, after a moment.

'A sort of special hug with someone you love. Ask Luc to show you.'

She sighed. 'Ha ha. You can joke all you like. I know you're only doing it because you're freaking out. I meant between you and Tom, as well you know.'

'It's OK,' I said. 'Nice.' Which was true, it was – when we did it. A bit like watching a repeat episode of *Friends*: comforting, and I knew exactly what was going to happen next.

'Hmm,' she said doubtfully. 'Just nice?'

'Vic, we've been together a couple of years. That's normal, in fact that's *good*.'

'OK, well maybe all this is just a panic reaction because Tom's decided it's time you two took things to the next level?' she continued. 'Maybe you're just not ready for that yet?'

I shook my head. 'He hasn't said anything about that for months, I'd have told you if he had. He *was* all fired up about starting to look for somewhere to buy but then Paulo moved in and it's like the conversation never even happened.'

'Al,' said Vic slowly, 'do you think there's a chance you might never be ready – for him?'

'I . . . don't know.'

The words floated lightly on the air around us but I suddenly felt indescribably heavy and sad, because as I heard myself say them I realised, for the first time, that I actually *was* having serious doubts about me and Tom. This wasn't just him annoying me with a bit of anal attention to detail or me frustrating him with my cavalier approach to household security, but a real, actual problem. And yet there was no question at all that I loved him. I did, definitely. When I thought about the people I loved – my mum and dad, Fran, Phil, Vic – I knew I felt that way about Tom too.

I looked ahead at him again. He and Luc had stopped and were waiting for us, flopping down on to the grass. Suddenly, I wished I'd never said anything, not made it real, but kept it in my head where I didn't have to do anything with it. Maybe that was why my mouth had said the lie in the first place; I was forcing myself to deal with something I didn't want to have to face.

'I know you love Tom,' Vic said carefully, as if reading my mind. 'I love him too. I love you both. But you know, I also think he loves you quite a lot more than you love him, and I'm not sure that can ever really work long term.'

I looked at her, shocked.

'I'm sorry. I would never have said anything all the time I thought you were happy, because who am I to question it if it works? But it's obviously not working, is it? Regardless of this Bailey – he's just a symptom, not a cause.'

I said nothing. I didn't know what to say. I felt very confused.

'And I don't deny that it's not all horribly complicated by Tom being good looking, nice to be around and basically willing to do anything for you.'

'And that's a bad thing how exactly?'

'It's not – it just makes it even harder because he's ninety per cent perfect. It'd be easy to walk away if he was a complete bastard and not right for you.'

'Oh come on, Vic, no one is one hundred per cent perfect.'

She considered that. 'You know, you're right. If someone's not the one for you, they're not the one. It's academic by how much they miss the mark, twenty per cent, two per cent, who cares? They're still not hitting the spot. You and Tom are both so lovely, you deserve to be with the right people, even if that isn't each other. And don't ask me how you know if he's the one, because if you have to ask, he isn't. It's as simple as that.'

She couldn't say anything else because we caught up with the boys, but I wasn't sure how much more I could listen to in any case. I felt as if a huge weight had sunk on to my shoulders. What had started as a light chat about a crush had suddenly mutated into something else entirely – a dark genie filling the air around me with heavy smoke as it barged its way out of the bottle.

I tried to smile at Tom. He had taken his socks and shoes off and was wiggling his toes happily in the sun. 'I'm hot,' he said. 'I can't believe it's only April. Hurrah for global warming. I think we should go and get a glass of something cool and celebratory.' I glanced at his feet and noticed he had one rather long toenail – gross.

'You need to cut that,' I said, nodding at it.

'But then how will I play the guitar?' he responded, quick as a flash, and I laughed. See, *he* could be funny too! He made me laugh! And Vic was right – he *was* kind, thoughtful, reliable . . .

And yet somehow I knew we were never going to be

the same again. My clumsy confession about my crush on Bailey had seen to that.

Everything had already changed irrevocably and I wasn't sure how, or if, we were going to be able to get it back.

Chapter Eleven

'It goes beyond selfish,' Tom rants, getting up, the cheap hospital chair sliding away from under him and hitting the wall. 'It's actually *dangerous*. We don't know if there are decisions that need to be made about Gretchen that are being delayed because of him not being here! How is it that—'

I'm bordering on losing it completely. 'Tom, he missed a plane! Please! For God's sake!'

'You wait,' Tom says, shaking his head. 'He'll rock up here and it'll come out that he wasn't even in bloody Spain, the lying bastard. He's totally responsible for—'

'Oh *Tom*!' I explode desperately, my voice cracking. 'Just stop it!'

We're interrupted by the nurse, who appears at the door. 'It's fine for you to go back through now,' she says, looking at Tom, and then me, a little uncertainly, obviously having heard our exchange. 'If you're ready?' Tom shoots me a hurt look and then gets to his feet. 'Yes, we are.'

But I'm not. I don't want to go back in there at all. I can't. I can't do it. I can't sit there next to her with him – just waiting – not knowing what really happened. And worse still, Bailey is going to arrive at any minute. What's Tom going to do when he actually gets here?

I stand up on wobbly legs and we walk out of the room and up the corridor together, slowly. The room is getting closer and closer, my heart starts to thump and I feel another sluice of sick and panic pulse through me.

Then we turn the corner and there she is again. Everything starts to feel blurry, but I manage to sit down next to the bed and Tom sits next to me. We don't say anything. The nurse is writing something on a chart at the far end of the room. Everything has regained a sense of calm efficiency.

Gretchen, in fact, looks no different than before the alarm sounded. Her eyelashes are resting on her cheeks and her hands are either side of her on the sheet. She is perfectly still. A drip, feeding into a needle embedded in a vein that runs along the back of her hand, is sending a curious, clear liquid drifting into her bloodstream. I try to focus on a bubble rising to the surface of the solution in the bag that hangs from the drip stand. It vanishes without trace and, so help me God, I wish, *wish* that she would just do the same.

'Is it OK to touch her?' Tom asks the nurse, almost in a whisper, and she nods.

'It's fine.'

'I won't hurt her or anything?' he hesitates.

'No,' she says kindly.

I watch him reach out and very gently stroke her pale cheek, softly, like you would to a sleeping newborn baby. Then he reaches down and takes her hand in his, but it's limp and unresponsive. Her eyelids don't flicker – she doesn't move at all. It's painful to see him touch her, but I am in no position to say anything. I look away instead and focus on a tiny bit of tinsel that is still stuck on the far corner of the ceiling, left over from Christmas. I can't imagine having to spend a Christmas Day here. I hope whoever was lying in this bed then is all right now; safe at home with their family.

'I've never seen her so quiet,' Tom laughs, but it is the saddest little sound, like a shattering of ice as someone deliberately smashes the surface of a shallow puddle. There is nothing behind it, no warmth. 'I don't understand, Al,' he whispers. 'She had everything ahead of her. Absolutely everything. It was all just coming good. Why would she want to do this to herself?'

'I don't know. She probably didn't either.'

I feel sick as soon as the lie is out of my mouth. I can't look at him. I just tell myself that it's what Gretchen would want.

'How is she now?' Tom looks worriedly at the nurse.

'There's not really any change,' the nurse says. 'Once her next of kin arrives . . .'

'Yes, I know,' Tom says tiredly. The nurse looks sympathetic and sits down silently at the back of the room, her thin wedding ring catching the light.

'He could have flown there and back by now, surely?' Tom whispers to me, beginning again, angrily tight-lipped.

Oh PLEASE! In spite of myself I resort to giving him a fierce warning look, and he shuts up. I look down at my hands with relief.

'So when you found her,' he suddenly asks, as ever needing somewhere to channel his energy, 'did it look like she'd taken a lot of the pills? I suppose she must have, to have a heart attack like that.'

I look up sharply. 'I've told them everything, Tom,' I say, glancing at the nurse. 'Don't worry.'

96

'Yes, but no one is telling *me* anything,' he says unhappily. 'Was it her lithium? Because that's really dangerous.'

'I don't know what lithium looks like. They were just pills. I gave the bottles to the paramedics. It all happened really fast, Tom – there wasn't a lot of time to think.'

'Bottles? There was more than one?'

'I don't know – I can't remember.' I'm starting to feel woozy, the blood is rushing round my veins. 'She was unconscious – I was frightened.'

The nurse coughs pointedly and then says, 'Perhaps you would like to discuss this outside?' and Tom says, 'OK, OK – sorry.' She drops her head and resumes writing again.

'Thank God you *did* go over there.' He reaches his hand out and grabs mine, squeezing it tightly before letting it go again. 'You're such a good friend to Gretch. You'd do anything for her, wouldn't you?'

I hear the nurse's pen pause at that. Maybe it's just coincidence. I just stare at the floor, not looking at either of them.

'At least bloody Bailey managed to do one thing right,' he continues. 'Imagine what would have happened if he hadn't phoned you and asked you to go over to check on her?' He shudders.

We fall silent.

But as Tom sits there, thinking, a slow look of puzzlement spreads across his face. 'But, hang on –' he says. 'How did you get into the flat if she was unconscious?'

Oh God.

Out of the corner of my eye I see the nurse's head look up quickly, and I run a rather shaky hand across my face. 'I . . .'

But before I can answer, to my relief, the door opens suddenly. We all turn and, finally, there is Bailey, standing in the doorway, much as Tom did earlier, panting slightly. Tom's lip curls and he turns away. My heart, however, leaps involuntarily and delightedly at the sight of him. I quickly stand up. He is wearing a hoodie under a jacket, loose jeans and trainers. He has a big bag slung across his shoulder and a look of panic and fatigue on his tanned face.

'I'm so sorry!' He moves quickly over to me, pulling me into a hug and planting a kiss somewhere vaguely in the region of my hairline. I see Tom look to the floor and a muscle clench briefly in his jaw. 'I got here literally as soon as I could.' He releases me and takes two steps towards the bed, where Gretchen is lying. 'Oh shit!' he says in shock and puts his hands on his head, elbows wide, at the sight of his little sister. 'Oh Gretch!' His voice cracks. 'What the hell have you done this time?'

Chapter Twelve

'You know this gig tomorrow?' Gretchen walked unhurriedly up the street behind me, languidly smoking a fag. 'What time is it? I've completely forgotten.'

'It's at two,' I said absently, stopping to look at my list, feeling a bit stressed out. I'd not had an easy time of it since we got back from Paris. To all intents and purposes nothing had changed on the outside, but inside I was struggling to get a grip on how I felt about the me and Tom situation. I kept swinging between thinking I was being ridiculous to allow myself to become so unsettled by a crush, to worrying that my refusal to acknowledge my feelings didn't mean they would neatly go away if I just buried my head in the sand. I didn't know *what* to do or think, because I was so confused, but I couldn't stop agonising over it; even when I was focusing on something else entirely it was lurking in the back of my mind like a circling pike just under the surface of the water.

As Vic was on holiday in Spain, I called Fran and arranged to meet her for lunch in the hope that she'd have some helpful big-sisterly advice, but she blew me out at the last moment with some sickness bug she thought she'd picked up at work.

'Well can I come and see you at home instead?' I'd asked her hopefully.

'Not unless you want to spend the morning in the bog holding my hair back and seeing what I had for breakfast,' she said graphically. 'I feel like shit, Al. I'm sorry, but whatever it is will have to wait.'

I almost even called my mum instead, but seeing as she was a firmly paid-up member of the Tom fan club and had muttered darkly – on more than one occasion – about the unfairness of her being the only member of her fifty-plus yoga group not to have grandchildren, I wasn't convinced she'd find herself able to offer me unbiased advice.

'Are you nearly done, Al?' Gretchen yawned, dropping her fag butt and grinding it out with her heel. 'I've got to tell you, I love hanging out with you, but this isn't the most exciting way to spend a morning. You're not supposed to take the client to buy props you're going to be using in her shoot, you know.' She nudged me and I couldn't help grinning at her. I really wanted to talk to *her* about it, but I didn't know where to start – Bailey was her brother!

'Not everything is about you, you know,' I teased.

'More's the pity,' she said. 'Come on then. What's left on your little list, Rabbit?'

I looked at her, puzzled.

'As in Winnie the Pooh?' she said. 'Christopher Robin? You should know that: "We're changing the guard at Buckingham Palace, said Alice."'

'My grandpa says that to me,' I said delightedly.

'Ah,' she said, 'that's nice. But seriously – list, focus.' The studio was rotating her presenting gig with a new girl and so she had an enforced day off. I knew she was bored, I could tell. She'd quickly tired of lethargically trailing around after me for something to do.

'OK, OK. All I need now is the rope,' I said, 'for the lassos. The PR girls are sending over the kids' outfits, including the hats and the horse masks. Half an hour and we'll go and have lunch, OK?'

'Urghhh!' groaned Gretchen melodramatically. 'I *hate* my life. *Why* do I have to be photographed surrounded by a load of children dressed like cowgirls and small horses?'

'Because the magazine, whose idea the shoot is, is read by about six hundred thousand people a month and they thought it would be a "cute" idea.' I folded the list and shoved it in my jeans pocket. 'At least it's me doing the shots – it could be a lot worse. I promise I'll make you look good. This could be really good for both of us, you know. Did you tell them you wanted to use me?'

'No, I didn't actually,' Gretchen said honestly. 'My agent suggested you, but you got it on your own merit. So tell me again, what exactly are we doing tomorrow?'

'*We're gonna make twelve five-year-olds look like cowgirls and Gretchen like a fuckin' grown up sexy cowgirl, because she's a kids TV presenter hitting America.*' I did an impression of the stylist I'd spoken to earlier on the phone. 'This magazine is quite literally jumping on your LA bandwagon.'

'Yeah, but I'm not going to bloody *Texas*, am I?' exclaimed Gretchen. 'This "going to America" thing seemed a really good idea at the time, but I'm nowhere near getting any actual offers and now every magazine I do seems to want to dress me up as a giant apple or the Statue of Liberty.'

'They were ideas three and six on the list, in fact,' I laughed, 'both of which I managed to talk them out of.'

'Well thank God for you,' Gretchen said, linking arms

101

with me and looking appalled. 'Can we just hurry up and buy this rope so I can hang myself with it? My job completely sucks. Oooh, look! I like the dress in that window over there. Let's just take five – c'mon!' And without waiting for an answer, she dragged me across the street.

Half an hour later we had managed to find somewhere to buy the props, which was lucky, as by then Gretchen had very firmly lost interest in shops that weren't selling something she could wear. Despite claiming to be hungry enough to eat a buffalo, en route to a café she swore served the best pizza she'd ever had outside of Italy, she suddenly broke off left and came to a stop outside a small shoe shop I hadn't even noticed we were passing.

'I *love* this place, I'd forgotten it was here! Have we just got five minutes?' she asked hopefully.

'Yeah sure,' I said, although all these five minutes of hers were really adding up. In we went. I sat down patiently, quite glad for the chance to rest the heavy loop of rope across my lap.

'So, I meant to say, you've been very sneaky-quiet about your Paris trip.' She inspected the shoes, took one off the shelf, kicked her own off carelessly and slipped her foot into the prospective new one. 'Explain to me again how it is that you said it was "properly over" with this Tom bloke, but then he whisked you off on some extravagant European love trip?' She raised an eyebrow and looked at me pointedly. 'For the record, you can't go away like that again – it wasn't fun here without you.'

I smiled, then hesitated, wondering if I should just tell her the truth. Well, maybe not all of it. An edited version perhaps.

'We just went to see our ex-flatmate together,' I said. 'A birthday- rather than love-trip. It was sweet of him.'

'Very nice indeed, all things considered. You must have stayed on pretty good terms post-split?'

I glanced away guiltily. 'He's very important to me, yes.'

'Hmm,' she said sardonically. 'So there wasn't, in fact, any dropping down on one knee in the shadow of the Eiffel Tower then?'

I paled. 'God no!'

'Do you like these?' she said, looking up questioningly and wiggling her foot.

They were nothing special. 'They're OK,' I said absently, 'but they're pretty similar to your other ones, with the buckle?'

'True,' she conceded, 'but they're brown. These are black,' she looked at me naughtily and I laughed.

'Well, that makes all the difference.'

She grinned and then turned back to look in the mirror. 'You know what I think?' she said slyly. 'I think you're hiding something from me.'

My mouth fell open. Was it written all over my face? But just that little bit of probing was all it took. I was, it seemed, more desperate to confess everything to her than I'd realised.

'You guessed? How?' I said. 'OK, so I *might* have a bit of a crush on someone.'

'What?' She looked perplexed for a moment and then her eyes widened. 'Really? How very naughty! Who is he? I'll take these please!' She beamed at the shop assistant, kicked the shoes off nonchalantly and turned to me expectantly.

I took a deep breath and said, 'Your brother,' and then did a half shrug and smile as I waited.

But unlike when we'd been in the café, when she'd been all twinkling eyes and suggestive nods, she just sort of blankly stared at me for a moment and then said, 'Oh, right,' before abruptly turning away and starting to busily look through another row of shoes. She picked up a strappy, purple number with a three-inch heel and said, 'I'll take these too – in a five, please,' to the assistant, who was still hovering, now rather awkwardly, in the background.

'Don't you want to try them on first, see if they fit?' I asked. 'Remember the Louboutins?'

'No I don't, thanks,' she said shortly, not looking at me. 'In fact,' she called after the assistant, who had scampered off, 'I'll take *them* in the black too.'

'Are you pissed off with me?' I said carefully, knowing that she was, without really understanding why. She'd encouraged me before, offered to put in a good word. What had changed? My heart sped up a bit as I realised that I'd completely unwittingly steered us into the first disagreement of our friendship. 'Have I upset you?'

She looked up at me, eyes all wide and innocent. 'No!'

'Is it because of what I just said? About Bailey?'

She laughed airily. 'You can't possibly think you're the first friend of mine to fancy my brother? It's been like this since I was fifteen – maybe even younger.' She picked up another shoe, inspected it and then threw it down carelessly. I felt incredibly stupid. 'Anyway, I hate to be the bearer of bad tidings, but he's just started seeing someone.'

'Oh.' I felt my expectant heart pop with disappointment and plummet through the bottom of my sensible, old shoes.

'She's Brazilian,' she added, turning to look at me unfalteringly. 'From Rio, I think.'

'Right.' I looked down at the rope on my lap. 'Well, that's nice for him.'

We said nothing more, just waited in silence until the assistant came back and put Gretchen's three boxes down

104

on the counter and rang them through. The only sound in the small shop was the churning of Gretchen's receipt as she yanked her credit card out of the machine. 'Enjoy your shoes,' the girl said, looking uncomfortably at Gretchen, then at me as I stood up.

Gretchen swung the shop door open with unnecessary force and it clashed off the wall, almost hitting me as it rebounded. 'Oops! I'm so sorry!' she said immediately to the girl and pulled a face. 'Bit overexcited about my new shoes!'

Once we were back out on the street I said, 'Look, let's just go and get lunch and we can talk abo—'

'Can't, I'm afraid,' she said briskly. 'We took much longer than I thought we would getting all your stuff. I've got to get over to the studios now.'

'But it's your day off.' I looked at her as I adjusted the rope more comfortably on my shoulder. 'Gretch, I'm getting the feeling you're really unhappy with me and—'

She exhaled shortly. 'Nope, I'm not. I've just *really* got to go.'

'But I—'

'For fuck's sake, Alice!' she exploded. 'The only bloody problem is the fact that you keep saying there's one when there isn't! I'm fine, but I'm now going to be late for a work meeting. Just like you said earlier – it's not always about what *you* want and *you* need, OK?'

'Gretchen,' I said in disbelief, 'what on earth are you talking about? I was joking when I said that. Can't we just—'

'Look, please,' her voice suddenly wavered, 'can we just leave it? I'm sorry. I didn't mean to get shitty with you. I'm just . . . I'm just a little stressed out, OK?'

'What's up?' I asked immediately, my own stuff forgotten. 'You can tell me.'

'It's nothing,' she said. 'Nothing major anyway, I promise. I'm just tired.'

I looked at her critically. Come to mention it, she did look pretty knackered under her make-up. 'Is there something I can help with? Is it work?'

'Seriously,' she insisted. 'Don't give it a second thought – I'm just being a twat, just ignore me.'

She stepped out into the middle of the street, waved and a black cab immediately swerved over to her, indicator flashing.

'I'll see you tomorrow, OK?' She leant forward, kissed me on the cheek briefly and jumped into the cab. Her eyes were shining as she slammed the door shut and I suddenly realised she was near to tears.

I watched her lips move silently as she sat back on the seat and gave an address. I tapped on the window to get her to stop. Something was very badly up – I'd never seen her like this. I mimed undoing the window but she just pretended she hadn't seen me. She smiled and waved cheerily, even though I saw a tear unmistakably spill over and run down her face. The cab jerked away and I instinctively stepped away, watching her staring furiously ahead, refusing to meet my eye. Then she disappeared round the corner, leaving me standing on the pavement, clutching my rope.

Chapter Thirteen

She ignored my calls for the rest of the afternoon and by the time I tried her again when I got home, her mobile was switched off.

'That's about the seventh time I've seen you check your phone tonight,' Tom said as we got ready for bed. 'Something wrong?'

'Gretchen's a bit out of sorts,' I confessed. 'I'm worried about her and she's not picking up calls.'

'I'm sure it's nothing,' he yawned. 'Though I wouldn't know, I guess – having not actually met her.' He pulled the duvet back, got in and reached for his book. 'God, I'm so wrecked! I've never known a work schedule like this . . . but it's going to pay off.' He patted my hand and smiled. 'You'll see. Anyway, I know it's slack that I've not met Gretchen yet. When things calm down a bit I will, I promise.'

'It's really not a problem,' I said quickly. Seeing as Gretch thought he was only my flatmate anyway, I wasn't exactly in a rush to introduce them.

'I'm going to the gym after work tomorrow,' he said, 'so

I won't be back until late. Why don't you bring her round to have dinner here or something?'

I shook my head. 'I'm doing a shoot with her tomorrow so I'll see her then – and I'm sure you're right, it's probably nothing to worry about. I expect she's just gone to bed early to get some beauty sleep.'

I must have still looked worried though, because he put his book down and reached out an arm to me. 'Want a hug?' he said.

But I wanted to take my make-up off first before I settled down, and by the time I came back from the bathroom, he had fallen asleep with his arms folded and his book open on his chest. Relieved, I closed it and slipped into bed beside him, turning the light off.

I slept badly, dreaming about engagement rings slipping on my fingers that then exploded my hands – which was pleasant – so the following morning I arrived to set up the studio, feeling tired and like I needed at least another three hours in bed to deal with the day ahead. I wasn't sure how best to handle Gretchen. Should I act like nothing was wrong? Not mention yesterday? I didn't want her to think I didn't care about what was obviously bothering her, but equally I didn't want to upset her again, especially not just before she was having a set of pictures done.

But then I discovered that I had a more pressing problem. The studio had already taken delivery of the rack of clothes for the shoot. When I unwrapped them, however, I realised we'd been sent the wrong rail. It was full of exotic and very expensive haute couture destined for – I checked the label – *Coco* magazine. I had a moment of complete panic but then took a deep breath and checked my watch. I had ages before anyone was supposed to arrive. There was plenty of time to sort it.

Which was lucky because when I phoned the PR company who had sent the rail, they couldn't have given less of a shit. 'The labels fall off all the time,' one of the girls said carelessly down the phone. 'I expect they just got mixed up and *Coco* got your stuff. We could get it picked up and sorted tomorrow, I suppose?'

What, a day *after* my shoot? An hour later, I was trying to calm myself down in the back of a ludicrously expensive people carrier, bombing across town, having asked the driver to get to *Coco's* offices as fast as he could. I'd never worked for them before, but knew that they liked to be seen as *the* directional magazine, meaning their fashion department probably consisted of scouts and muses that scoured the world looking for the very latest designers, seeking out women weaving exquisite fabrics by candlelight on mountain tops so remote one would have to trek on a camel for five days to reach them. And I had to explain the rack of couture they thought they had was in fact twelve mini cowgirl outfits and a novelty horse mask.

I wrestled the rail from the back of the taxi outside the swish, glass-fronted building, out of which impossibly glamorous people were drifting. They stared at me coolly as I, glowing rosily, pushed through into the stark, air-conchilled reception.

'Can I speak to someone on fashion at *Coco*?' I puffed to the *über* cool receptionist who had an asymmetric fringe. It looked like an optical illusion when she raised an icy eyebrow at the sight of a sweaty me hanging over her desk.

Eventually, after some embarrassing explanations, I was ushered into a large lift and told someone would meet me on the fourth floor. I stepped out into a corridor lined with hundreds and hundreds of framed magazine covers, all of which had *Coco* blazed across them. No one was there, so

I pushed my rail round the corner . . . into a scene little short of office carnage. There were about thirty desks in the open plan office and a lot of shouting coming from one in the middle, where a man was saying loudly into a phone, 'Robert, I don't care. I've got a load of plaid stuck in Morocco and everyone waiting in the middle of a bloody desert for it.' In another corner, a group of very overexcited women were huddled round a very camp man, cooing, 'Who's the birthday boy?' as he opened a small pile of presents. He pulled a pair of huge sunglasses out of some wrapping and screamed 'OH MY GOD – I literally LOVE THEM! They're so FUCKING *COCO*!' He shoved them on and inexplicably the women began to sing, 'It's gotta be . . . so *Coco*, it's gotta be . . . so *Coco*,' to the tune of Sinitta's 'So Macho'.

I wanted to leave. Instantly.

Another woman barged past me, clutching a loose sheaf of pages and throwing them over her shoulder as she discarded them one by one, muttering, 'No, no . . . definitely no, her knees sag . . . possibly her, get the agency to send her arse over.' She shoved the picture at a timid looking girl trotting alongside her, who nodded and rushed off like the white rabbit.

No one took any notice of me at all.

Eventually, after what felt like hours, a girl looked up from a desk and said boredly, and without smiling, 'Can I help you?'

I explained the situation and, after much hilarity (how I laughed), at the fashion desk, which is what the bunch of singing women and the gay bloke turned out to be, we swapped rails.

'You know, that is just *brilliant*,' the gay bloke gasped, as he wiped tears from his eyes and sat back into his chair, exhausted by all the activity. 'You had a whole rail of

McQueen in the back of a taxi and we had a whole load of mini Dolly Parton outfits – and no one noticed! That's just delicious! Giddy up, horsey.' He held the now infamous horse mask up to his face and everyone screamed with laughter.

'Seriously though,' he let the mask drop for a moment, 'I've just had a *roaringly* brilliant idea.' He sat up sharply and seemed to stare into the distance. There was a sudden low murmur in the office. Everyone fell quiet, as if anticipating a life changing moment. 'What about . . . what about we do the leather shoot as a next generation cowgirl concept – the *evolution* of leather. We could hang these funny little miniature outfits of hers,' he nodded at me, 'from tree branches – along with a load of horse masks. God, it could be a kitsch nod to the Wild West meets *The Godfather* meets urban warfare. Saddle up, cowgirl, Daddy's back in town!' He slapped the table gleefully. 'Someone start sourcing a farm location, I need one for tomorrow. Come on, people: *Can we do this? I SHOULD COCO!*' he shouted and people started jumping up in a flurry of activity. 'Darling, can we appropriate your sweet little costumes for one more day?' He turned to me.

I suddenly remembered exactly why I wanted to be a travel photographer.

By the time I got back to the studio at 1.42, having literally wrestled the outfits out of his very manicured hands and been told I was a brassy bitch harlot who offended his very eyes, I found twelve overexcited children, their chaperones, the stylist and a hair and make-up girl all waiting for me. I was hungry, tired and we hadn't even started. I wanted to cry.

But just as I was considering shouting 'Look over there!' and then legging it out of the door, Gretchen walked in.

She was wearing a bright red version of the waiting-list-only Lucky dress, which with its cute capped sleeves would have looked demure if she hadn't teamed it with black patent open-toed heels. She looked like Red Riding Hood with an agenda that was going to end badly for the wolf. She filled the room with smiles and loud 'Hellooooo!'s and 'I'm so sorry I'm late . . . *Hi, girls!*' she called over to the children, who immediately got up, ran over and gathered round her, happily shouting things like, 'I know who you are! You're on my TV!' and 'Gretchen, Gretchen! Come and see my dress!' One of them, standing next to me, jumped up and down on the spot three times, shouted, 'It's her, it's her!' and was then promptly sick on my foot.

Gretchen dumped her oversized bag down on the floor and it fell open to reveal several paper bags completely stuffed with pick 'n' mix.

'Oh how sweet,' said one of the chaperones. 'Did you get them for the girls?'

'Um, yeah,' said Gretchen. 'If you like. Go for it, kids!'

Squealing like piglets, including the one that had just puked on me, they all dove in and began to squabble about who got what. Gretchen laughed and walked over, looking just like her normal self.

'Hey, Al, you OK?' Her face creased into a look of concern at the sight of me.

'I've just had a run-in with some horrible bitchy git at *Coco* magazine,' I said and laughed, but it came out a bit high and squeaky at the end.

'What happened?' Gretchen listened intently as she pulled up a chair next to the make-up mirror and I sat down on it. 'You need to get that shoe off, Al – it honks.'

'It's so stupid, I shouldn't even care. They had our clothes and we had theirs. He wanted to keep the kids' outfits for

112

reasons too stupid to bore you with, but when I said he couldn't, he called me a harlot and the whole office went quiet to listen. He told me I'd never work in fashion again.' I steadied my voice as I slipped off the shoe. 'Not that I even bloody want to.' Gretchen pulled a tissue out of a nearby box, picked up the shoe and hurriedly dropped it in the bin. 'Now that's friendship,' she patted my shoulder, 'I wouldn't do sick for anyone else.' She peered at my leg. 'I don't think any has gone on your trouser leg. Thank God for cut-offs, eh? Just don't give that silly queen a second thought, he probably has a miserable life perpetually dieting to fit into trousers he's permanently too fat for.'

'Well, it was his birthday,' I said. 'So I hope someone gets him a big massive cake he can't allow himself to eat.'

'Oh, well that explains it,' she said instantly, 'he's another year older too . . . you were just wrong place wrong time. With any luck the cake will completely choke him for being mean to my best friend, the bastard.'

'Thanks,' I said gratefully. She thought of me as her best friend? That was so nice! I was torn between wanting to hug her and feeling bad for dumping my stress on her when *she'd* been upset the day before. 'Anyway, enough about me. Are *you* OK?'

She waved a hand airily. 'Yeah, sorry about yesterday . . . and I'm sorry I didn't call you back either, I just had massive PMT. In fact, can you use every trick of the trade today, because I'm so bloated I feel like ten-tonne Tessie *and* I'm craving sugar like you wouldn't believe, but,' she lowered her voice and whispered, 'those horrible little rug rats are eating all my sweets!'

I laughed. 'Let's get each other through this, shall we?'

She nodded. 'But only if we can go out and have a glass or three once it's done.'

'Deal,' I said. 'Except I've got no shoes.'

'We'll think of something,' she said. 'We always do.'

By quarter to four, the kids' sugar rush was showing no signs of letting up. They were all completely out of control and running about the place like small Tasmanian devils on speed, not helped by the fact that the stylist had stuck the *High School Musical* soundtrack on, very loudly, to which they were all dancing and singing like crazy. To give her credit though, Gretchen had firmly thrown herself into proceedings and was also leaping around like a lunatic, making the kids giggle with delight.

By five o'clock she was still going strong, but the children were fading fast.

'You've been amazing today,' I laughed, wrapping her in a grateful hug. 'Well done. I think we should go and get that drink – I've got all I need.'

'Except a shoe.' She pointed, still dancing to the background music, at my foot. 'The stylist asked me why you were only wearing one, I told her it's your creative "thing" and she bought it – the prat. Why don't we get a cab and swing past yours before the bar, so you can grab a replacement?'

That was fine by me, as I knew Tom was gyming it after work so wouldn't be at home.

Half an hour or so later we pulled up outside the flat and, having unlocked the front door, I rummaged around quickly in the jumble of mine, Tom's and Paulo's shoes – aware the taxi meter was running. I was just dragging on a pair of pumps when Tom appeared at the top of the stairs. 'Hi,' he called down.

'What are you doing here?' I said in amazement, looking up at him.

'Well, that's nice!' he laughed. 'Love you too. My meeting finished early and I couldn't be arsed to go back to the office, but all my kit is under my desk. I'll go for a run tomorrow instead. How about you?'

'Gretchen and I are just zipping out for a drink, post-shoot.'

'She's here?' he said instantly. 'Oh right, I'll come down and say hello.'

'No! It's fine, we're just –' I began, but he was already halfway down and practically out of the door. Panicking, I followed him.

Gretchen had unwound the window and Tom extended his hand through the gap. 'Hello, Gretchen, I'm Tom,' he said easily.

She took in his work outfit and said, 'Oh hi! Alice has told me lots about you.'

Tom laughed and said what everyone says to that: 'All good, I hope?'

I held my breath. She knew *something* had been – might still be – going on between Tom and me, but she also knew I had an inappropriate crush on her brother. Yet she said immediately, 'Of course – so good it was almost hard to believe.' She held his gaze steadily. 'Just finished for the day then?'

'Yeah, I work for a consultancy in the city.'

'Oh, which one?' she asked politely.

'Holland and Grange,' he replied, hands in pockets. I guiltily ran round the other side of the taxi and jerked the door open, desperate to be gone.

'I'll see you later, Tom,' I said. 'Sorry to dash – meter and all that.' Checking that Gretchen wasn't looking, I blew him a quick kiss.

'Have fun,' he said. 'Nice to meet you, Gretchen.'

'You too,' she said.

We pulled away and she turned to look at him curiously over her shoulder, watching him walk back into the flat. 'Well,' she said, 'he wasn't what I expected *at all*.'

Chapter Fourteen

'Honestly, Al, I didn't mean anything by it, it was just one of those throwaway remarks people make.'

'OK, so what *were* you expecting him to be like?' I pressed insistently. It was really niggling me that she'd obviously had some preconceived idea of Tom, but wouldn't tell me what that was. I'd certainly never described him to her – we'd barely discussed him at all! She'd clearly imagined my 'flatmate' to be far less . . . conventional.

'Oh, let it go,' she said without malice. 'Let me just zip to the loo, then I'll get us a drink. Bottle of white?'

I waited at our table for what felt like ages before she returned. She plonked two glasses and the wine down and said, 'You *so* owe me.'

I immediately reached for my purse. 'You're absolutely right, sorry. How much was it?'

'What?' She looked puzzled, then it dawned on her. 'Not the drink – I've just called Bailey and told him about your little crush.'

I stared at her, flabbergasted. She'd done *what*?

'Turns out the girl from Ipanema was more of a fling than a serious thing,' she said slyly, pouring me a very full glass and passing it over.

Despite my shock and panic that events had taken such an alarming leap forward without my knowledge, I was unable to help myself. 'What did he say?' I whispered.

'He was very flattered,' she said.

I felt my insides curl up and wither like burning paper. I wanted to die – how incredibly embarrassing. He was *flattered*? That was tantamount to a carefully phrased fan mail response: 'Mr Clooney was very *flattered* that you sent him a picture of your breasts and some of your underwear, but will in fact be filming until the end of 2008 and will be unable to accept your kind offer to marry him at any point this year.'

She must have noticed the look on my face because she said, 'That's not a bad thing, Al. Just watch this space. That's all I'm saying.'

Watch this space? There *was* no space – it already had Tom in it. 'But Gretchen—' I began urgently.

'Hush up, Al, I've got it all under control,' she said smugly.

'But—'

'Oh brilliant!' she exclaimed, as she noticed something over my shoulder. 'Look, they're setting up karaoke!'

I glanced over to a small stage at the front of the bar where a man was fiddling with a microphone. 'You'll do a song with me, won't you?' she said eagerly.

For a moment I saw myself singing a mournful rendition of 'I Will Survive' under a lonely spotlight – Tom, betrayed and hurt in the audience, staring angrily at me; and Bailey, arm slung round a model type, smiling pityingly before blowing me a kiss and sauntering off. Urgh. Oh why the fuck had she told Bailey I fancied him?

'No, thanks,' I said faintly.

But Gretchen wasn't taking no for an answer. An hour later she was still saying 'Oh pleeeease?'

Since our earlier arrival, the bar had filled out and become fiercely hot. I was already a little dehydrated from the wine and was starting to feel like I was stuck in a sauna where someone was steadily pouring other people's sweat on the coals. I desperately wanted some air. In fact, I just wanted to go.

'I think we should call it a night, Gretch,' I said.

'Oh but look!' She nodded delightedly up at the stage, where four girls were now energetically bouncing around to 'Wake Me Up Before You Go Go'. 'They're having a wicked time. Come on!'

'Gretch, please! I really don't want to.'

'Tell you what,' she knocked back the last of her drink, 'I'll sing with them on my own.'

'You don't even know them!'

'They won't mind. Wait here for me?' She handed me her empty glass.

'All right,' I said reluctantly. 'Then I think we ought to get going, OK?' She was doing amazingly well for someone with himping PMT. I'd have been lying on the sofa crying at RSPCA adverts, eating a whole packet of biscuits and then randomly shouting at Tom for no apparent reason.

She bounded off and I watched as she climbed on to the stage in her heels and red dress, to admiring whistles from the audience – some of whom immediately pulled out their camera phones to sneak a picture. She put an arm round one of the girls, who at first looked a bit surprised but then smiled widely, pulling her new celebrity friend into the group – probably pissed.

Gretchen had obviously decided she was going to sing

lead vocals, however, and pushed her way to the mic, which didn't seem to annoy the girls much, apart from the leader of the pack, who was looking a little irritated as Gretchen bounced away energetically next to her. Luckily the song started to wind down and, as everyone began to clap and cheer, I looked down to check in my bag that I had enough money for a cab. But then I heard Gretchen say through the mic, 'No, no – play that one again!'

I looked up to see the girls leaving the stage, shooting curious glances at Gretchen. She was ignoring the bloke who had set up earlier and who was now leaning in and trying to talk to her. 'No!' she repeated clearly through the mic. 'Just that one again – go on! Once more!' And she leant forward and flicked a button on the monitor. The first bars of 'Wake Me Up' began again and there were a few catcalls and whistles, but she ignored them and began to sing.

The bloke, irked, reached over and flicked the switch off. The music died. 'Hey!' Gretchen said, annoyed. 'Put it . . . now.' The mic became muffled as she let it slip. It squealed slightly while they gesticulated a bit and she was waving it around. The bloke tried to grab for it, but Gretchen moved smartly out of his way and shouted, 'Fine, well I don't need the music . . . I'm going to sing anyway and you can't stop me.'

What was she *doing*? I couldn't help grinning – nutter. I put my hand over my mouth and tried not to laugh as she launched into an a cappella version of 'Wake Me Up'. There were a few shouts of 'Get OFF!' and 'Put a sock in it, blondie!' from the audience.

But she ignored them and began to wave her arms around, kicking her legs from one side to the other as she sang. It was a bit like watching my slightly drunk dad dancing to

120

'New York, New York' at the end of a wedding reception, only with slightly more coordination and much better legs.

She was starting to get a little puffed out. The organiser walked on stage and put his hand out on to her arm. As he touched her, she suddenly stopped moving and shouted 'DON'T touch me,' and glared at him furiously. Alarmed, the organiser backed off to the edge of the stage, hands in the air, and gestured to one of the barmen. He nodded and picked up a phone.

Gretchen, meanwhile, had bizarrely gone completely still and was clutching the mic in the middle of the stage, having closed her eyes firmly, still singing. I didn't understand what she was trying to do – make the point that she'd finish when she was good and ready? It wasn't that she had a bad voice, it was actually beautiful, surprisingly low and sultry, but I had now realised something was not right. She was clutching the mic as if her life depended on it. People in the audience had fallen quiet and were starting to whisper to each other curiously. Everyone was just looking at her. I saw one woman tap the side of her head and roll her eyes at her friend.

'Wo wooo wo wo wo, wooo wo wo wo woooooo . . .' She'd started to do the guitar solo and then I realised she wasn't going to stop and this wasn't funny any more. Suddenly completely sober, I saw a door open at the back of the room and two grimly determined-looking bouncers appear. I grabbed our bags and started to weave through the audience and push my way to the front. The barman was saying something to the bouncers and pointing at Gretchen. They nodded and started to walk towards the stage. I got there first though and reached out to put my hand on her arm. She was still singing.

'Gretch? *Gretchen*. You've got to stop.'

Everyone was staring at us as a bouncer climbed the steps on the left-hand side of the stage. I protectively grabbed her and pulled her towards me. She dropped the mic and opened her eyes, appearing astonished to find herself there. 'I just want to sing,' she said. 'Let me sing.'

'Don't touch her!' I said warningly as the bouncer advanced on us and I dragged her off the stage. Pulling her through the crowds, her tottering to move faster in heels, I shoved her up the stairs past the cloakroom and she started giggling uncontrollably, as if we were playing a game. I pushed her through the door and the night air hit us as we fell out on to the street. She stumbled and I grabbed her hand to steady her. 'Gretchen, are you OK?' I asked worriedly.

She looked up at me and, in the neon lights of the bar sign, I saw that her pupils were huge, like pools. She just giggled again. With a sinking feeling, I realised why she'd been gone so long in the loos. She was high as a kite.

I eventually managed to get us a taxi – Gretchen had begun to sing again under her breath. Having given my address I sank back into the seat, exhausted, and said nothing for the next few minutes. There was so much I wanted to ask I didn't know where to begin. I thought again about her being near to tears the day before; PMT my arse – there was obviously a lot more to it than that, something she wasn't telling me. I racked my brains. Was it bloke-related, perhaps? But then the last person she'd actually dated had been that boyband prat, and that had been ages ago.

Gretchen stared out of the window, eyes glittering brightly as if she was waiting for the next party trick. Finally she said pleasantly, 'Are we going back to yours then?' as if we were stopping off after a charming night at the theatre.

I looked at her in disbelief. 'Yes, we are.' I closed my eyes for a moment. I just wanted the day to stop. I'd had enough.

'Ohhhh look!' she suddenly said excitedly as we passed it. 'There's a church! Let's stop and go in!' She reached for the door handle.

'Oh!' she said in disappointment as it clicked redundantly in her hand; it was on auto lock. The driver glanced in his rearview mirror in annoyance. 'I can't get out. Make it work, Alice, I want to have a chat with God. I need to tell him some stuff. Let's go and see God *right now.*'

'Gretchen!' I reached out quickly. 'The car is moving! Don't – it's dangerous!'

But she kept clicking furiously and in the end I had to grab her hand and pull it away. She just laughed and threw herself back in the seat breathlessly, tapping her fingers rapidly on her leg. Then she started humming under her breath.

I looked at her in frightened disbelief. What on earth had she taken in that toilet cubicle? I wasn't naive enough to think that someone who worked in her industry would be completely squeaky clean, but still – she was practically delusional. She wanted to talk to *God*?

As the church disappeared from view, however, she settled down. We arrived back at the flat five minutes later and I eventually persuaded her to come in, my voice much calmer than I actually felt. I knew Tom would long since have gone to bed as it was a school night, so the coast was clear – but Paulo was still up watching TV, doing bicep curls with enormous dumb-bells.

He looked up when we came in and then immediately set his weights down appreciatively at the sight of Gretchen. He pushed his damp-with-sweat, dark hair off his face and then offered his hand to her, having wiped it first on the front of his T-shirt. '*Hola,*' he said disarmingly, and I saw her take in his well-developed shoulders – over-developed in my opinion – and absurdly flat stomach. 'I am Paulo.'

'Hello, Paulo. I am staying the night.' She smiled seductively and then giggled.

Ohhhh no no. That was the last thing anyone needed. 'Night, Paulo,' I said firmly and took Gretchen's hand. I led her into the hall, quickly pulling our bedroom door to, so as not to wake Tom. She just saw the outline of his body in bed as she peered over my shoulder into the dark room. 'He's very lovely, Alice,' she said slowly. 'Can I have him now you don't want him?' She hiccupped gently. 'I think he's perfect.' Tom? Perfect? God, she really was out of it. 'Or I'll have the other one. Wassisname – Mario. I don't care. He's very pretty. Is he single?'

'Yes he is, but it's time to lie down now, Gretch,' I said quietly. 'You can sleep in here.'

I opened the door to my old room, now my office, and cleared the junk off the unmade bed.

'Nice "bedroom".' She mimed inverted commas and laughed restlessly, flopping down on to the mattress. Then she yawned so widely I saw the teeth at the back of her mouth. 'I want to sleep now.'

Perhaps she was just drunk after all. 'So do you think you'll be able to get some rest?' I said and she nodded.

'What about you? Where are *you* going to sleep?' She giggled.

'I'll kip on the sofa,' I lied, and made a mental note to be up early, before her, so she was none the wiser. 'We'll talk in the morning then, shall we?' I said, pulling a duvet over her. It hadn't got a cover on it but she didn't seem to care, her eyes were already shut. I closed the door gently behind me.

* * *

124

The following morning I woke up with a start, having overslept. Tom had already left for work and I quickly got up, my head throbbing, and dragged on my dressing gown. She wouldn't be up yet, surely? She'd been out for the count. I checked my watch — I had an afternoon shoot, luckily. That would give me plenty of time to get her up and find out what on earth last night had been all about.

I tiptoed over to my office and pushed the door open a crack.

The bed was completely empty . . . She'd vanished.

Chapter Fifteen

She was simply nowhere to be seen. In the sitting room there was no note, no nothing, only her patent shoes . . . sticking out from under the sofa, unsettlingly reminiscent of the Wicked Witch in *The Wizard of Oz*. Slumped alongside them was her handbag. I actually got on my hands and knees and had a quick double check under the couch but, unsurprisingly, she wasn't there. Where could she have gone without shoes and her bag?

I walked back into the hall and slap into Paulo, who was dressed in a snug T-shirt, distressingly low-slung tracksuit bottoms and enormous basketball trainers. '*Hola*, Alice,' he said quickly.

'You haven't seen Gretchen—' I began, but he tapped his watch and said, 'Very late for the gym, sorry.' He glanced briefly at his bedroom – the door was pushed to – and then clattered rapidly down the stairs, banging the front door behind him.

What was he looking so evasive for? It wasn't as if I'd

accused him of abducting Gretchen into *his* room under the cover of darkness . . .

Oh shhhhiiitt.

No, that was impossible. She couldn't have. She hadn't said so much as a sentence to him the previous night! They had *barely* met.

Even so, I found myself curiously tiptoeing over to his room.

Very, very slowly, holding my breath and clutching my dressing gown together with one hand, I creaked the door open with the other and peered in.

The bed was unmade, but empty. Oh thank God for that. I exhaled heavily.

But then that still didn't solve where the hell she was. There weren't enough rooms in our flat *to* get lost in.

I looked everywhere and, even though I knew it was pointless because this wasn't some bizarre game of hide and seek where she was going to gleefully stick her head out from under the sink and shout 'I won!', I looked again.

She had simply disappeared into thin air. I sank back on to the sofa and tried to think sensibly. I couldn't, so I rang Tom.

'Well she definitely wasn't in your old room when I got up this morning,' he said. 'Hang on a minute, Al – yes, I'll be two seconds,' he told someone in the background. I could hear phones ringing, the hum and bustle of an office, then he came back to me. 'Al, I've got to go, things are really hectic here this morning. I'll call you later, love you.' And he hung up.

I sat there pondering whether I should call the police, but wasn't sure what I would tell them. 'My best friend got drunk and possibly high last night, I put her to bed and now she's gone.' They'd tell me to bugger off.

I went and picked up her bag, peering into it. It contained her phone, purse, some make-up, a hairband – nothing that gave me any clues. I reached for her phone, it was on.

And then it occurred to me. Bailey. I could phone him. His sister had disappeared and I was worried about her. He ought to know.

Ohhh, but I didn't want to phone him. He knew I fancied him. I was going to look like a teenage stalker. Thanks very bloody much, Gretch, I thought crossly as I went through her address book and his name slid into view. I paused. I *so* didn't want to do this, but she *was* missing . . . ARGH! Taking a deep breath, and before I could change my mind, I hit call.

'Grot, *please* fuck off,' said a sleepy voice. 'I'm still in bed . . .'

Oh God – suppose he wasn't alone . . .

'It's Alice actually,' I began, trying to focus only on the matter in hand. 'We met at the café?'

'Oh right!' he said quickly, and I imagined him sitting up. 'I'm so sorry! Hang on – you *are* on my sister's phone, aren't you?'

'Yes.' I took a deep breath. 'I'm afraid something's happened . . .'

I waited nervously in the coffee shop for him, clutching Gretchen's handbag, in which I'd also placed her shoes. At half ten the door opened and in he walked, looking subdued and a little tired.

I couldn't help it. My heart spontaneously leapt at the sight of him and I nervously pushed my freshly washed hair off my face and smoothed a wrinkle out of my black, slightly-lower-cut-than-normal top, as I tried not to think about the fact that Gretchen had told him about my crush. There were far more important things to worry about. I half stood up awkwardly and held the bag out to him straight away.

'Hi, Alice.' He managed a faint smile. 'Oh, this is hers, is it? Thanks.' He took the bag from me and set it down on the table between us. Then, pulling out the chair opposite, he sank down heavily. 'I'm so sorry that you've got caught up in all of this.'

'It's OK.'

'It's not OK actually.' He sat back and looked at me steadily. 'It's very frustrating and, well, sad I suppose. She hasn't had a setback like this for a while and you almost manage to convince yourself that she's fine, but then . . .' He sighed. 'You're reminded she's not at all. Poor little scrap.'

I hadn't got a clue what he was talking about.

'She must have come off it to have ramped up like this. She hasn't done a bunk for a while now.'

'Come off what?' I asked.

'Her lithium,' he said, surprised by my confusion.

I must have looked totally blank, because he stared at me and then said, very slowly, 'Oh holy shit — she hasn't told you, has she?'

'Lithium?' I echoed, as that rang a bell somewhere. 'I've heard of that.'

But Bailey was looking at the table and had covered his face with his hands, muttering 'Shit, shit, shit' through his fingers. He exhaled, lifted his head back up and said simply, 'Gretchen's a manic depressive. I thought you knew. I'm so sorry.'

I stared at him, utterly at a loss for words.

'I assumed . . .' he trailed off awkwardly. 'It's just she talks about you a lot, says how good you are for her. I thought

129

she would have said. She's usually pretty upfront about it – although it's cost her lots of friends in the past. Maybe that's why she didn't say anything this time, she was worried about how you'd react. Oh fuck it, I'm *such* a wanker!' He looked furious with himself. 'Where's the waiter? I need one of your huge spoons,' he said, trying to lighten the mood but failing miserably.

My mind had spun into motion and was spooling back through the previous night; her singing and trying to get out of the moving taxi . . . So she hadn't been drunk or on drugs? She was a manic depressive? Why hadn't she told me?

Bailey was looking at me carefully. 'You look pretty taken aback. Don't take this the wrong way, but do you actually know what manic depression is? You don't need to be frightened, Alice, she's not a nutter.'

He waited but I said nothing. I could only see her fingers squeezing on the door handle over and over again in the back of the cab. What if it hadn't been locked? What if . . .

'Can I try and explain it to you?' Bailey said gently. 'You know what it's like to be high, right?'

'Not really,' I said. 'I did some blow-ups at university, or whatever they are.'

'You mean when someone blows smoke into your mouth? That's a blowback.' He smiled slightly at my mistake. 'The reason I ask is this . . .' He paused and took a deep breath.

We both sat still and quiet for a moment while he appeared to gather his thoughts.

'Imagine,' he said eventually, 'you've taken a drug. It makes you feel ecstatically happy and like you love the world. You feel like there is nothing you can't do. You don't need sleep, you have so much energy you can barely sit still. You start to have these fantastically colourful ideas and schemes that before you wouldn't have believed you could make happen . . . But now you feel *anything* is possible. Money, other people, it's all irrelevant – you're not inhibited any more, constrained by nothing and no one. In fact, you feel at your most attractive – *everyone* wants to listen to you; you feel seductive and like you want to be seduced all at once. You just want to dance and dance, then run and run. It's like speeding down an open road at sunset in a convertible, wind rushing wildly through your hair.'

I caught my breath, it sounded wonderful. I wanted to do all of that – with him.

'But then,' he continued, 'it starts to go too fast. It feels like someone has glued your foot to the accelerator and you can't take it off. You go speeding dangerously across intersections, your ideas start to feel jumbled and confused. You feel frightened and the people around you start to make you cross or scared.

'With no warning at all you find yourself under the darkest, blackest clouds you've ever seen, but you have no idea where you are or how you got there. All that frenzied energy starts to whirl up and up . . . thunder is starting to rumble in the sky over your head – there's a crack of lightning and it makes you think you're hearing and seeing things that you can't be sure are real. You feel this demented confusion and fear pressing on you so heavily you scream, but then people are reaching out and pinning you down. You don't know who they are, so you try to protect your-self, you hit out, but they hold you down, even though you try to fight and stay in control . . .'

I sat frozen to the spot, the background noise of the café seemed to drain away. All I was aware of was him and what he was saying.

'Then you wake up, not remembering how you fell asleep,

131

under this heavy, relentless rain that won't stop and you feel more sad and hopeless than you have ever felt in your life; you can't see how it will ever end. You start to remember all the horribly embarrassing things you did while you were high; you feel deeply ashamed and you don't want to see anyone. It's as if you have nothing to offer the world – and it seems it doesn't have much to offer you either.'

A sweetly smiling waitress appeared next to us and asked in a light, sing-song voice, 'Can I take your order?'

'Er, coffee, please,' I said, completely thrown by her interruption.

'Me too,' Bailey said. 'White. Thanks.'

She bustled off and left us in silence.

'Gretchen's brain does everything I've just described to you, on its own,' Bailey ploughed on determinedly as he held my gaze. 'She doesn't need to take anything to induce those feelings, although undoubtedly the drugs and alcohol she *does* take don't help. Basically, she's got this chemical imbalance in her brain. They don't really know what causes it or why it suddenly becomes an issue – it might be hereditary, they're not sure. Anyway, she was diagnosed with manic depression about three years ago.'

'Has she disappeared like this before?' I managed eventually.

He nodded.

'So do you know where she is?'

He shook his head. 'We'll just have to sit and wait. Hope she rings us, or that someone else does. There isn't really anything more we can do.' He shrugged helplessly.

I looked at him searchingly, trying to imagine how I would feel if Phil was lost out there somewhere, confused and vulnerable, somewhere where none of us could reach him, gather him to us and simply protect him. Bailey dropped his gaze and stared hard at the table.

'You just have to wait?'

He nodded.

'That must be very difficult.'

A desperate laugh escaped him. 'Like you wouldn't believe. You want the phone call, but you dread it at the same time, in case, God forbid . . .'

We said nothing for a moment. The pause seemed to go on for ever. I wanted to reach out, put my hand on his, but I didn't want him to misunderstand the gesture.

'So, when she turns up,' I said eventually, encouragingly, 'what happens then?'

'I'll try and get her to go back into a psychiatric hospital.'

I took a sharp intake of breath, immediately picturing white walls, echoey corridors, barred windows and strait-jackets. I couldn't help it.

'It's not like you think,' he said quickly, catching sight of my expression. 'It's completely voluntary and it's a private hospital. She doesn't become sectioned against her will or anything, but she has to go in because at certain points in the cycle I described to you, she has no control over her moods – there's a risk she could be so desperate to get some control back that she might try to take her own life, or not be *aware* that she's trying to take her own life. Suffice to say that I don't want to go into detail, but that has happened in the past.'

The waitress reappeared and inexpertly dumped our coffees down, jerking some of the dark liquid into the saucers. 'Oops!' she said. 'Enjoy!' And disappeared again.

I was completely horrified by what Bailey had said. I almost couldn't believe it. Gretchen? Beautiful, fun, fearless Gretch? It was like stepping into a lift, but finding the lift wasn't there where I expected it to be – just a vast empty space beneath my feet.

'It's just a precaution, Alice,' he said quickly. 'It sounds horrific, but she's been there before and come out of it. This will probably happen to her again at some point in the future and, in spite of everything I've told you, it really *is* manageable, I promise you. The imbalance can be addressed with drugs. As long as she takes them, and has regular counselling, she's totally normal. Trust me, I'm something of an expert now. I think I've read every book and studied every website.' He tried a smile.

'Last night . . .' I was struggling very slowly to get to grips with everything. 'She was behaving . . . quite erratically. Was that why? She'd come off her medication, you think?'

'It sounds like it, yes,' he said. 'I'm just sorry I was so indiscreet and just blurted it out like that — she's going to kill me.' He looked devastated. 'She's such a private person as it is. Urgh, I'm such a twat!' He covered his face. 'It just didn't occur to me that she wouldn't have told you. You seem so in control, just the sort of person she could rely on.'

'I really haven't known her that long,' I said slowly. 'We are very good friends, but . . .'

'I thought girls were supposed to talk about everything?' he tried gamely, shooting me a look, and for a foolish moment I thought he was referring to my being attracted to him. His smile faded quickly though. 'Then again, I suppose when is the right time to talk about something like that?'

When indeed? Poor, poor Gretchen.

'You're not going to walk away, are you?' he asked urgently. 'I know it's a lot to take on board and it sounds really heavy, but she needs good friends around her right now, Alice.'

I looked at him. 'Of course I'm not going to walk away.'

'Thank you.' He looked hugely relieved. 'She will get through this, I promise. And thank you for ringing me . . . and meeting me.' There was a pause and then he said, 'I was actually going to call you anyway.'

My heart thumped expectantly. His hand was resting opposite mine on the table. I wondered what it would feel like to have him touch me.

'Gretchen told me—' he started.

'Yes, well,' I interrupted quickly, flushing. 'She shouldn't have. I'd just like to point out I don't usually adopt the tactics of a fifteen-year-old, i.e. "My friend fancies you."'

'I was just going to say Gretchen told me you and your boyfriend split up.'

'Oh,' I said, wondering if there was a hole nearby I could crawl into.

He laughed. 'Don't look like that . . . OK, OK. I have to come clean. She *might* have discussed you with me, I think she wanted to make sure I didn't miss my chance again. I wanted to call you the day after we first met, but Gretchen explained you were in a serious relationship. You're quite right, she shouldn't have interfered, but I'm glad she did.'

I was in a serious relationship? Had she been a whole lot more astute about Tom and me than I had realised?

'Will you come and sit with me outside?' he asked. 'Have you got time?'

I'd have stopped it completely for him.

We paid up and he walked ahead of me, throwing the door open and stepping with relief into the sunshine. He found us a bench in Leicester Square amid Londoners clustering on the grass, busily unwrapping lunchtime sandwiches. They were tipping their faces gratefully up to the sun like flowers, snatching a couple of moments of peace away from office phones and incoming emails.

'So,' Bailey said, trying to adopt a lighter tone as he sat down, 'what inappropriately heavy subject shall we pick for when I next take you out? China's human rights record perhaps?'

'You seem to be managing to stay very calm about everything,' I said, thinking, *when you next take me out?*

'I have to. What's the alternative?' And at that, he smiled a slightly wobbly smile. I think it was that flash of raw vulnerability that made me overcome any worry I had about misinterpretation. I instinctively reached out, picked up his hand and simply held it – because I knew he needed me to.

He didn't say anything. We just sat there and held hands quietly. I was scared to move in case any shift made him feel he should let go, but he didn't.

Eventually, though, the moment started to change shape, and what had begun as my innocently comforting him started morphing into something that began to make my heartbeat pulse loudly at my wrist. I was still holding his hand. We were holding hands. I glanced round the square casually but I was barely breathing. People were sitting at tables outside cafés and bars, laughing and smoking languidly. It could have been Paris – if I'd squinted and blocked out the black cabs, postboxes and pint glasses on tables. I thought of Paris, and then I thought of Tom.

'I have to go.' I turned to Bailey.

'OK.' He looked at me and I suddenly realised how close we were to each other. 'Thanks for holding my hand,' he smiled. 'It's been a while since anyone actually listened like that. It was very nice of you. But then you're very nice full stop.'

And then it happened.

He leant forward and kissed me, right there, like we were

the only people in the square. I froze for a second, but then, then I very tentatively kissed him back and I forgot everything else except how it made me feel. My mouth started tingling as my tense shoulder muscles relaxed, and I felt his hand resting lightly on my leg. I could smell his skin and feel the warmth of him as I started to fall . . . Just for a second I lost myself totally and I didn't care who was watching; if the whole of London had ground to a halt and was standing, just staring at us. Had the world only ten seconds left before exploding, I would have died happy, going out on that kiss. It was as if every nerve in my body sprang to life and cried out for him to carry on.

But *Tom*, what about *Tom*? I pulled back quickly and Bailey looked at me, totally bemused.

'We shouldn't be doing this,' I said guiltily.

'Why?'

I stalled. 'Gretchen's missing and—'

'No, no,' he said, 'you've got to grab these little bits of happiness where you find them. I know it's not the most uncomplicated of situations, but I actually think Gretchen would be thrilled at the thought of her matchmaking coming off.'

I remembered her comments in the shoe shop that time and wasn't so sure. And yet she'd told Bailey that Tom and I had separated, and that I was attracted to him . . . I was confused. But then, it sounded like she had been, too – poor thing. She was literally all over the place.

'I want to see you again,' Bailey said. 'Can I? Once I've sorted Gretchen out?'

And I nodded. It was an instinctive thing, I didn't even think about it.

'You promise?'

'I promise.'

'I'll call you then,' he said. 'As soon as she turns up, so you know she's safe, and to arrange something for us.'

Us. There was going to be an us.

Stunned by what had just happened and what I'd agreed to, I stood up and barely whispered, 'I'll look forward to it,' before turning and walking away.

I could feel him watching me. It felt good.

Chapter Sixteen

'You've done *what*?' Vic said incredulously.

I closed my eyes and sank down on to the carpet in my bedroom. 'Kissed Bailey.'

'When?'

I cringed. 'Two days ago.'

'*Two days ago*?' A clunk carried down the phone line, there was a pause and then I heard her swear in the background before she said, 'I'm back, knocked my drink over. What the fucking fuck?'

'You were away! I couldn't call you and tell you on holiday, could I? Vic, I've been going out of my mind. I've felt so horrifically guilty, and even worse, he's just called me to ask me out.'

'Just now? What did you say?'

'Nothing. He left a message because I couldn't bring myself to pick up. He was all "Gretchen's back and are you free tomorrow night?" What am I going to do?'

'Gretchen's back?' Vic said. 'Where's she been? On holiday too?'

'Not exactly, she's –' I began, and then I heard Tom shout, 'Hi, Al, I'm home. Where are you?'

'Shit, Tom's here. Hang on,' I hissed.

'Al! Don't you dare hang up!'

Tom appeared in the doorway, looking more excited than I'd seen him for months.

'I've got some amazing news,' he said. 'How would you,' he paused for dramatic effect, 'like to spend the next . . . Oh, you're on the phone. Sorry.'

'Tell him I'm crying – that I've just had a row with Luc,' Vic instructed.

'Vic's had a row with Luc,' I said.

Tom pulled a face. 'You want a cup of tea?' I shook my head. 'Don't be too long, OK? I want to finish what I was telling you before Paulo gets back.'

'He's gone,' I said once he was out of earshot.

'Right,' she said. 'Tell me again what happened.'

Ten minutes later, well into a heated debate, Vic was absolutely adamant that it was all going to end in tears.

'So you had a perfect kiss. Keep it that way – hold on to the memory but *walk away*! I'm telling you, from everything you've said he sounds gorgeous, perfect and lovely, so there's bound to be something really wrong with him.'

'There isn't. He's amazing,' I insisted. 'What happened to your "you deserve to be happy, even if that isn't with Tom" stuff?'

'You barely know this bloke!'

'You barely knew Luc,' I shot back. 'And three months later you moved to another country for him.'

There was a pause.

'But he's Gretchen's brother!' she said, changing tack. 'What'll happen if you and Mr Perfect eventually split up? Gretchen'll be caught in the middle and you'll be wanting to ask her what he's up to, who he's shagging and she won't want to tell you because she'll feel loyal to him . . . Or he'll turn out to be some dick that you have to see every time she has a birthday or party. It'll properly bugger your friendship up. Not that I give a tiny rat's arse about that.'

'I know you don't like Gretchen,' I sighed.

'I don't know her,' Vic said quickly.

'Yeah, well, there's some stuff going on there too.' Then I repeated what Bailey had told me about Gretchen.

'Oh God, Alice,' Vic said.

My bedroom door gently pushed open again. 'Are you nearly done?' Tom asked. 'I really want to talk to you.' Then we both heard the doorbell ring. 'What the—? I'll get it.' He rolled his eyes and slipped back out noiselessly.

'Please don't start anything with this girl's brother,' Vic implored. '*Please*.'

'I already have, so I *have* to tell Tom, don't I? It's the only honourable thing to do. I'm not a cheat and I don't want to treat him this way.'

'It was a kiss, Alice — it's not like a rampant shag back at yours or his and it's certainly not worth ending a relationship over. You're not kids, and Tom's one of your — our — best friends!'

'But I promised Bailey I'd see him again!' I stared at the ceiling. It looked all nice and simple up there. 'And I know I want to. That's the real problem; it wasn't just what the kiss meant then. It's what it's going to lead to and I can't do that to Tom. You know him . . . you know that would kill him.' I paused. 'Actions have consequences and I just have to deal with that. I'm sitting here like I've got a decision to make and I haven't. I made it the second I kissed someone else.'

'Fine. Finish it then, but *do not* tell him there's another

141

man. What the hell will that achieve apart from making him feel like shit – you'll just lose him as a friend, too. You're going to have to lie, tell him there's no one else and then not start seeing Bailey openly for at least another couple of months.'

'That's just taking the easy way out!' I said, chewing on a nail. 'Isn't it?'

'Of course it's not, you dick! You only want to tell him you kissed someone else to make yourself feel better – that's not fair to him. You've got to just live with what you did and make it as OK for him as possible. That's what you do if you care about someone. But you know what, Al? You should *never* end a relationship with someone to be with someone else. End it because it's not working and you're not happy, but not just because you want to swap new for old. It never works. You know what colour grass is on the other side of the fence? It's just green. That's all. Does Gretchen even know about all this?' Vic asked suddenly.

'No idea. All Bailey said in his message was she's back. He did say that he was going to try and get her to go into a psychiatric hospital for a bit when I saw him. I assume she's there, I haven't spoken to her yet.'

'Jesus.'

'Don't tell anyone,' I said immediately. 'I shouldn't even have told you, really.' I took a deep breath. 'Right. I won't say anything to Tom about the kiss. I'll just do the decent thing and end it.'

'I can't believe you're actually even talking like this – like two years with him mean nothing. How can you walk away just like that and . . .'

I'd asked myself the same questions for two days and I was still nowhere closer to an answer, except for the simple truth. 'I kissed someone else,' I said with my eyes closed.

142

'If I was really happy, I'd never have done that. Not in a million years.'

'But *he* kissed *you*! And people slip up all the time! They get drunk, they—'

'I was completely sober, Vic. Just wish me luck.'

'Luck,' she said sadly and hung up.

I got to my feet, straightened my skirt and walked out into the sitting room. Was I actually going to do this?

'Tom,' I began – but the words died on my lips as I saw, to my utter astonishment, *Gretchen* perched on the edge of the sofa and Tom standing frozen in the middle of the room, his mouth slightly open, holding, bizarrely, a fish slice in one hand and a tea towel in the other. He was just staring at me, like he was seeing me for the first time.

'Hi, Al!' Gretchen said merrily, as if she'd seen me only the day before and hadn't, in fact, done a mysterious bunk in the meantime. Hadn't Bailey said she'd need to be hospitalised when she turned up? She looked totally normal, but then I wasn't sure how someone with a mental illness was supposed to look. 'I was just saying to Tom how he and I shouldn't mind that you and my brother are going out with each other now. We'll all have to be terribly grown up about it, won't we?'

I felt my stomach lurch, knot and then fall away from me. Horrified, I swayed slightly on the spot and for a minute thought I was going to faint. Tom hadn't moved a muscle.

Gretchen looked at me, then at Tom. 'What?' she said innocently.

I don't remember who told her to go. I think he did.

After the sound of her feet running down the stairs and the bang of the front door, when it was just us standing at

143

opposite ends of the room, facing each other, Tom finally said, 'Whatever happens next, don't lie to me, Alice.'

I heard a low whimper and realised it had come from me.

'What the hell is going on? What's she talking about, you and her brother going out?'

I shook my head desperately. 'I don't know! I met him for coffee, that's all! What did she say to you?'

'You met him for coffee?' With all the precision of a business hotshot in training, he leapt on that. 'When?'

'Two days ago.'

'You didn't tell me!'

'I've hardly seen you!' I said truthfully. 'I was going to tell you tonight but Vic rang – you and I have barely had a chance to say hello!'

I saw him look at me hesitantly, worried and wanting to believe me. Suddenly understanding Vic's little white lie theory and thinking I saw a chance to claw the situation back, I said, 'I promise, Tom, whatever she told you, she's got the wrong end of the stick. I told her brother I'd see him to discuss Gretchen. She's not well, I've just found out she's—'

But he ignored me. 'So it was just an innocent coffee?'

Out of the corner of my eye I saw a wisp of smoke drift through the top of the oven. Whatever Tom was cooking was starting to burn.

'The oven, Tom.'

'It's only a pizza, leave it.' He looked at me steadily. 'It was just an innocent coffee?'

My eyes started to swim with tears. He was asking me outright. 'Yes,' I said. Which was true – that had certainly been my intention.

'Absolutely nothing happened?'

I just stood there, like a rabbit frozen in the headlights. I didn't know whether to dash towards a lie and protect both of us or face the truth and take the hit. I hesitated just a fraction too long.

He looked at me in disbelief. 'Something did happen, didn't it?'

I nodded slowly, whispered 'Yes', and the tea towel slipped from his fingers and fell to the floor.

I saw his chest rising and falling as he stood there, looking at me. 'Tell me.'

'I kissed him.'

He flinched like I had physically struck him, and a look of surprised pain flashed across his face. Walking over to the small rickety table his mum and dad gave us when they got their new one, he leant on it for support, not looking at me. 'I was going to tell you I'd met up with him, Tom!' I burst, 'I promise – ask Vic!'

The minute the words were out of my mouth I knew I'd made a huge mistake. His head snapped up. 'You've discussed this with other people?'

'Only Vic,' I said pleadingly as he put his head in his hands.

Smoke was more determinedly escaping from the oven. 'Tom, the pizza—' I said timidly.

'FUCK the pizza!' he shouted suddenly, making me jump.

'You know what happened to me today?' he exploded. 'I finally got offered a six-month placement in New York. They first hinted I might be in with a chance before Christmas and I was so excited because you'd just come back from America and loved it – I thought it would be really great for us: you can work from anywhere; we'd have six months in another country, a subsidised apartment tax-free, where we could save loads to buy our own place when we got back! I didn't say anything because I didn't want to get your hopes up, but I've been working my arse off to prove to them that I'm New York office material and today, *today*, I found out they've OKed it – they want me to start in May. I said I'd have to check with my girlfriend first, but I thought you'd be over the moon. I pretty much said we'd go, as long as you agreed. Jesus!'

'Oh Tom . . .' I said. So that was why he'd not said anything more about getting a mortgage or registering for property details; all the time he'd been waiting and working to surprise me. I reached my hand out and moved towards him. 'But sweetheart, that's in, what, two weeks? I couldn't just drop everything and go,' I said truthfully, trying to make things better. 'I've got clients booked. I've worked so hard to—'

He stepped back quickly. 'Don't touch me,' he said brokenly. Then, to my horror, I saw tears well up in his eyes. 'I was doing all that while you were busy kissing Gretchen's brother and then talking to Vic about it?' he whispered incredulously. A tear angrily spilled over and ran down his cheek.

Pushing past me, he strode out of the kitchen and into our room. I followed him and watched as he grabbed a bag from the bottom of the wardrobe and began to shove random things in it, including one trainer, the other of which he left under the bed. He didn't notice and I didn't point it out.

'What are you doing? You're not going? Just stay and talk to me. Tom, it was the first and only time it's happened. It was just a kiss! I promise you!'

He ignored me, marching out of the room, grabbing his keys and wallet from the side in the kitchen, pausing only to glance at the oven, before switching it off.

'Open a window in a minute or the fire alarm will go off,' he said.

Then, picking up his bag, he walked straight past me.

'Tom! Please don't go,' I begged. He wasn't actually *leaving*? 'Tom, *please*, wait!' I heard his feet on the stairs and seconds later the front door slammed. He had gone.

In the silent and slightly smoky flat I stood there stunned, jumping only as the fire alarm shrilly sprang into life with an ear-piercing shriek.

Chapter Seventeen

The high-pitched mechanical bleep bounces off the hospital walls, my eyes are wide with fear as the alarm relentlessly sounds and I'm starting to shake. Not again – oh God, not again. Tom's face is ashen as he looks first at the nurse fiddling with the tubes above Gretchen's head and then at Gretchen herself, the only person untroubled by the noise.

Bailey looks absolutely petrified, he's not even been in the room long enough to sit down yet and now this. 'Don't panic!' the nurse says loudly, moving smartly round to the other side of the room and pushing a button. The noise dies immediately. 'It's not her heart. A tube needed reconnecting,' she explains. 'The alarm has to go off so we know about it, that's all.'

Seconds later, as we are recovering ourselves, a doctor arrives to give Bailey a rundown of what has happened and an update on Gretchen's current condition, so Tom and I are again removed to the relatives' room. Tom is now extremely agitated. He isn't the only one.

'He won't remember everything they're telling him, this

is ludicrous!' He paces the room. 'He's just arrived, you don't have to be Brain of Britain to see he's not going to take it all in. One of us should be with him – if not me, you,' he says, which must cost him.

'Be patient, Tom, he'll be back in a minute.'

'Patient?' He looks at me incredulously. 'If that were your . . .' But he bites his lip and manages not to finish the end of his sentence.

The nurse pops her head round the door. 'Tom? Would you like to go back through now?'

Without waiting for me, Tom practically shoves her aside so he can get past her through the door. I stand up to follow as the nurse comes all the way in and says casually, but with an assured, no-nonsense tone to her voice, 'Let's just give them a minute.'

I sit back down, but instinctively know something is up.

The nurse sits down too. 'So, how long have you and Gretchen been friends?' she asks chattily, absently twisting her wedding ring.

I look at her, frightened and wary. 'Over a year now. Why?'

'Not long really then.' She puts her head on one side, clean light hair gleaming, and waits.

'We're very close though,' I say to plug the gap. 'You know how you just click with some people?'

She smiles. 'Absolutely, kindred spirits and all that. I've known my best friend since school. Love her to pieces but she drives me crazy sometimes. I expect Gretchen does you, too?'

I don't say anything. I just glance out of the window. 'Sometimes, yes, she does,' I say eventually. 'She can be *very* difficult . . . but then she's a manic depressive.' I look back at the nurse. 'Although I'm sure you already know that. So she can't help some of the things she does.'

'I understand,' says the nurse. 'It must be quite hard for *you* sometimes though.'

She has no fucking idea. 'Harder for her, I think.'

'Of course, but equally it can be very painful watching someone you care about struggling to keep going, especially when it appears they really don't want to. You found Gretchen, didn't you?' she asks gently. 'In her flat?'

'Yes,' I say very quietly. I've seen this coming. 'The front door was slightly open,' I say. 'I let myself in and there she was.'

'I wonder why she left the door open?' the nurse says.

'She wasn't in her right mind,' I respond quickly.

'Had you spoken to her yourself, then?'

I dart a glance at the door. 'No, I mean, I assume she wasn't – to have done something like this.'

I stand up quickly, I just want to leave. She puts a hand out. 'It's a really horrible condition, Alice, but very distressing to see too. I'm just trying to give you the opportunity to talk. There are groups we could put you in touch with and—'

'*She's* the one that needs help,' I say swiftly. 'She's supposed to be able to control it, it doesn't *have* to be like this.' I suddenly find myself speaking with more energy than I should have at this time of night, especially given what has happened. 'It can be treated. You can take pills to level yourself out, make the moods less extreme – I can think of plenty worse things. It's only when you *don't* take your medication, when you're selfish enough to stop because you don't think you need it, even though you've been told by people who love you and other people who are experts that you need to take it – that it becomes a problem.'

The nurse looks slightly surprised by my outburst, but not thrown. 'It's very normal to feel angry, Alice,' she says, and suddenly I'm aware I've balled my hands up into fists so tight that my knuckles have gone white. 'It's a common reaction and—'

But it's too late – I've tumbled over the edge. All the shock, fear and anger are rushing up and through me. I can see her sitting slumped there in the sitting room, then frozen in the hospital bed . . . My pulse pounds at my temples, pushes at the back of my mouth.

'It's just selfish!' I finally and tearfully explode. 'She *knows* what she's doing – this *isn't* something that she has no control over! *She* chooses not to take her treatment, even though she knows what will happen. She knows that Bailey and Tom and . . . oh shit!' I scrabble for a tissue as my nose begins to run. I'm a mess of snot and hot, furious tears of frustration and anger. I'm so angry with Gretchen, and myself, that I'm shaking.

I also know I've said too much already, and I want to stop. I want to get away from this nurse. I stumble to the door and almost throw myself down the corridor. I hear her call, 'Alice!' behind me, but I ignore it.

When I get back to the room, just Tom and a new nurse are in there. I don't know where Bailey is.

'Are you OK?' he asks, curious, looking at my tear-stained face as I slump down next to him.

'Fine.'

'Do you know something I don't?' he says sharply. 'Bailey is still with the doctors. What? What is it, Al?' He reaches a hand out and clutches at my arm.

'Nothing's wrong, Tom,' I say wearily, suddenly feeling totally exhausted. *Liar liar, pants on fire* . . . Nothing's wrong? It's never been more wrong in my entire life.

I sit forward and put my head in my hands for a moment and try to regain some composure. What the hell am I doing here? How has this happened? Tom leans towards me and rubs my back for a second, rather awkwardly. I sit back up.

'Better?' he says uncertainly and I nod my head, although to be honest I'm not really.

'You probably need something to eat,' he says. 'I expect . . .'

But I'm not listening, because right at that precise moment, although I think I might have imagined it, I'm sure I see a tiny movement of a finger on the sheet. *Did Gretchen just move her hand?*

Oh holy Christ.

I look immediately at Tom, but he's staring at me intently. She did, I'm sure she did. Oh my God. *Oh my God*.

I start to shake, but try to make out like everything is normal and I haven't just seen anything. At all. Is she coming round? She can't! She simply *can't*.

'You look pretty pale,' Tom says. 'I mean even if you just have a bar of chocolate I think it'd do you good. Want me to give you some change?'

The nurse who has just been quizzing me appears in the doorway. 'Alice, could I just –'

And then we all see Gretchen lightly twitch her head. Unmistakably. An alarm starts to sound again as I jerk my chair backwards and jump to my feet like I've had an electric shock. The chair bangs off the back of the wall behind me with a plastic crack. I can't take these fucking sirens going off every second – it's shooting what's left of my nerves to pieces.

'Shit!' Tom exclaims in shock and then a huge smile spreads over his face. 'Did you see that?' he shouts, twisting to me then twisting back eagerly. 'She moved!'

I cover my mouth with my hand and run from the room. I can hear the nurse calling my name again.

I slam down the corridor and into the ladies' loos, smashing

152

into a cubicle, and dry retch over the bowl. My teeth start to chatter. I think I am moaning 'Fuck, fuck, fuck . . .' I can't be sure. I hear the main door open and the nurse say 'Alice?' more calmly this time. She pushes on the door and because it isn't locked and it's a very tiny space, the door bangs lightly into my arm and I can see her face through the slit.

'Alice, are you all right?'

'Is she coming round? She is, isn't she?' I blurt desperately, then I say it. The words are out of my mouth before I can stop them. 'She can't wake up – she just can't!'

The nurse, to give her credit, does not look horrified. She just says very slowly, 'You're very distressed, in a heightened situation, but . . .'

I barely hear her. I can see Gretchen swallowing the pills again. Oh God, oh God. It doesn't make me a bad person, it doesn't. She asked me to help her . . .

'Help her?' the nurse says and I realise I've just said all that out loud.

There is a pause that seems to last a lifetime.

'Alice,' she says eventually. 'You didn't *help* Gretchen to do this, did you?'

I look at her and I can see, under that calm exterior, her mind racing through textbook phrases . . . *assisted suicide . . . helping a severely depressed person to die, however good the intentions seem . . . illegal . . . carries prison sentence . . . more than a decade. Taking your own life by your own hand is not illegal. Helping someone to do it is.*

'Is that why you don't want Gretchen to wake up, Alice?' she says.

I make a sort of strangulated noise and then blurt, 'I never wanted this.'

'Of course you didn't,' she says softly. 'What you're feeling is very normal, Alice.'

No it isn't! Nothing about this is normal – nothing at all – it's totally fucked up! How can she tell what I'm feeling is OK?

'You're right,' she continues, like she's sneaking up on a dangerous cat she wants to trick into a basket, 'it doesn't make you a bad person. It's very hard to watch someone you love in pain and struggling.'

I watch her creep closer and suddenly I feel exhausted. I just want it all to be over now. I can't do this any more. I'm so sorry, so sorry.

'I thought . . . and she had this plan and I said it was stupid and wrong,' I'm struggling to get the words out, gulping my breath and shaking, 'She said she'd do it anyway and I had to help her . . . she swallowed them . . . and I didn't do it. She was waiting and I didn't, I just sat there and—' I gasp. 'Oh God, oh God. She'd just keep doing this over and over. Hurting herself, hurting those who love her. Is it wrong not to want that for any of us?'

I look at the nurse, utterly terrified.

'Did Gretchen ask you to help her die? Is that why you don't want her to wake up, because you're scared it'll all come out?'

I shake my head vehemently. 'No! She –'

But then I hear the door open. The nurse turns her head and I hear a male voice – it's Tom. 'Is she in here? Al?'

'I'm here!' I say desperately and then the nurse is standing back and Tom's opening the door. 'It's OK!' he says. 'It was just an alarm because she moved her head – but that's a good thing, sweetheart – a really good thing. Don't be scared! It's going to be all right.' He looks at me, his face knitted with concern.

I sniff and tip my head back, trying so, so hard to get

myself under control. 'I'm sorry!' I say and tears rush to my eyes again.

'Don't be ridiculous!' he says. 'You're shattered, it's practically the middle of the night . . . Come on. Come back in the room with me.'

I can't! She's waking up! But I can't stay here either – not with this nurse.

He holds a hand out and without looking at her, my head lowered, I slink past and bolt from the room. I wonder what she is thinking and who she is going to tell. I didn't actually admit anything though, did I? Very nearly – but not quite.

Thank God for Tom.

Chapter Eighteen

The walk back to the room feels like the longest one in the world. I put one foot in front of the other, watching them taking me there. I know that she won't be able to just sit up and talk, that she'll be drowsy and confused, but it won't be long until she *does* know where she is. I have to go, I have to . . .

We round the corner and Bailey is back, listening earnestly to a chiselled-looking doctor, nodding and saying, 'I see.' The doctor looks brisk and impersonal, his features are rather too hard, but the younger new nurse at the back of the room seems to have come over all coy and distracted, so perhaps he is the hospital hottie. He glances briefly at Gretchen as he discusses her. She is mercifully still again and I get the immediate feeling he regards the physical manifestation of a bunch of symptoms as an irritation. Gretchen is just another body to him, a mass of cells. And we are hangers-on who are rather getting in the way.

'So that's about everything, I think,' he says, looking again at the notes in his hand briefly before murmuring smoothly,

'Thank you, nurse,' and passing them to her as if they were an empty martini glass.

He prepares to sweep out of the room when Tom says clearly and firmly, 'So is Gretchen now showing signs of improvement after that earlier scare?'

The doctor looks at Tom as if someone vaguely familiar has approached him at the golf club whose name and status he can't quite remember, but he's pretty certain isn't worth bothering with. He glances at Bailey enquiringly and Bailey says, 'It's fine, I'd like them to be aware of everything that's going on.'

At that, I see a flash of irritation on the doctor's face, because he's going to have to repeat himself. But then just as quickly he fixes it into an expression that must have been labelled 'Concerned Assurance', when he reached in and pulled it out of the box marked 'Doctors' Faces for Unimportant Friends and Relatives'.

'Hello,' he nods in introduction, 'I'm Dr Benedict. Gretchen has ingested a severe mixture of drugs and alcohol,' he says with some pace. 'They have induced the early feature of coma and, as you have already seen, unfortunately that carries a significant risk of cardiac arrest. There are also a number of adverse side effects, including a risk of respiratory depression and renal failure, among others. It is however positive that she has exhibited signs of movement and—'

Then he stops because an alarm goes off again, but this is our third time now so we are used to it.

'As if on cue,' he says dryly and glances behind him as the nurse reaches across Gretchen.

We wait for a second. 'You all right there?' he asks, slightly tersely, waiting to continue.

'Her sats have just dropped,' the nurse says, 'I'm going to have to suction her.'

157

'Is that a good or bad thing?' Bailey looks at Dr Benedict, desperate for some assurance, but he's scanning the monitors swiftly as the nurse is concentrating on some sort of tube and pump-like apparatus.

'OK, guys. I'm just going to ask you to step outside for a moment so we can clear her airways,' the doctor tells us firmly. Tom and I now know the drill well enough to move straight away. Bailey, however, starts to panic. 'Why? Can't she breathe or something? I thought she was waking up?'

Another nurse appears. 'Please can you just wait outside?' Benedict says to us and then adds irritably to a nurse, 'Shut that alarm down!'

'Come on, sis!' Bailey pleads desperately, ignoring him and looking at Gretchen. 'Breathe!'

'Bailey, come on!' Tom grabs him. 'Let them help her.'

'Get off!' Bailey shoves him off roughly. 'Don't do this to me, Gretch!' he says warningly, staring down at her, tears welling up in his eyes. 'Don't you dare do this to me!' He raises his hand up to his mouth and bites down furiously on a balled-up fist. 'I *know* you can hear me!'

Back in the sickly spearmint room, we wait silently. Tom and Bailey aren't speaking to each other, of course, and I have nothing I want to say. I am numb – both feet on the ground, hands in my lap – just staring straight ahead.

I don't know how long we sit like this, I've stopped noticing time. We are all lined up along one wall and I am uncomfortably sandwiched between them, strapped into a rickety rollercoaster car. I have survived one round of loops and dives but I can sense that this drift, along the flat straight bit, is about to end. We are picking up speed again.

Sure enough, Dr Benedict eventually appears, accompanied by the nurse who followed me into the loos. He explains in a calm voice that Gretchen's condition has unfortunately now 'significantly deteriorated'. I am aware that the nurse is watching me carefully.

No one says anything, but one of the boys, I don't know which, makes a frightened gulping sound.

Dr Benedict waits for his words to sink in and then continues. 'Unfortunately secondary complications often arise and Gretchen has now developed respiratory difficulties. We've removed a mucus plug using suction. Did she have a cold, flu, maybe a chest infection before she—' He stops briefly, clearly thinking of a way to avoid saying 'tried to commit suicide' and plumps cleverly for 'was admitted?'

Tom nods. 'She had a cold.'

'She's also a smoker, I believe?' Dr Benedict says. 'When a patient is in a coma and ventilated they are unable to do things like clear mucus build-ups from an infection, as we would do normally by moving and throat clearing. Her blood gases were also quite poor and we've had to increase her oxygen support to sixty per cent.'

'But she was waking up!' Tom says quickly. 'We saw her move!'

Benedict's eyes alight on him. 'As I said, she has now developed a secondary complication. While it seems Gretchen was recovering from the effects of her overdose and her earlier heart problems, we are now actually going to have to sedate her because we don't want her to fight the intubation as she regains consciousness; that's the tube in her mouth so she can breathe,' he adds when Bailey looks blankly at him. 'We now have a new set of priorities.'

'Could she die?' Bailey pales. 'Could these complications kill her?'

Benedict does not falter and looks Bailey in the eye. 'She

159

is very seriously ill, yes,' he says. There is a painful silence. 'But we'll know more in the morning.' He doesn't hold eye contact while saying that, however.

'How long will she be sedated for?' I can't not ask.

'As long as she requires significant oxygen support,' Benedict replies. 'Then, all being well, we could lower her oxygen support and gradually stop her sedation. Then we would remove her ventilation. But let's see where we are tomorrow.' He gives what I imagine he thinks is a concerned yet reassuring smile. Do they practise them in the mirror at home, I wonder? I am not fooled.

Tom and Bailey stand up, so automatically I do too. 'Thank you,' Bailey says dully and one by one we file out of the relatives' room.

I am halfway up the corridor when I realise I've left my bag under the seat, so I double back alone. My footfall is soft and tired. The owners of the two voices I hear drifting back out to me clearly haven't heard me approaching. I pause. It's Benedict and the nurse.

'I was talking with the best friend . . .'

The nurse doesn't sound soothing any more. She sounds urgent. My heart stops.

'I think she might have had something to do with the suicide attempt. She started to tell me about a "plan" they had but then her boyfriend walked in, only he's not her boyfriend and—'

'Nurse,' Benedict interrupts boredly, 'I'm starving and due home for dinner. What exactly are you saying?'

'The friend, she's called Alice, said she didn't want Gretchen to suffer any more.' The nurse doesn't sound in the least bit thrown by Benedict's brusque tone; instead she is determined, convinced. 'She said that she didn't want her to wake up. And I don't think Gretchen *was* unconscious when Alice found her – she said the front door was open, but that doesn't ring true . . . And she became agitated when I suggested she might have been involved.'

I hear Benedict snort. 'Hardly surprising. Relatives tend to get a little touchy about unfounded allegations of a very serious nature.'

'Dr Benedict, I didn't *accuse* her of anything. I think she was on the verge of confessing that she helped her do it. That's assisted killing – murder!'

Benedict laughs a light, patronising laugh. 'Don't you think you might have been watching too many TV dramas?'

'But I'm supposed to tell someone if I think something illegal is going on, or think there is something or someone that could be harmful to the patient,' the nurse persists. 'Well, I'm telling you!'

Benedict sighs. 'OK. Run me through what she said . . .'

Oh no. Oh no no no!

'She started to say they had a plan! What if she meant a plan to help Gretchen die? She said Gretchen asked her for help.'

No, I didn't! Did I?

'Help her to do it? Or help to *stop* her doing it?' Judging by the tone of Benedict's voice, I imagine he is shrugging and looking at the nurse like she is a half-wit. 'What did this girl *actually* say? Did she say, "I helped her commit suicide"?'

'No, but—'

'Well, what *did* she say?'

'Nothing exactly, but . . .'

'Nothing exactly,' Benedict repeats in disbelief.

I start to exhale . . . he doesn't believe her.

'I asked if she'd helped her and she said no, then she was about to—'

'So actually she *denied* it?'

'But don't you think—'

'No,' Benedict says crossly. 'I try not to unless absolutely necessary.'

I start to back away in relief but then I hear her say very firmly and insistently, 'Dr Benedict, I know something is wrong.' There is a pause and I imagine he has stopped and turned to look at her.

He sighs and I hear him say, 'OK, OK. Just keep an eye on everything if it makes you feel better. Monitor her.'

'I would, but I'm going off shift, that's why I wanted to tell you.'

'All right, *I'll* monitor things, and when I go I'll tell someone else to. Leave it with me.'

I hurry away at that – I'll come back for my bag. I walk quickly back up the corridor. Thank God that interfering nurse is leaving, but is that doctor going to be watching me? Will he actually tell someone else when he leaves? He sounded like he was just saying it to shut her up, but still, still . . .

Tom and Bailey are sitting and staring at Gretchen, who actually now looks very calm and peaceful, not at all like she is fighting to stay alive. I sit down.

The only sound is the *bleep, bleep* of the machines and people walking up and down outside. I try to focus on that, rather than worrying about the nursing staff. The sound of everyday life going on beyond these thin, nondescript walls makes me flinch. I count up to seven bleeps, but then Bailey suddenly blurts miserably, 'I knew I was going to miss the plane. We had an end of shoot party last night – I overslept and I knew I wouldn't make it on time so I called and went on standby.'

Tom looks at him in disbelief. 'This happened because you went to a *party*?'

162

'If I could go back in time, I'd get that plane and spare all of us this, I promise.' He shoots Tom a haunted look. 'You can't blame me any more than I blame myself, for what it's worth.'

Tears rise to my eyes as I look at him sitting there, holding himself responsible when I know it is not his fault at all. *Oh what have we done, Gretchen?*

'You went to a bloody party!' Tom repeats, unable to believe his ears.

'Yes, but—' begins Bailey.

'Stop it, please!' I cry, finally reaching my absolute limit and jumping up.

I shove my chair back and run from the room as fast as I can.

Chapter Nineteen

'I'm just so, so sorry,' Gretchen whispered so quietly I could barely hear her. She was lying on the sofa bed in Bailey's flat. I was seated opposite her. 'I didn't realise. I didn't mean to mess everything up . . .'

It was the first time I'd seen her since she'd appeared at the flat and wrought havoc. She was a little thinner after two weeks in a psychiatric unit, and seemed somehow a smaller version of herself altogether – fragile and subdued – but then I'd also never seen her completely without make-up, in a simple T-shirt and what looked like pyjama bottoms. She looked exhausted and stripped back.

'I know you didn't mean to,' I said, trying to settle back in the seat and make it look like I was more relaxed than I actually was.

'It's just you'd said you two were a casual thing, I didn't think . . .' She trailed off, looking devastated. 'But I shouldn't have said anything. I'm so sorry.'

Simultaneously I remembered Bailey saying to me, 'Gretchen explained you were in a serious relationship.'

But then, if there was any confusion and ambiguity, I had only myself to blame. This was exactly the kind of pointless hurt and mess that resulted when you weren't straight with people. If I hadn't behaved like a child and had just been honest with Gretchen – and maybe myself – from the word go about Tom and me, it wouldn't have all ended so bitterly. *She'd* been very ill when she'd randomly turned up and put her foot in it, not in her right mind. What was my excuse? I still couldn't even think about Tom standing there in our kitchen and staring at me without wanting to cry.

I cleared my throat and adopted a bright, chatty tone. 'So how are you feeling? Bailey,' it felt odd using his name like that with her, 'told me they've played around with your medication a bit. Has it helped?'

'A little, maybe . . . So are you and Tom still speaking?'

I shook my head and said with difficulty, 'He's gone. I bought you a couple of DVDs.' I reached for my bag. 'I thought we could watch them together. I haven't seen—'

She hauled herself up on the bed. 'What do you mean he's gone? Gone where?'

'America.'

'*America?*' She froze, like I'd said the moon, and then looked absolutely desolate.

I nodded. In spite of my best efforts, my voice had become a little unsteady. I needed to get a grip, I was supposed to be here to cheer her up, for God's sake, and she already felt bad enough about what she'd done. I looked away so she couldn't see my face and made a show of rummaging around in the bag.

'When was this?' she said.

'He left me a letter.' I got the DVDs out and began to unwrap the cellophane.

The envelope addressed to me had been waiting on the table at home, the day after he walked out:

Alice,

Came back to get the rest of my things. Passport, etc. You weren't here and that's probably best.

You were and are very important to me. I love you very much and all I wanted was to make you happy. I'm sorry that I wasn't able to do that.

I don't think you would ever set out to deliberately hurt me, but I also hope you'll understand why I can't talk to you for a while now.

I go to New York shortly. I've spoken to Paulo and we've agreed I will pay rent for the months while I'm away. With holidays etc I arrive back towards the end of November. By then I'm sure you will have found somewhere else to live. I hope you agree that it's fair of me to ask you to be the one to move out – I can't find somewhere new very easily from over there. Paulo will help find someone else to take your old room.

Be happy.

With my love,
Tom.

'I'm so sorry, Alice,' Gretchen said again. 'If I could go back in time and not say it . . . I never meant to, to—'

'Gretch, I know,' I interrupted, finding it too hard to talk about any more. 'You didn't do it on purpose.' I stood up to put the DVD on. 'And at least it was a clean break. In some ways it's probably very helpful that he had the opportunity to just up and leave.'

She was silent for a moment. 'It's certainly made things much easier for you and Bailey.'

I sat back down. I hadn't meant that. I meant it was surely better for Tom to be able to just walk away from the situation, although I couldn't deny his leaving had meant Bailey and I had a certain freedom we might not have otherwise had.

Vic had pleaded with me not to rush into anything. 'Al, it's so important to have a break in between relationships. You need to confront the end of you and Tom – mourn it, get over it – do whatever you have to do to be free and move on. And don't you think it would be a good thing to have some time to yourself? Pick up with some of the girls? I saw that group email about a picnic in Richmond Park. You haven't replied – you can't be working on a Saturday?'

'I'm not,' I said. 'And it's got nothing to do with Bailey either. It's Dad's birthday, they wanted us all to go home, but Phil can't make it and neither can Fran, so I *have* to go.'

'Well, I'm pleased you're not working – but just don't keep turning down invitations,' warned Vic, 'or people will think you're not interested and stop asking you. This is the perfect opportunity for you to get back in the social mix, Al, decide where you *want* things to go, not just where you get swept to. If Bailey really likes you, he'll wait until you're ready.'

But he didn't want to wait and I was so flattered and delighted that he wanted to see me again so badly, I found I didn't want to wait either.

We went for dinner at a tiny little tapas place that I had never even heard of and talked for hours about the places he had been to and countries I wanted to see. He'd reached over the table and held my hand, gently caressing the inside of my wrist with languid fingers. Then, in the back of the taxi, me very aware of the slight space between us, he had rested his hand on my leg. We jolted as the cab went over a speed bump and he grinned as I was thrown towards him. 'That's much better,' he said and then he kissed me again.

The journey was the fastest I've ever known – all I was aware of was his hand on my thigh, my breath quickening and his kiss becoming deeper as we twisted around on the back seat so we could face each other.

'Are you coming in?' he said to me as the taxi pulled up outside his front door and he kissed me softly on the tip of my nose. 'No pressure.'

I hesitated, and then shook my head. He nodded understandingly and said, 'I had the best evening. Text me when you get home – let me know you got back safe.'

So I did, and got a text back saying, 'I'm lying on my bed thinking of you x'. I clutched my phone to me with delight and longing. He was so unbelievably sexy. Several heady days at work followed, where I found it hard to concentrate and even forgot a booking completely. I temporarily sobered up when I dreamily drifted in to open up the studio and found a very cross client waiting for me. By Friday, I was so completely overexcited about meeting him again, I took some of the worst shots of my professional career; just about acceptable, but dull, dull, dull. It bothered me a bit, but not enough to redo them. Instead I rushed home early, so I could take my time getting ready before slipping into my brand new matching underwear, specially purchased for the evening ahead. Just in case.

It didn't stay on for long. After another meal and two bottles of red wine, my resolve, and any guilt I might have felt about Tom, fell away completely. 'I don't want you to think I do this sort of thing with just anyone,' I said afterwards, lying in his bed and his arms.

'Of course not,' he said, 'but you do it very well nonetheless.' He kissed my neck.

'No, really.' I closed my eyes and exhaled as I tried to concentrate. 'I don't . . .'

He stopped kissing and looked at me. 'Are you saying I'm special?' he teased.

I laughed. 'Very. But just stop talking. Kiss me again.'

'Alice?' Gretchen said. 'You need to press enter on the menu to start the movie.'

I shook my head and sat up a bit in my chair, dragging my attention back to the TV screen. I picked up the remote and pointed it quickly at the machine.

'You don't have to sit here with me like this, you know. I'm sure you've got somewhere else more fun you could be,' she said as I pushed play, then I shook the remote and banged it on my palm before trying again. The opening titles finally began.

I shook my head determinedly. 'I want to watch this movie with you,' I said, and turned it up. If truth be told, I had been invited to a launch party by a client that I ought to have gone to, but I knew Gretchen was just sitting in on her own, and Bailey had made a point of asking me to drop by and see her.

I'd expected her to go straight to their parents' home once she'd come out of the psychiatric hospital, as I would have done in her position, but Bailey had quietly explained that wasn't an option.

'They'll just clash,' he explained. 'Mum will try and take over, which will be fine at first, but then she'll start making all these plans for Gretchen – with the best of intentions obviously,' he held up a hand, 'but Gretchen won't be able to handle it. It'll just blow up, Gretch will take off again . . . It's just not worth it – at least if she's here I know where she is.'

'So she's going to live with you?' I asked, slightly surprised.

He nodded. 'Very short term though. She'll start getting better and stronger as the medication kicks in – then she'll get bored and want to go back to her own flat. That's what happened last time. It won't get in the way of us having . . . space . . . together. I promise.'

'I wasn't worried about that at all,' I said quickly. Jesus, if coming out of a psychiatric hospital wasn't enough to earn you everyone's full focus, care and attention I wasn't sure what was. She had every right to be coming first as far as he was concerned. If it were Phil, or Fran, I'd be doing exactly the same thing.

'She'll be gone before you know it,' he said and pulled me to him.

'I'm sorry to be here, getting in your way,' she said one evening, about two weeks into her living at Bailey's. I'd called over to see her after I'd finished work because she'd sounded particularly low when I'd rung her earlier in the day. She was dressed but had no make-up on and I wasn't entirely sure she'd brushed her hair. By the side of the sofa there were several half full bowls of cereal and almost empty mugs that had stinky fag ends floating on the surface. She climbed over them and settled back into position, tucking a blanket back round her even though it was a pleasantly warm evening.

'How can you be getting in my way when I've come to see you?' I teased gently, sinking into a chair to her left.

'Oh?' she said. 'So you've come to see me? I assumed it was Bay you were after.'

I hesitated. She seemed to have come out of her earlier low mood only to move into a rather touchy one. 'It's always nice to see both of you,' I said reasonably, to make her feel less like an invalid at hospital visiting time, but equally, valued. 'Anyway, you can do what you like, it's your brother's flat.'

'But your boyfriend's,' she countered swiftly.

We lapsed into silence.

'Shall I open the curtains? It's a bit gloomy in here.' I half got to my feet.

She shrugged non-commitally and then winced as I drew them back and bright evening sunshine flooded the room.

'So what have you done today?' I asked, sitting down.

She glanced at me, then back at the TV. 'Not much. Had a therapy session. You?'

'I took a photo of a dog sat next to a bag of feed. Big day,' I smiled.

She smiled so briefly I barely saw it.

'So, any calls from your agent?' I ploughed on determinedly.

She nodded, picked up the TV remote and flicked channels. 'She's still in damage limitation mode. We're going with the story that I'm taking time out to address a booze problem. I can't present like this.' She motioned down at herself with disgust.

'You can't just . . . tell the truth?' I suggested. It was hardly her fault she was ill; after all, no one would expect her to be working if she'd got pneumonia or something.

'People don't "get" mental illness,' she said flatly, still flicking, images and colours jerking around on the screen in front of her. 'They say they do but they don't. They can't see it — you look normal, so you can't be ill, right? Anyway, a booze problem might apparently make me more interesting, more

171

edgy, less kiddie-friendly,' she shook her head in disbelief, 'which is pretty fucked up.'

At least she wasn't going to be out of work for ever though, by the sound of it, which had to be a good thing surely? Her mobile began to ring on the blanket next to her, she picked it up and glanced irritably at the screen. 'Oh fuck off, Mum,' she breathed, looking at the number and then letting it drop heavily back down beside her.

'Answer it if you like,' I said, 'don't mind me.'

'I don't want to speak to her,' Gretchen said tonelessly and stared straight ahead.

'So where's Bailey?' I said, finding that I needed another conversational avenue to explore. It was hard to find neutral topics that weren't controversial – she'd not really done anything with her day that she could talk about.

'He had some stuff to pick up from the library. He said he'd be back by seven. So what are you two up to tonight then?' She looked at me briefly then turned back to the TV.

'Not sure, just a meal I think.' I deliberately downplayed our plans as I felt guilty to think we'd be going out and leaving her on her own. 'How about you?'

She laughed. 'Me? Well tonight I'll be watching TV and answering the phone to my bloody parents who will be ringing every five seconds, as you can see.' She waved in the direction of her now silent phone. 'Mum's hosting some sort of thespian gathering in our garden tomorrow – they're doing a play next year and this is the pre-rehearsal get-together. She wants me to go. In fact,' she changed channels again with energy, 'she wants me to be *in* the play.'

'What?' I wrinkled my nose.

'Yup,' she gritted her teeth. 'Because after eighteen-odd years in the business, that's *really* what I've been aspiring to

– some sad amateur production of "We're All Crap In A Village Hall!" Apparently, it will "do me good". She won't stop going on and on about it. *That's* why she was ringing just then – trying to wear me down. She's going to fucking finish me off at this rate.'

I didn't know what to say. Poor Gretch.

'You see?' She turned to me. 'Just in case you were wondering why I didn't tell you about my illness, this is why . . . because no one bloody understands. She thinks I *want* to be like this!' She gestured wildly around her. 'If I could do something about it, I would. She has no fucking idea.' She glowered and crossed her arms fiercely, flicking the channels violently before finally flinging the remote away. 'I just need a little space and time to get through this bit, that's all.'

I tried hard not to, but I felt a little hurt at being lumped in with everyone else. 'You could have told *me*,' I said eventually. 'I wouldn't have liked you any the less and I could have helped. Been there more for you.'

'Helped me?' she pounced immediately. 'Helped me do what?'

Thrown by her directness, I didn't know what to say. 'Listened?' I hazarded. 'Helped you find better treatment?'

She looked sideways at me, tiredly. 'Don't make this about you being annoyed that I didn't tell you, please. I can barely deal with my own feelings. You'll have to sort all that out yourself.'

My mouth fell open with embarrassment and shock. 'I wasn't—'

'Yes, you were. I'm not saying it's wrong, Alice. It makes people feel good about themselves, being needed.'

Hurt and completely chastened, I closed my mouth. The intensity of her mood was making the room small and uncomfortable. I decided it would be better to go and leave her alone.

'Sorry,' she said two seconds later, as I was about to make my excuses. 'That was shit of me. I didn't mean to take it out on you. You *have* helped, you've been there loads.' She shot a quick look at me. 'You've been amazing, coming round after work all cheerful even when I've been a totally miserable bitch. Like now.'

'You haven't been, you've been ill.'

'Yes I have actually. I didn't *want* to tell you,' she said, looking down at the blanket. 'It's been very hard to keep friendships going alongside my . . . more reckless phases. Friends in the past have found my behaviour hard to cope with, even when I've been honest with them. I've found it easier on the whole to try and keep it under wraps. I didn't want to lose you too.' Her eyes filled and she looked quickly away, her voice bleak. 'It's not the best, feeling like you're the only one going mad in a world full of sane people.'

I felt an overwhelming rush of affection and sadness as I watched her internal struggle. I just wanted to hug her. I got off my seat and knelt down next to her, moving a cereal bowl.

I picked up her hand and grasped it firmly. 'There's nothing you could do that would make me not be your friend,' I said firmly.

She couldn't look at me. 'I'm so sorry,' she whispered, tears spilling over. 'I've let you all down so badly.'

'You haven't at all,' I said gently.

'I'm so embarrassed and ashamed. That night at yours . . . I would never, you know, with Paulo if . . .' She trailed off, face flaming. I tried to hide my shock. She'd slept with him? I just shrugged and half smiled. 'These things happen.'

'I know I shouldn't have stopped taking my medication,' she fiddled with the edge of the blanket urgently with her other hand, 'but I missed the hypermania. I like the person it makes me become. You feel beautiful . . . all lit up inside like a human firefly, flitting from place to place – everything you touch bursts into life. It's like being in a plane while reaching out of the window at sunset and touching the underside of a sunburnt cloud; I can just feel it flow through my fingers.'

But at what cost?

She twisted the edge of the blanket up into an agitated peak. 'The lithium makes me thick and numb. I don't feel anything – I just want to *feel* again. And I'm boring, people who used to ring me haven't rung me for ages and I can't ring them because I've got nothing to say . . . mostly because I've done nothing, felt nothing.' She looked desperately sad.

'You've got me,' I said. 'And Bailey.'

'I know,' she sniffed, 'but that's not fair either. Bailey's always had to be there, no matter what I've done. I don't deserve him.'

I suddenly wondered if our getting together had made things worse, two of the people she relied on starting something new and exciting. Had she felt left out, lonely?

'Are you OK with me and Bailey being together?' I asked eventually.

'Of course,' she said quickly. She pulled her hand back and reached for a tissue. 'It was me who set you up, remember?'

I smiled at her and she almost managed a smile through her tears.

'I hate that you're seeing me like this, all pathetic and crying like a baby,' she said. 'But I'm also so glad you're here.'

Chapter Twenty

'Alice, what the fuck are you doing?' Gretchen exploded, as I picked up a plate she'd left on the sitting room floor to take it out to the kitchen. I'd arrived at Bailey's late on Friday night after an exhilarating shoot in Barcelona, desperate to tell him all about it, only to find him out getting a takeaway, her in her usual place on the sofa and the sitting room in a tip. It wasn't exactly the start to the evening I'd had in mind. Was it only two months since she'd flipped out? It felt more like two bloody years.

'I thought I'd make us a cup of tea, so I'm taking the plate out as I'm going to the kitchen. It's no big deal,' I said, as calmly as I could manage.

'I'll do it in a minute!' she said crossly. 'I'm not an invalid, despite what everyone thinks.'

I bit my tongue, put the plate back and sat down. These new bursts of bored, irritable self-absorption were pretty trying. While I was glad that she was noticeably less depressed, appeared to have more energy and was becoming restless – all of which could only be good signs – I wished she'd hurry up and get there faster.

'Sorry,' she said immediately. 'I'm just bored, really crazy bored – I know you were just trying to be helpful. How was Barcelona?' She attempted to look interested.

'Oh, amazing!' I began, my eyes lighting up. Then I saw the wistful and sad look on her face. 'But very tiring,' I lied, 'and uncomfortably hot.' I racked my brain for a more neutral topic. 'Hey, guess what? I found out my sister is expecting her first baby!'

Fran's news was the talk of the family, particularly with Mum, who was over the moon. She'd rung to summon me for lunch, incandescent with family pride.

'I thought you could bring this new Bailey with you,' she'd said, magnanimous in her disapproval, 'as long as he doesn't mind having to meet Frances and Adam at the same time too. I'm doing lunch for them because Frances is in that totally knackered stage, you'll know when it happens to you, and I'm doing a veggie pasta because she can't bear the smell of cooking meat. Already! Amazing, isn't it?'

I was pretty certain 'this Bailey' absolutely didn't want to be subjected to meeting the majority of my nearest and dearest to talk babies, especially so early in our relationship. Neither did I particularly. Being around family was all we seemed to do.

'Wow, that's great news,' Gretchen said uninterestedly, clearly not caring less about Frances. We lapsed into silence for a moment and then she suddenly got up quickly. 'I think I'm going to stay at mine tonight.' She slipped a foot into her shoe. 'I know Bailey thinks I'm not ready yet, but I am.'

I folded my optimistically shaved legs up and under me. She wasn't going to hear any argument from my corner.

177

It would be a novel experience to have a Friday night on my own with Bailey. Rocking up at his after a long day at work, craving a big glass of wine – and sex – only to find Gretchen curled up on the sofa miserably, refusing all food except the odd biscuit and staring at the TV like she wasn't really seeing the picture, was seriously losing its appeal. And because I was her best friend, it wasn't even like I could say, 'I'm sick of your sister hanging round at yours *all* the time, can't you tell her to sling her hook?'

I didn't even *want* to be staying in, as it went. I wanted to be going out with Bailey, going to fun places, the dating stuff you were supposed to do at the start of relationships that I'd never had with Tom either because we'd been living in the same flat when we started seeing each other. Bailey, however, was nervous about Gretch being on her own for long periods of time, so when we did go out, I felt like we were having to rush back for the babysitter. In fact it was worse – we *were* the babysitters. Bailey and I would hold hands chastely while we desperately waited for her to go to bed, so we could make out on the sofa. Except I was more than ten years too old to be satisfied with that sort of stolen moment. Was it *that* selfish to want some time with my new boyfriend that didn't involve her?

'Anyway,' Gretchen said, as if she'd read my mind, 'you two badly need some time on your own. Tell him I'll text him to let him know I got back to my flat OK.'

'You're sure you'll be all right?' I said, immediately feeling like a total bitch for thinking such mean thoughts.

But she was already halfway out the door and answered me only with a resounding slam.

Two weeks later, when she'd apparently had several successful off and on nights at her own place, I tentatively suggested to Bailey that perhaps we could have a weekend in Paris, a sort of 'Let's start again, shall we?' gesture, coupled with showing him off to Vic of course.

He agreed, once he'd checked in with Gretchen that she'd be all right. 'Just do it,' she said. 'It'll be the perfect test for me – three whole days on my own. Look, if worst comes to the worst, I promise I'll call Mum and Dad. OK?'

I, however, had no doubt in my mind that it was the right thing to have done when I finally woke up next to Bailey in our anonymous, private hotel room. He kissed me slowly like I was the first woman he'd ever seen and the last he wanted to love. Could things finally be turning a corner? God, I hoped so.

'Thank you for being so patient for the last couple of months,' he said, looking at me as he stroked my head. 'You are without doubt the most incredible, strong, beautiful woman I've ever met. How did I ever manage before you?' Then we had sex that was so good I actually felt like the woman he'd described.

'How did he ever manage without you?' Vic repeated, later that afternoon. 'He said that?'

I nodded. 'I know! I almost melted. So? What do you think?'

'I think it's very nice of you to drag yourself out of bed long enough to meet us for coffee during your Paris bonkathon. Thank you,' she said. 'I feel honoured.'

'I meant,' I said quietly, as we walked around Lafayette, 'what do you think of him?' I motioned to Bailey, who was admiring the department store's impressive galleried roof, being pointed out to him by Luc.

'OK, OK, I like him!'

I smiled, relieved. 'Good. Me too. And don't you think he's gorgeous?'

'Heartbreakingly,' she said.

'Do you think we'd have pretty children?' I said dreamily.

She paused and said carefully, 'I'd leave all that sort of thing to your sis for now. I'm not sure Bailey is the sort I see with children. A great fun uncle perhaps, but he's already done quite a lot of looking after already, hasn't he?'

We walked in silence for a moment while I decided firmly she was wrong, but I'd keep it to myself.

'I heard from Tom last week,' she said, changing the subject. 'He's OK. Started dating.'

Which oddly made me feel very strange. I'd not really allowed myself to think about Tom.

'Thought you might like to know,' she continued, pulling a stray bit of dark hair out of her mouth. 'In fact I think he was hoping I'd tell you, poor old bloke. I take it he still hasn't contacted you yet?'

I shook my head.

'Give it time, he will. I'm sure of it.'

'Did he ask about me?' I said.

She nodded. 'He asked if you and Bailey were . . . together.'

I winced.

'I didn't say I was meeting you today,' Vic said, 'that would have been way too much for him, but I did say I thought you were dating. I wasn't more committal than that. That's when he said he was seeing people.'

I didn't say anything. She reached out and squeezed my hand.

'So,' she said, wisely changing the subject again, 'was that girls' night at Tanya's fun? I sort of wish sometimes that I didn't still get included in the emails. I know everyone does it to keep me in the loop, but it sucks knowing you're all there having fun without me. Damn Luc and his smooth French ways!'

'What email?' I frowned. 'I didn't see anything.' There was a brief pause and then Vic said kindly, 'I'm sure it was just an accidental oversight, Al, or I think maybe I'd explained to Tanya that you were taking some time out to look after a pal. How is Gretchen, by the way?'

I was subdued when we arrived back in England on Sunday night, already missing Vic's easy company while knowing Gretchen was waiting for us back at the flat.

When we walked in through the door, however, I thought perhaps we'd come to the wrong place. The whole flat smelt faintly of polish and effort; fresh flowers were in a vase in the sitting room and food was waiting for us on the table. But it was the difference in Gretchen herself that was most apparent.

She literally looked like a different person. Her hair was bouncy and gleaming, she was wearing make-up and a dress I didn't recognise. She was positively glowing with excitement. It was as if the other Gretchen had simply packed up and left town. She looked like her old self again.

'Come in and sit down,' she said shyly. 'I've made you dinner. And I've got some news.'

'I know it's the right thing for me to do,' she insisted later, as I cleared our plates. 'Acting and singing is the way forward, no more presenting, and this three-month summer workshop I've booked will be the perfect kick-start. I'm so excited! It starts in August. You two have been so great, but I need some routine and structure back. I can't sit around here or at mine all day like Miss Haversham.'

'That's great, Gretch,' Bailey said warmly as he reached

behind him for the giant cake we'd brought back for her. 'Sudden, but great.' He got up and grabbed three bowls and spoons, then sat back down, cut himself a large slice and dug in. 'So where is this course?' he asked through a mouthful.

'New York,' she said.

Bailey paused. 'But, sis, I can't just get on a plane if you flip out again or come off the lithium.'

She looked at him patiently. 'I can see why you might worry about that. But don't. It's not going to happen. I promise you. Look at how much better I am. I've already lined up a therapist out there . . . I did that before I even found somewhere to live! I'm going out way before the course even starts so I've got plenty of time to get settled. Everyone thinks I was poised to go out there anyway, so I might as well actually do it. It makes perfect sense!'

Bailey looked doubtful. I, on the other hand, was holding my breath with hope. It was the first time in ages she'd been this animated, and might Bailey and I also be about to get the chance to be a proper couple? Just us? She could have said she was going to swim to America and I'd have offered to blow up her armbands myself, I was so keen for her to grab the opportunity with both hands.

'Talking of somewhere to live. My flat.' She reached into her pocket and pulled out a key. 'I'm not rocked about leaving it empty for so long and, Al, I know you have to move out of your place soon anyway . . . I'm planning to stay on in the States until the end of the year, so you'd be doing me a massive favour and it would be rent-free, of course. Help you save some cash for your own place. Would you stay there for me?' She shoved it across the table and it slid straight into my lap.

'I can't deny she hasn't got it all worked out,' Bailey said to me later in bed. 'But she doesn't even know anyone in New York! What am I going to do if I get a call from some hospital saying she's been admitted? I've already turned down so much work these last few months to be here for her. I can't start flying across the Atlantic at the drop of a hat. Do you think I should persuade her to stay?'

'No, I don't think so,' I said slowly. 'She's probably right. She needs a challenge. And she does seem a lot more stable. I think we have to trust her.' I was actually really proud of her – she'd been so patient, come such a long way to get herself to where she was. I couldn't help but feel sad for me that just as I was getting my friend back, she was leaving. But then, it had been such an intense last couple of months, I sort of needed the space from her too.

'I think it'll be great for her,' I said. 'And New York! The lucky thing!'

I still can't believe I was so stupid.

Chapter Twenty-One

Bailey eventually finds me in the hospital chapel.

'Don't just leg it like that again,' he says. 'It really freaked me out. What are you doing down here anyway?'

He has a point. The chapel is cold, dingy and the walls are saturated with desperate prayers. It's hard to imagine anything good coming from this little room set aside for people who are holding out for a miracle, or looking to find comfort from a habitual faith. There is a small plastic Jesus, arms outstretched, balanced on a table, alongside a book with a pen next to it, a sort of religious request book. 'Pray for the soul of Mary McCarthy', 'Make my dad better please'. But at least there are no doctors, and no watching nurses.

'I think I walked past the same man in a dressing gown three times, it was like I was on some sort of medical Escher staircase,' he says conversationally. He twists a chair round behind me, so it's facing the opposite way. Then he sits across it and reaches his arms round my shoulders and neck. 'Don't cry,' he says and kisses the back of my head.

Actually, him doing that makes me feel even more like crying. 'How'd you know I'd be here?'

'I didn't,' he confesses. 'Tom suggested it.'

Oh.

He peers over into my lap. 'You're reading the Bible?' He reaches an arm round before I can close the book and grabs it.

'"Lord, how many times shall I forgive my brother when he sins against me? Up to seven times?" Jesus answered, "I tell you, not seven times, but seventy-seven times,"' he reads aloud. 'Hmm,' he says. 'Seventy-seven. That's a fuck of a lot.'

'Bailey! It's a chapel,' I say quickly.

He looks around the craphole of a room. 'Al, I'm not sure God is here any more than if I was sitting in a cupboard full of cleaning equipment. Who are you down here forgiving anyway? Gretchen? Me?'

I shake my head. 'Of course not – it's really not your fault. Tom's just scared, he's looking for someone to blame.'

'I wasn't just talking about me missing the plane. No one should have to sit at the bedside of their best friend with two ex-boyfriends of all people. It isn't reasonable.'

I try to smile. 'No it isn't – you're damn right there.'

'I'm so very sorry for all this, Alice. For everything. I really am.'

There's not very much I can say to that. It won't change anything.

'Try not to blame Gretchen,' he says. 'It really isn't her fault either.'

I say nothing.

'Although admittedly, things weren't exactly easy for us, were they? If we had more time together at the start . . . if she hadn't been so low and needed us both so much, perhaps things would have been different . . .'

185

Oh please don't. I don't need this on top of everything else.

'You were so amazing through that time, you know,' he says. 'She wasn't exactly easy, but you were incredible.'

No I wasn't. She was my friend, who needed help. It's what you do, isn't it?

'I *am* truly sorry though,' Bailey says, staring at the plastic Jesus. 'I wish it could have been different. It's just once she went to the States and I had the opportunity to start working again . . . you know I couldn't turn the offers down, Al, I was so strapped for cash by then. We barely saw each over those three months, did we? I felt like a tax exile. And I guess,' he sighs sadly and shrugs, 'that's the downside of my job. I *have* to be away a lot. It's just the way it is.'

'We really don't have to do this, Bailey,' I say. Mostly because I don't want to – it's still too fresh to be discussing it. I can hear myself now on the phone to him in LA, in Cape Town, in Timbukfuckingtu and God knows where else, an unfamiliar, unwelcome needy tone creeping into my voice as I said, 'I miss you.' Quietly worrying but trying to squash it as he replied absently, 'I miss you too, but I'm working hard and it feels good to be doing stuff again. Listen babe, I've got to go, still got some things to write up. I'd like to get it down while it's still fresh in my head, you know?'

'So, do you forgive me?' he says, snapping the Bible shut with one hand and giving it back to me.

'There's nothing to forgive,' I shrug. 'People fall out of love. It happens.' Then I feel foolish and embarrassed because he never actually said he loved me. I just loved him.

'You're so great, Al.' Bailey shakes his head admiringly. 'Nothing ever fazes you, does it?' He shivers. 'Can we go back up now? It's really cold in here. And it's creeping me

186

out a bit.' He shudders as he stares at the statue on the table.

'It's not cold, you baby!' I force a smile. 'You're just used to more exotic temperatures.'

'I'm not away that much,' he scolds.

I raise an eyebrow.

'OK, I am.' He sighs. 'I might have to reappraise that a bit now though. I thought Gretch was doing so well. But . . . anyway. I'll just have to scale down again for the time being. Articles on "A hundred weekends of fun in Britain" here I come!'

'You're going to do that, just to be around for her?' I can't keep the incredulity out of my voice. He *has* to be away, doesn't he? It's just the way it is, isn't it? Apparently not . . . not when he doesn't want it to be.

'Of course!' Bailey says in surprise. 'She's going to be really low when she wakes up,' he adds determinedly, as if there is no other alternative, she *will* get better. 'You remember.'

I know he's her brother and he'd do anything for her, and that's how it should be. If Gretchen shouted for him on the highest hill in the middle of the loudest storm, he'd get to her somehow. I think it's lovely that he has such a generous, big, kind heart that still remains full of hope that he can love her better; it's one of the many reasons I fell in love with him. You should be there for your family. It just really, really hurts to have it so obviously pointed out that I am not as important to Bailey as Gretchen is – and I never will be. She will always come first with him.

'When I see her just lying there in that hospital bed, full of all those tubes, I just want to rip them all out of her,' he suddenly says, 'even though I know she won't be able to breathe without them. She looks so tiny, so vulnerable.

I can't tell you what it feels like to see someone you love like that. I actually feel my heart physically wrenching in my chest.' He shakes his head. 'You want to do anything you can . . . do it *for* them, and it breaks me up that she was in a place so bad that she could do this to herself, even when she knows what it will do to me if one day – God forbid – she ever succeeds. The only way I can even vaguely deal with it is by telling myself that she would never do it if she was rational. Never.'

His eyes become shiny and he continues, 'I know she's a grown adult and I know she's not perfect by any means, but you know, when I look at her, Alice, I just see a little girl. She was a right pain in the arse when we were growing up, but she always, always smiled when I came into the room. She used to follow me around everywhere. She was all, "*Bailey! Let me! Muuuuuummmmm!*" he mimics. "*He won't let me play!*" He does a short little laugh. 'I'd be racing off upstairs with one of my mates at that point of course, mean git, but she never gave up – I'd hear her stomping up the stairs determinedly after me. She just wanted to be around me, I think.' He pauses, letting himself swim about in happier memories, then adds, 'I'd let her play now if she wanted to.'

A sudden tear angrily shoots out of the corner of his eye and courses down his face, but he wipes it away quickly. 'I should have been there, Alice! That's what big brothers do!' He falls silent for a moment. 'It was me who was with her the first time. When she was seventeen.' He has never told me this before. Neither has she.

'Her boyfriend dumped her. Usual story – first love, huge passion and all that. She was really, really low and Mum sent me up to get her from her bedroom because she wasn't coming down for tea. She was on her window ledge in the dark. You know, all I can remember is seeing the window flapping around in the wind, in the space. I spent twenty minutes trying to talk her down, but she jumped anyway.'

'Oh, Bailey!' I reach out and clasp his hand for all I am worth. I would do anything to make it better for him. Anything.

'She only broke her ankle and three ribs – I don't know how. We thought she was just in a state over the break-up, but I can see now that was when it was starting. It was totally terrifying and I'm so sorry that you had to find her, Alice, I really am. But don't hate her for it. She really doesn't know what she is doing.'

He looks at me so sincerely, but I still can't say anything to that.

'I wouldn't blame you if you did, I mean even Mum can't do it any more. She hasn't got anything left. It's just turned her into a wreck and she hasn't got it in her to watch Gretch fight again . . . I think Dad might persuade her to come down tomorrow.' He rakes a hand over his tired face. 'I don't get it myself. If it were my child I'd walk into the mouth of hell and snatch them back from the edge of oblivion if that's what it took,' he says, suddenly fierce.

Finally he tips his head back, forces his eyes shut and says, 'When this is all over, I'm going to take her somewhere hot where she can sink her toes into some warm sand and just have a cold beer. Simple stuff.'

I know he means it too – he would trade every single good experience of his life, every laugh yet to come out of his mouth and every possession he had, as long as she is all right.

'Bailey,' I say quietly, 'can I ask you something? Did Gretchen ever ask you to end our relationship?'

He looks astonished. 'No! Why?'

So Vic was right – he just hadn't got enough strength for anyone else to need him, and to be fair, by then I *had* become clingy. Vic was indefinitely loved up in Paris, Gretchen was in New York where there was also a five-hour time difference, Tom was gone, my family had become obsessed with landmark baby scans, Fran moving to a bigger house, the next midwife visit. I was lonely, but I can see how my saying 'I miss you' repeatedly to Bailey during overseas phone calls added up to make him feel overwhelmed with responsibility for yet someone else's happiness, when all he wanted was a bit of fun. We might still be together now if I'd made absolutely no demands on him whatso-ever, just been there for him when he needed me – his strong, reliable, caring Alice.

'Sorry,' he rubs my arm briefly, 'I didn't mean to go off on one, bending your ear like that. I feel much better now though, thanks,' he says gratefully. 'Come on, Ally pally!' He stands up and holds out a hand. 'Let's go. I'm done with this chapel. It smells funny too.' He wrinkles his nose. 'Gretchen needs us up there.'

'I'll be back up in a minute, I promise,' I say.

He nods, gets up easily and walks to the door. 'Thanks for listening, Al,' he says. 'It so helps that you know Gretchen as well as you do. She, we, owe you so much. Thank you.' And he leaves.

With trembling hands, I turn from the page in the Bible on forgiveness to the one on envy. I read the words over and over again, focusing so hard that I can see the grain of the paper as the words brand my brain:

In envy and selfish ambition, there you find disorder and every evil practice.

James 3:16–18

Chapter Twenty-Two

'Take a big breath, sweetheart, now tell me what's happened?'

'He dumped me! We finally get some time just us and he's ended it!' I was hunched up against a wall in Gretchen's flat, crying into the phone.

'What, literally just now?' Vic said.

I tried to get my voice under control. 'He got back from Rio yesterday—'

Vic snorted. 'As you do.'

'. . . And asked me to meet him as soon as I could. I didn't think anything of it, I just thought he wanted to see me.' I looked around desperately for another tissue. 'He said he needed to get out of the flat to stop himself falling asleep,' I continued. 'So we met in Hyde Park for coffee, then went for a walk. I was all overexcited to have him back and all chatty.'

'Of course you were,' Vic agreed sympathetically.

'I was kicking the leaves around and gibbering on about how I've always wanted to go to New England and see the fall there, all sort of "Don't you think the colours are amazing? Go on, you kick them too."' I closed my eyes with the humiliation. 'Oh I feel so *stupid*! *And* he's going to think I meant we should go together, which is even worse.'

Vic waited patiently.

'He was really quiet, but I thought it was just jet lag, so I said I'd kick for him, but I kicked a lump of dog shit by mistake.' I tried to laugh, but found I couldn't.

'Oh no!' Vic, to her credit, didn't laugh at all.

'It was hidden under a pile of leaves. I was wiping my foot on the grass and saying I'd wash it off when we got back, but he said it wasn't working and I said it was, and I lifted my foot up to show him I'd got almost all of it off and *then* he said, "Not the shoe, us. *We're* not working."'

'Ouuuucchhh,' groaned Vic. 'What did you say?'

'I don't really remember. Nothing much at first.' I huddled over the phone. 'He walked me back here, which must have been weird for him, what with it being his sister's flat.'

'That was the bloody least he could do!' Vic said, outraged.

'But when we got back and I knew he was going to go and that would be it, I tried to persuade him he was making a mistake.' The pain and rawness of the fresh memory – him just standing there, resolute, as I hopefully laid out reasons why I was worth staying with – made me start to cry afresh.

'It doesn't get more soul-destroying than that,' Vic said.

'I know,' I gulped. 'Holding on to just a small shred of dignity would have been nice.'

'Break-ups are never pretty . . .'

'I kept on and on until he lost patience with me. And then I asked him if there was anyone else. It really wasn't my finest hour.'

'And? Is there someone else?'

'He says not, and that he'd never do that, he just couldn't give me what I need or want. He said it wouldn't be fair to pretend otherwise.'

'Well at least he admitted he wasn't man enough for you after all and has serious personal shortcomings,' Vic said crisply, 'but he was the one that pursued *you* and was all "I can't wait for you," and "Let's just grab happiness now". Urrggghhh! I *hate* headfuck men like him!'

'And then, then I asked him to stay anyway, just for one more night,' I blurted, my heart breaking. I didn't want to admit the depths I'd sunk to – even to her – but neither could I stop my confession.

'Oh, Al . . .' Vic fell silent for a moment.

She waited as I cried quietly, the sound echoing round Gretchen's flat. Then, gently, she said, 'And did he stay? Is that why you're calling me now? Has he just left?'

I shook my head, which was stupid of course, because she couldn't see me. 'He refused to stay.' I tried to laugh and blew my nose a little bit. 'Which just about finished me off. He got all sulky and started looking at his watch and saying over and over again that he had work to do. Eventually I got so upset I just shouted at him to fuck off if it was that important to him, and he did.'

'Well let's be thankful for small mercies,' Vic said. 'At least he, and you, did one thing right. That's what you have to hold on to, Al – that ultimately you told him to fuck off.'

'Only because he pushed me to it.'

'Doesn't matter,' Vic insisted. 'You still told him. Did Gretchen know he was going to do this? You've rung her, I take it?'

'I tried to,' I admitted, 'but it's so hard to catch her, what with the five hours time difference and everything. She was out last night and it's too early to call again yet – it's six on Sunday morning for her, she'll be in bed. You were so right, you said this would happen if we broke up and it has.'

'Yeah, well, I take no pleasure in that.'

'You were right about everything. That's part of the problem too – I'm so fucking *angry* with myself for all this.' I tearfully scrunched up my tissue into a ball. 'When Tom and I broke up you said have some space and get back in the mix. But instead,' I threw the tissue away angrily, 'I spent every waking minute at Bailey's with Gretchen and him for the first two months, which, OK, wasn't really his or her fault because she was ill, but then she goes and he starts poncing off everywhere . . . and what do I do then?'

Vic waited, knowing that I didn't expect her to answer.

'I wait around like some saddo on standby for him to get back from each trip – I make *him* my priority.' I began to rant. 'I turn down a shoot in Italy because otherwise I'll be leaving the country when he's coming home for two days. I take loads of boring home-based jobs that mean I'm always around at the drop of a hat. I mean, what the fuck was I *thinking*?' I yanked another tissue out of the box violently. 'It's so pathetic!'

'Come on, Al, we've all done it,' Vic said. 'You fell head over heels for him and what you thought he was going to offer you, so you threw yourself into it. You're not the first person to realise that living your life for someone else is a crap idea. At worst, you gave up six months to a bit of a dickhead. But you'll never make that mistake again.'

I listened as I dried my tired, puffy eyes and then blew my sore, red nose.

'When you're busy working and getting on with day-to-day bollocks – actually *living* the situation – it's hard to step back and look at the bigger picture and see where you're going wrong. I don't know a single person who hasn't thought, "I really should phone one of the girls and arrange to meet up, but hey, I'm tired and it's been a bitch of a day. All I want to do is go home, have some tea and collapse with my other half." I know I have. This is a really sad thing to admit, but half the time I'm too knackered even to use Facebook to keep up with people. I only go on it to have a nose at other people's photos. Now that's bad.'

I snorted slightly and then did a big sniff. 'You're not just saying that to make me feel better?'

'Of course not! Stop beating yourself up. You've got so much going for you, Alice. You're amazingly talented, you've built up a really successful business and now you're free to take whatever jobs you want! Start chasing the ones you're really interested in again – the travel ones.'

'I should, I know,' I said. 'I am at least really lucky to have a job I love – I know that.'

'Atta girl!' she said briskly. 'You never have to see the creep ever again. The rest of your life starts here. Now what are you going to do today? I don't think you should be on your own, because you may feel angry now, but you're going to get all sad again later.'

Later? The tears were already welling up. She was right! I might have seen him for the last time. We'd had our last ever kiss. Oooohhhhhhhhh! That hurt.

'Why don't you go and see your mum and dad? Stay at theirs perhaps?'

'I've got a job tomorrow first thing I need to be here for – a nice calm one, actually. Just me, a client and a box of nail varnishes. Thank God.'

'OK, well just go for lunch. Listen, I'm sure you've thought of this,' she said, 'but it's Halloween today. That's quite a big deal in the States so bear it in mind if you're trying to get hold of Gretchen later. Now, I want you to get off the phone and call your mum. OK? Call me tonight when you get home again.'

I hung up and had another cry while I wondered where he was and what he was doing. Then I came worryingly close to sending him a really shit text to 'check he was all right' and just to say that I hoped we could 'still be friends' and that I hadn't meant to tell him to fuck off.

But then I thought about what Vic had said, and I made myself hit delete instead. I dialled my mum and dad quickly. It would take me two hours to get there, but it *would* be nice to have a hug and a cry at home.

Mum tersely answered after barely two rings. 'Frances, for the love of God – it's *just Braxton Hicks and I am about to leave*! The more you keep ringing me, the more it slows me down.'

'It's not Frances,' I said, doing a sorry-for-myself sniff. 'It's me.'

'Oh, Alice,' she said. 'Don't sniff, blow. Now listen, I'd love to stop, but I can't – your sister is utterly convinced she's in labour and is in danger of having her baby on the kitchen floor, although I might add this is now the fourth time in two days we've been here.'

That explained why Fran hadn't called me back yesterday just after Bailey had left.

'Not only that, but Dad and Phil are at each other's throats because Phil had some friends over last night and now there's a hole halfway up the back fence. Philip!' she said crossly, 'don't make that hand gesture at your father! It's very rude . . . yes, he does know what it means actually and that's not the point. I've got to go, darling. Thank God for you. I should have had you first and stopped after that. I'll call you later. Philip, speak to your sister.'

'Yo, Al,' said Phil. 'What's new? Dad's going *mental* here and Frances has lost the plot too, she keeps ringing and, like, *wailing* down the phone, it's really freaky. Oh my *God*! All right! Al, I've got to go. There's, like, some insane old man just shouting at me and saying I've got to go and fix the stupid fence – even though it's *nothing to do with me*. I'll put him on.'

Then my father took the phone and said tightly, 'Hello, Alice. We're all a bit fraught here today, I'm afraid. Philip, as I'm sure you've realised, still hasn't got a job and has taken to a nocturnal existence that involves lying on the sofa scratching himself, eating anything that sits still long enough, drinking my whisky, and is now apparently wantonly destroying the house for his amusement. Yes you *did*, Phil!' he roared and I had to hold the phone away from my ear. 'What kind of bloody idiot do you take me for? The football was *right by it*!'

So, instead of going home, where they'd all apparently gone mad, I spent most of the day on-off crying in bed, which wasn't quite the start to the rest of my life I would have chosen, and then discovered a random bottle of peach schnapps under the kitchen sink at about five p.m. As a direct result, things later took a turn for the worse.

With shaking fingers, which could have been nerves or the first sign of my liver packing up, I dialled, and held my breath as the unfamiliar overseas tone began. Shit! It was ringing! I wasn't even sure he'd still have the same mobile number, let alone if it would work in America. I waited.

All afternoon, every time I'd thought of Bailey, who until yesterday had been my boyfriend – who I could have called any time I liked – I'd felt myself collapse with pain and longing on the inside. But like some masochistic mixer, through my increasingly fuzzy haze I'd started to think guiltily about Tom, too. Had he felt like I felt now? Had he had to go to another country and act like everything was OK, be bright and cheery, start a new job in a city he didn't know *feeling like this*? Oh poor, poor Tom.

It was a sloppy, curdled cocktail of guilt and heartbreak that I could barely stomach and, by eleven p.m., I'd been beyond reason and just felt very, very sad. I wanted Bailey and I missed Tom, too. It had seemed perfectly sensible to call him in America to apologise for breaking his heart.

He answered with a happy 'Hello?' It was like six months of not speaking had never happened. 'Hi,' I said in a whisper of a voice. 'It's me. Are you awake?'

'Alice?' He sounded very surprised, as well he might be, but not altogether displeased, which I took as a good sign – but then I was so hammered I would have taken a smack in the face with a road sign as encouragement.

'I just wanted to say that I'm sorry,' I slurred, as I wandered around Gretchen's living room on her cordless phone. 'So very, very sorry. Bailey dumped me, I thought you might like to know, and it's not nice, is it? I felt bad, because you are a lovely person, Tom – lovely, kind and generous with a big heart. And I miss you very much. I'd like to hug you actually,' and I started crying at that point. 'You're a good hugger.'

'Alice, are you drunk?' he said clearly.

'Of course not,' I said carefully, eyeing the almost empty schnapps bottle. 'I know how I feel, because this is me talking. And not, I would like to tell you, the booze.' I cleared my throat, aware that I was actually having a tiny problem speaking, and wobbled over to the sofa. 'I'm fine. Really.'

Then I thought I heard a voice in the background. A female voice.

'Alice, I can't really talk to you now because I'm about to go out.'

I sat down suddenly. 'With a girl?' I asked, remembering Vic saying about him dating Americans.

'Yes,' he said uncomfortably. 'A sort of Halloween party thing. I can call you in the morning my time if you think it would help?'

'No, no,' I said, shaking my head, suddenly feeling very sad and confused. Everything was all wrong. There was his oh-so-familiar voice, but he was in a room I'd never seen, in another country – with some other girl. 'I'm, er, going out with Gretchen tomorrow night,' I lied, suddenly wanting to prove I had a life too and wasn't some raddled alcoholic saddo getting drunk alone on a fruit liqueur, 'so I won't be in.' I felt tears well up in my eyes again and struggled to keep my voice under control. 'It's nice to talk to you again though. When you get back, do you think you might want to have a drink with me?'

'Sure,' he said awkwardly. 'We can sort something.'

'You can never have too many friends, eh?' I tried a laugh, but it came out like more of a bleat.

He softened. 'I wasn't ever not your friend. I just needed time, that was all. Al, go to bed. And put a waste bin next to you, OK? Promise?'

The kind concern in his voice was enough to finish me off completely. 'Will do. Bye then,' I blurted, hanging up. I lifted my head tearfully and caught sight of my worse-for-wear reflection in the window. I barely recognised myself. I simply didn't know the desperate, inconsolable girl sitting alone in a vast empty room, staring back at me. That night I very firmly cried myself to sleep.

Thank God I had work to get up for the following morning.

I found the peace and quiet of the empty studio – before the client arrived – calming, and for the millionth time thanked God I didn't work in a busy, loud office where I had to appear sharp and dress to impress. Looking slightly dishevelled was part of the creative package and seemed almost expected by the clients. Luckily, the day's job was an easy one – even feeling as crap as I did, it was impossible to mess up photos of nail varnish. Once we got started I became quickly absorbed by the curves of the bottles and the colours of the liquids. By the time my mobile rang in my pocket just after lunch, I was on track, focused – and would have ignored the call, except it was Gretchen.

'Hi,' she said sympathetically, sounding just like her old self. 'I'm so sorry, I got back last night to find all your messages and by then it was too late to call you. So my stupid brother has made the classically stupid decision to let you slip through his fingers, has he?'

I exhaled, stepped away from the studio lights and the client, who was fiddling neurotically with one of the bottles again – even though I'd patiently asked her all morning not to touch the set-ups – and sat down on a chair right at the back of the studio so fast my hungover brain sloshed around in my head like dirty fish-tank water. 'He told you,' I said quickly. 'What did he say?'

'You must be feeling like shit,' she said sympathetically. 'I'm so sorry, Al.'

'I've felt better,' I wobbled, and then lowered my voice so that the client wouldn't hear me. 'And oh God, Gretch, you wouldn't believe it. I called Tom and he was there with some girl in the background, just about to go on a date.' I closed my eyes with the shame. 'Oh, I really wish you were here!'

'I will be in just four weeks. That's all. Just hang on in

there and *I'll* look after *you* when I get back! We'll go out and have some fun – some *us* time. Cheer you up.'

Her words were incredibly comforting, reminding me immediately of happier times. 'And don't worry about ringing Tom,' she said. 'We've all been there – get dumped, call the man that was always your safety net for a bit of reassurance, cry, etc., etc. It's no big deal.'

Thank goodness for her and Vic.

I closed my eyes. 'Do you think he got off the phone and said to her, "Sorry about that, that was my drunken English ex-girlfriend who cheated on me"?'

There was a pause, and then she said carefully, 'No, he didn't. He just said you were upset and a bit pissed. To be honest that's why I didn't call straight back, but I'm here now.'

At first I thought I'd heard wrong, then I wondered if I was *still* pissed.

I sat up a little straighter and then said, 'What?' stupidly, unable to take it in. 'You were at Tom's? What?'

'Alice, whatever you do, don't hang up,' she said. 'I want you to let me explain.'

'What were you doing there?' I said, utterly confused. 'You don't even know him! He said he was going on a date with some American girl.'

'No, he didn't say that. You assumed it,' she said gently. She took a deep breath. 'He was going out with me . . . well, *is* going out with me.'

I froze completely as everything carried on regardless. The client knocked over one of the bottles and nail varnish began to spill gloopily everywhere. The studio door opened and a delivery man came in carrying a parcel . . . everything normal. Except what Gretchen had just said.

She was *what*?

'Alice —' she began. But before she could say anything else, in complete shock, I fumbled with the phone while still holding it to my ear and cut her off. I stared at the wall in front of me.

Tom and Gretchen?

Going out with each other?

He'd met her *twice*. How was she at his flat?

I had a sudden violent picture of them in a glossy, spacious loft in Manhattan — Tom hanging up the phone on a drunken me, turning to a beautifully manicured Gretchen sitting on a sofa and saying sorrowfully, 'Poor old Alice,' but then holding out his hand to her and saying, 'Shall we?' Her standing and looking at him lovingly and him leaning in to kiss her . . .

I felt the stab of something so sharp slice through me, I gasped.

And oh God — I closed my eyes tight — I'd lied to him and said I was going out with her tonight to make it look like I had a life . . .

And all the time, she'd been sat there with him.

Chapter Twenty-Three

By nine o'clock that night, back at the flat – her flat – I had a whole tape full of answerphone messages from Gretchen, alternating between imploring me to pick the phone up, to angrily insisting she'd done nothing wrong, to reminding me how important I was to her – after all, who'd fixed me up with her brother? Given me her flat to live in rent-free? The last one simply said she wanted to explain.

Before I'd had the chance to pull the phone out of the socket and throw it across the room, it rang again and I nearly snatched it up, only deciding not to right at the last minute. It wasn't her voice that filled the flat after the bleep, however – it was Tom's. I collapsed on to the sofa and stared at the phone as I listened to him calmly talking from the other side of the world.

'Al, it's me. I'm so sorry that Gretchen was placed in the impossible situation of deciding whether to tell you about us over the phone.'

About us? I let out a cry.

'We had agreed Gretchen would tell you once we were back in the UK, but er . . . things don't always pan out as you imagine and . . . Anyway, you're Gretchen's best friend – you've been through so much together and you not letting her explain all this is devastating her.'

My jaw fell open. Devastating *her*?

'I hope you'll agree to see her when we get back, give her the chance to talk it through so you can see that *no one* set out to hurt you. Call me if you want to talk, but I'll understand if it's not right now.'

'Did you know? Did you know he was seeing her?' I demanded, having called Vic the second he hung up.

'Of course not!' she said quickly. 'Al, it's not that I don't want to discuss this with you, I do. But could I possibly call you back in just five minutes? It's just Luc and I were just finishing a DVD when you rang and he wants to go off to bed—'

'Oh I'm sorry,' I said immediately. 'I was just so shocked, and . . . I just needed to . . .'

I heard her take a breath. 'Hey, don't worry,' she said. 'It's no problem. I can finish the movie up in a bit. Luc can watch it now and I'll catch the end tomorrow or something.'

'Can you even believe it?' I said in disbelief. 'First Bailey and now this?'

'I know,' she said, softening. 'It must be horrible.'

'How could she do this to me? You never, *ever* do anything with a friend's significant ex – it's an unwritten rule!'

'I agree that it's a fucking outrage after all you did for her,' Vic said. 'But *please* – I'm begging you not to rewrite history. For your own sanity you *have* to remember that you and Tom split up because of Bailey, *not her* . . . Both she and Tom were free agents, and they both thought you were seeing someone else. It's not nice and I understand that it hurts, but would you be minding so much if you were still with Bailey and you'd found out about this? Don't get me wrong, I think it's perfectly natural to be a bit jealous, but—'

'I'm not jealous!' I interrupted. 'I think it's *weird*, it's *horrible*. I've told her secrets, stuff about Tom – sexual stuff about him – and now she's sleeping with him herself! And I did actually love Tom, OK so I wasn't *in* love with him and I know I hurt him really badly, but you don't just stop loving someone overnight. It'd be hard to get used to the idea that he had a full-on new girlfriend regardless of who she was – but it's Gretchen? I mean, what the hell? How can I be friends with her now? How can we ever sit down and have one of those girlie chats about what's annoying her about her boyfriend? We can't, can we?'

'Well, you couldn't when you were dating her brother either,' Vic said. 'This is why . . .'

I knew she was about to have a big 'I told you so' moment, so I carried on regardless. 'I told *her* when I liked Bailey, and when she flipped out at first, I just stepped back. She has categorically never said anything to me about Tom like that. Nothing! She didn't even tell me she'd bumped into him!' I sat down, my head spinning. It felt unreal, like a sick joke, and yet I'd heard the proof – from both of them.

Vic said nothing, just listened.

'And what do you suppose they say to each other about me?' I whispered. 'What will he have told her and what will she have told him? Both of them know really personal stuff about me that I don't want them sitting round and talking about . . . and do you think they both feel sorry for me that I just got dumped? I can't handle them pitying me. I don't want that!'

'I'm sure they're not saying anything, Al. You're just having a really rough time and it's making you think stuff that normally I know you wouldn't,' Vic tried to reassure me. 'Tom is a good person, he's not like that. To be fair, Al, he didn't have to ring you to explain — lots of blokes wouldn't have done.'

'Because of what happened with Bailey?' I said.

'Well, partly, yes,' she said awkwardly.

'But I never wanted to tell Tom about him! I was going to do what you said — I was going to fib and protect him, if it hadn't been for Gretchen opening her trap. She had no business even being there, she was supposed to be in hospital for fuck's sake.' And then just like that, a realisation struck me between the eyes. Literally like an iron girder had swung through the air, smacked me in the forehead and knocked me clean off my feet.

'Oh my God, Vic. Do you think she *meant* to tell him?'

'I don't understand,' Vic said, confused. 'Meant to tell him what?'

'That Bailey and I were "going out". It very neatly split us up, didn't it? And she's now dating Tom. So obviously she finds him attractive.'

'I don't mean to be rude, but that's rather stating the obvious, isn't it?'

'My point is, when did she start fancying him? When she first met him? While he was still *my* boyfriend?'

My mind started to race as Vic considered the implications of what I'd just said.

She hesitated. 'It honestly sounds like they just met in America and it grew from there . . . I think maybe you need to—'

'What, randomly, in a city of millions of people? What are the chances of that actually happening?'

I stared at the wall, on which there hung a large Warhol-style print of Gretchen, recreating the Monroe shots, head tipped back and laughing, all in various colours. It was like looking at a tile game and starting to slot the pieces into place to make one, crystal clear picture.

'Out of the blue, she decides to do a course in New York, where she knows no one . . . but *does* know he's there, because I told her? And bingo! They just happen to meet and fall for each other? In a city that big?'

'Al,' Vic was starting to sound worried, 'you've had a shitty weekend and I get that you're upset and searching for reasons and explanations, but that's really fucked up. You're saying she went out there on purpose like some heat-seeking missile? She's not Glenn Close in whatsit – *Fatal Attraction*.'

'Well, she'd just had a stay in a mental hospital,' I said quickly.

'Oh Alice!' Vic said, horrified. 'Come on! You're bigger than that. I'm sure love and romance was the last thing on her mind. You said yourself she'd been really ill, done some horrendous stuff.'

'Yes, she had! Like tell Tom on purpose about me and Bailey!'

'What, so her illness was a handy excuse for her having put her foot in it?' Vic asked sceptically, which hadn't even occurred to me until then.

'YES!' I said. 'Of course! You're absolutely right!'

'Sorry, but *this* is what's actually crazy. Alice, please. You're losing the plot, I wasn't serious. No one could be that manipulative and calculating.'

'I can't believe this!' I said, not listening. 'I've got to go. I'll call you back.'

'Alice, *do not* call Tom—' I heard her begin to say, but I clicked off and began to dial furiously.

Chapter Twenty-Four

'So Gretchen fell for me in London, deliberately split us up and then followed me out to America?' said Tom slowly, in complete disbelief. 'Sorry, Alice, I don't buy it – I'm not *that* good looking.'

I didn't laugh. We'd been well into the phone row for twenty minutes, our past intimacy allowing us to believe it was acceptable to say exactly what was on our minds.

'It's ridiculous. I mean, come on!' Tom said. 'She and I,' he continued uncomfortably, 'really fought what was beginning between us . . .'

Clearly. They'd obviously fought *really* hard.

'Neither of us saw it coming.'

'Don't!' I said quickly. 'I don't want to know the details!'

'We never wanted to hurt anyone, but you were with someone else, remember?'

'Yeah, and look how you "accidentally" found out about that!'

I gasped as something else occurred to me: Gretchen being offhand and cross when I first said I liked Bailey, then suddenly swinging completely the other way and fixing us up. Had she pushed me together with Bailey just to get me out of the way?

'And it was Gretchen who set me up with Bailey – did she tell you that?'

Tom ignored me. 'Alice, me and Gretchen just happened. I was lonely out here, so was she. No one contrived to do anything deliberate at all – that's an insane thing to suggest! You need to take a time-out.' I couldn't believe he was trying to calm *me* down. I wasn't the loony! I looked at the prints of her on the wall again and had to restrain myself from throwing something at them.

'You've hit it on the head,' I responded, with all the ferocity of an electric shock. 'It's insane. Let's all feel sorry for poor innocent Gretchen: "Oh, did I just say something I shouldn't have? Wasn't me! It was the drugs, or the mental illness, or the depression . . ." *Bollocks!* Being a manic depressive isn't an excuse for bad behaviour. You can't just do what you like and then turn round and say, "Whoops, didn't mean to, that was the bad old naughty me!" She hides behind it when it suits her, so she can do exactly as she pleases – I just can't believe I've not seen it until now!'

'Alice, can you even hear yourself?'

'And don't you even care that she's mentally ill? Doesn't that worry you?'

'So you do want details,' Tom said patiently. 'Look, I never really got to know Gretchen in London, for obvious reasons, but despite her illness, everything you yourself told me about her is true. She's incredibly funny, generous, kind and spontaneous—'

'As well as manipulative, devious, will shag anything when hyper, goes on spending sprees like she's using Monopoly money,' I cut in viciously.

210

Tom took a deep breath and didn't rise. 'We just have a lot of fun together. As far as the manic thing goes, it hasn't been an issue. She was very frank about it from the start, she takes her medication . . . and sometimes she gets a bit ratty or a bit sad, but I just leave her to work through it calmly.'

'Gets a bit ratty?' I repeated in disbelief. 'Are you fucking kidding me? I've seen her try to get out of a moving car!'

'Al, please,' Tom paused. 'This isn't fair to Gretch . . . and this isn't like you.'

'So tell me how you just "met",' I said, like a police officer determined to re-examine the evidence and find the giveaway clue.

'Jesus, Alice,' he said, exhausted. 'She moved here, she didn't know anyone else. She had no idea how to find medical support, couldn't tell anyone on her course because she didn't want them to know about her condition. She remembered you telling her I was out here on second-ment and remembered what firm I was with. She was desperate – you know what it must have cost her to call someone she'd only met twice? And not exactly under the best of circumstances on the last occasion . . .'

'But that's just not true!' I burst. 'She told me and Ba—' I stopped quickly. 'Told me before she left that she'd already lined up a therapist. Why didn't he or she help her out with medical support? Why call you?'

'Maybe they let her down, maybe they simply didn't know – everyone out here calls themselves a shrink,' Tom said. 'It's embarrassing.'

Could he even hear *himself*? Since when was he an expert on psychiatry?

'Oh come on, Tom.'

'How would you know if I'm right or not?' he said, losing patience. 'You don't live here – I do.'

'She's manipulated both of us — and you're too stupid to see it!'

'What, she *made* you fall for her brother too, did she?' he snapped. 'Look, I'm a bloke, Al — you're right, I'm just not that complicated. We met, I liked her, I wasn't with anyone else. That's all. I accept that it would have been far more convenient to get together with someone *you* didn't know, but no one can help who they fall for. You proved that with Bailey,' he managed to say his name with difficulty, 'and that wasn't meant as a dig. It sounded like it, but it wasn't.'

'It didn't occur to you that it might upset me?'

'You want the honest answer, Al?' he cut in swiftly. 'Actually yes, at first it did, and much as I hate to admit it, there was a big part of me that wanted to get back at you. I mean, fuck, Alice, you took him to *Paris* with you?'

I gasped. 'Vic said she wouldn't tell you!'

'She didn't. I rang and Luc answered, let it slip by mistake. But I can honestly tell you that what I feel for Gretchen now . . .'

Hearing him talk about her like that made me feel nauseous. It was all *wrong*!

'. . . has nothing to do with that. Nothing at all. I'm not doing it to hurt you, Alice. I loved you.'

And that said it all — the past tense. I couldn't listen to any more.

I hung up and just sat there, paralysed.

How could she? How could *he*? But particularly, how could one of my best friends do this to me and not even tell me about it until after it had been happening for what appeared to be ages? I thought back over all the phone calls where we had chatted away aimlessly about stuff and nothing: her course, my work, the tutors she liked, my family news. And all the time she had met Tom and was dating him. Sleeping with him. I looked around me slowly, as if seeing her belongings through new eyes. I was sitting on her sofa, living in her flat, which, of course, had been her idea too.

I felt shaken by the frightening ease with which she'd expertly manoeuvred everything into position, but as I sat there, continuing to slot the pieces into place, a wave of anger, hurt, bitter betrayal and jealousy began to swell within me.

She was supposed to be one of my best friends. Everyone, everything that was important to me was now revolving around her.

I wasn't sure I could bear it.

Chapter Twenty-Five

I arrived back at Gretchen's silent flat and slung my copy of *Loot* on the table. It was oppressively quiet after the buzz and hum of having been on location in a busy restaurant in Mayfair all day, where the presence of other people and their chatter had comfortingly washed over me. There was no TV on or kettle just boiled, no one to ask me how my day had been. Just Gretchen's fucking Andy Warhol pictures laughing down at me. I decided to call Vic.

'*Salut*, Alice,' Luc answered, his calm, assured doctor's voice sounding in my ear. 'I hear you are having difficult times. I'm sorry for this. You would I think like to talk with Victoria? Or perhaps with me?'

'Er, it was actually Vic I was after,' I said, a bit confused by his offer. 'If she's there?'

'Of course,' he said politely. 'She is just finishing eating in fact. Here she is now.'

'Hi, Al.' Vic came on the line, speaking through a mouthful. 'How are you?'

'Going crazy,' I said. 'I have to get out of this flat, Vic.

You don't understand what it's like, feeling trapped in her space, but I literally can't find anywhere.' I looked around Gretchen's flat and shivered. 'Trying to move house in the run-up to Christmas is virtually impossible. Only truly desperate people are trying to find room at the inn.'

'Well, you're not desperate, not yet.' I heard her cutlery clatter on to a plate in the background. 'Thanks, Luc, that was lovely . . . I know you hate being there, Al, and I can totally understand why, but she's in another country and it's not like you're having to live *with* her. When's she due back?'

'I assume it's still the end of November – two weeks. If I haven't found anywhere by the end of this week I'm just going to have to get a hotel or sleep at the studio or something.'

'But it's Wednesday today!' Vic yawned. 'So you've got what, barely three full days?'

'I know. I've been scanning the papers religiously for short lets, long lets,' I said tiredly, 'but I just can't afford a one-bed on my own, so that leaves me with a flat share. Bearing in mind I've got a lot of expensive camera gear, trying to find one with some semi-normal people that isn't a crack house, or a mouldy hole with rickety windows you expect to see someone silently climbing through in the dead of night, isn't exactly easy. A few people have said some stuff might come up in the New Year, but that isn't much help now.'

'What about one of the uni lot?' Vic yawned again. 'God, sorry Al! I've just had a really long day at work. It's actually really tiring trying to focus on catching the odd word you can understand when people speak so fast. I really have to concentrate or it all merges into one big French blah. Anyway, the uni girls—'

'OK,' I said. 'Imagine how this would sound if you were one of them: "Hi, it's Alice here. Now, I know that recently I've barely seen you apart from the odd birthday drink, mostly because work's been really busy but also because I'm pretty lazy and it was easier to sit in on a Friday night with my then boyfriend than make the effort to meet up with you. Well, I'm not with him any more – he's going out with my so-called best friend, who's mad, and in fact I've just split up with someone else entirely! Oh, and did I mention I need somewhere to live? I was thinking your place might do the trick. See you Friday?"'

'I take your point,' Vic sighed. 'Fair enough.'

'Moreover it's embarrassing. I'm too old for this shit – begging a spare room. This whole me staying in her flat thing seemed such a good idea at the time, such a convenient, easy option. I never stopped to think about what would happen if we fell out. It never occurred to me that we would.'

I felt the now familiar mixture of sadness and anger swirling in my gut as I thought about Gretchen. I'd analysed our friendship for hours since I'd found out about her and Tom, and had come to the conclusion that anything she and I had must have been entirely built on sand. It had all fallen away as quickly as it had begun, to the point that I wasn't sure if it had ever really been there at all, even though it had grown to be so important to me. Was it my payback for expecting too much from someone who perhaps should never have been more than a cocktails and coffee buddy? She had, after all, once admitted she'd wanted to use me to expand her fashion contacts.

I wondered if, in her mind, it had ever really gone beyond that; if she'd meant what she said during her depression, about how she hadn't wanted to lose me. Whatever her motives for any of it, she'd obviously now got everything she needed from our relationship and was ready to move on to the next. I could now see how others before me could have fallen by the wayside, illness or no illness. But in quieter moments I just felt bereft, unable to see how she could have done it all: lied, manipulated . . . all when she *knew* Tom was special to me. I thought I had meant more to her than that.

Could I have done anything differently, given the chance? But done what? Asked on first meeting her if she was of sound mind? But then, it wasn't her illness that was the problem – it was her. How she'd *chosen* to behave. It was nothing more than bad luck, us meeting. She had just seemed a fun person. It had certainly proven to be a life changing friendship.

And in spite of everything, much as I was still angry with myself for wasting my time and energy, I had waited for her to ring and apologise again. She hadn't. Through silence, she neatly made her point that we were done.

'Of all the people to make friends with,' I said, trying to lighten the tone, 'I pick the mentally unstable social deviant. You know the only positive thing to come out of this utterly shit month is that I've lost about a stone without even trying.' I curled my feet up and under me.

'Perfect! You're thin, heartbroken – you should come to Paris!' Vic paused. 'You could stay here for a bit while you found your *pêche*?'

'And three-wheel it on yours and Luc's French bicyclette made for two? Thanks, but I need to start standing on my own two *pieds*. *Pêche* means fishing by the way,' I explained helpfully. '*Pieds* is feet.'

'Oh,' she said. 'No wonder buying stockings the other day was such hard work. Do you think you might just be better off moving home for a bit?'

217

'Four hours on a train on top of a working day?' I said. 'And if the commute didn't kill me, Fran would. She's round at Mum and Dad's all the time: cross, fed up of being pregnant and spoiling for a fight. Maybe I should see if a local church has a nativity crib where I can bunk down? If I can get a shepherd to sling his crook, I'm laughing.'

'I think you're being very brave, you know,' Vic said firmly, 'and I'm proud of you. I know it's hard not being part of the team any more when they *both* used to belong exclusively to you, and I think you're doing amazingly well. You're nearly there, Al. Chin up. Now, sweetheart, I'm sorry to cut this short but I've got to go now. I really am trashed and I'm on a long day tomorrow.'

'Oh are you?' Appalled, I suddenly realised that I'd been on the phone to her for ages and hadn't asked a single question about how she was. 'I'm so sorry, Vic. I've just gone on and on about me and not asked anything about what you've been up to.'

She hesitated. 'It's all right,' she said finally. 'You're having a tough time at the moment. I understand, honestly I do. You're going to be OK, Al – I promise.'

Her words comforted me later, as I sat worrying on Gretchen's sofa in the dark, watching crappy Wednesday night TV intently in my pyjamas, bed socks pulled up and no make-up on, eating my tea: a family sized bag of Doritos. I'd just got a text message that a flat I'd been going to see in the morning had been let earlier in the afternoon. Time, along with my options, was running out.

All thoughts slipped from my mind, however, as I heard voices the other side of the front door and saw the handle begin to turn slowly. Someone was out there trying to break in! For reasons best known to myself, I immediately turned the sound down on the TV, it was just an instant reaction. I froze completely rigid. Then I heard a key scratchily slip-sliding around the lock.

The door burst open and, like a bad dream, there they were: Tom and Gretchen, very real and right in front of me, piling in, laughing breathlessly, bags slipping off their shoulders. Gretchen reached for the light switch saying confusedly, 'The TV's on!' She obviously couldn't see me, immobile with shock on the sofa, but as the big light flooded the flat, she leapt out of her skin to find me sitting there motionless and exclaimed, 'Shit! Alice?'

Her arm dropped heavily by her side. She was totally floored to see me. She had obviously thought that I was so outraged, so hurt and betrayed, I had packed up and shipped out in a blaze of, 'I'm not living a second longer in her flat.'

'What are you doing here?' she said, astonished. 'I mean, I thought . . . well, I didn't think – we didn't expect . . .' She glanced at Tom, who was carefully putting his bag down and assessing the situation. He glanced back at her and that was enough. Just that, a shared coupled-up 'look' that didn't even need words.

She was wearing an oatmeal cashmere skirt – it looked expensive and understated, flowing over her slim hips and flaring gently out at the bottom, while her black polo neck clung to every soft curve. She looked groomed and sleek, the kind of woman the professional man would be proud to come home to, and I could see, as I glanced at Tom, he was that man.

His suit was no longer classic, but edgy. Over the seven months it had been since I'd seen him, he'd filled out. As he put his hands on his hips in an 'I'm anticipating trouble' stance, pushing his jacket open and causing his shirt to tighten over his pecs and tummy, I could see it was all lean, hard muscle. Someone had dealt with some pent-up hurt down at the gym, that was for sure. He had no tie on and his shoes weren't the staid Church's lace-ups he'd left London in, but were very 'Take no crap and if you have to ask, you can't afford them.' His hair was shorter and styled differently and he'd replaced his glasses with lenses, making his eyes look very clear and piercing.

It was, of course, just perfect that I was sat there looking such a pathetic state. I might as well have had a sign round my neck that said 'Please give generously.'

I took a deep breath and said, calmly and with as much dignity as I could manage, 'I didn't think you were back for another two weeks. I've been having difficulties finding somewhere to live. I'm sorry to have surprised you and I'm very sorry to still be here.'

There was a silence, then Tom coughed and said, 'Look, it's no problem. We can go back to mine, Gretch. Sort this in the morning. We *are* earlier, obviously. Gretchen's got this job thing and I transferred back too . . .' he petered out. 'Anyway, it's not important.'

'It's just not a great time to be moving, in the run-up to Christmas,' I said. 'Not that it is, of course, your problem.'

'All right, Tiny Tim,' Gretchen rolled her eyes and did an embarrassed laugh, 'I'm not going to throw you out. You can stay as long as you want, you know that. I'm just guessing you don't really want to live with me. Although there are two bedrooms, so . . .'

I stared at her. Was her medication too high or something? I didn't want to be in her flat full stop! She didn't really, either in her right or mentally unstable mind, think I'd want to live *with* her? Perhaps I could be on breakfast duty when Tom stayed over? Maybe we'd all stay up and watch movies together under a duvet eating popcorn, she and I with our hair in pigtails, and before they went off to bed to shag like rabbits, we'd all shout 'Goodnight!' like they did on Walton weirdo mountain.

Then I realised it was an act for Tom's benefit. Carefully crafted to make her look like the reasonable one, the one who had tried to be nice but had it thrown back in her face. Oh, I wasn't that green . . . how very Gretchen to think she could smother me with friendship. 'Thank you, but no,' I said quietly.

'I understand totally,' Gretchen said. 'This must be hard for you . . . I know you probably don't want to talk now. Well, I know you don't because you didn't call me back or anything when I left you all of those messages. But you can absolutely stay here until you have somewhere else to go. I'll just stay with Tom at his until you're ready to move.' She looked at Tom with wide, innocent eyes. 'That's OK, isn't it?'

'Of course!' he said, looking slightly put on the spot.

I had to hand it to her – she was even better than I had given her credit for. She'd just taken, what, five seconds to move herself into his flat, while giving him little or no say in the matter.

He looked at me and there was no guile or malice there. Just honest concern. 'We really do want to help, Al.'

'That's settled then,' Gretchen said quickly. 'It's the least we can do. I'll not trouble you while you're here. Just let me know when you've found somewhere. No rush.'

Of course there wasn't, the arrangement suited her down to the ground.

'I'll pop round tomorrow, just to drop off some things, if that's OK?' she asked, and I nodded.

And with her game, set and match in the bag – Tom picked up the remainder of them – they were gone.

I was up extra early the following morning. I knew it would be better to be out when she arrived, although part of me very much wanted to be there. But, despite my efforts, at eight a.m. I heard the door go and walked into the kitchen to find her kicking off her shoes, having let herself in. She'd wrong-footed me yet again.

'Oh good,' she smiled brightly, 'you're here. Sorry I'm so early – Tom had to go into work and I couldn't see any point in hanging around so . . . I picked up some post from downstairs for you.' She lightly threw a postcard across the room as she dumped her bag on the ground and began to remove her gloves.

I picked it up as it landed at my feet. It was a picture of a hippo with a small bird sitting on its back, and above it was the caption 'Friends'.

I flipped it over and read:

Dear Al. Hope you are OK. Let's have a Christmas drink, yeah? South Africa is hot, hot, hot! Love Bailey. xxx

'Sorry. I didn't know if I should hide it or not,' she said, head sympathetically on one side. 'I'm sure he meant well, Al, honestly . . . but it's fair to say he could have chosen a better card. No one needs to be told they remind someone of a hippo.'

That hadn't even occurred to me until then.

'I'm really sorry that it didn't work out between the two of you,' she said.

'Just don't bother, Gretchen,' I said, looking at her steadily. 'Tom's not here. You're wasting your breath.'

She sighed sadly. 'Oh, Alice. Don't. I was trying to be nice. How much longer are you going to keep grabbing the olive branch and hitting me with it?'

'How long have you got?'

'But Al, you finished with him. You didn't want him! Surely you want Tom to be happy, otherwise that's just . . . really selfish. It doesn't bother *me* that he went out with *you*.'

'Well it bothers me!' I shouted, suddenly angry. 'You were my best friend, Gretchen! You never even told me you liked him! He wasn't some bloke I saw for a month or two – I was with him for two years!' Had she actually just called me selfish? To my face?

'OK, I know that *now*,' she said warningly. 'But . . .'

'Oh come on, you knew that once you dropped your bombshell about me and Bailey! You totally knew he was a major part of my life.'

'But while we're on the subject, you'd been with my brother for about five months. If you still were, you and I wouldn't even be having this conversation and you know it.'

'Yes we would actually,' I said quickly. 'You lied to me, you manipulated me, you—'

'Oh you know what?' she said, closing her eyes briefly. 'I can't do this crap, it's beneath both of us. I tried to explain to you about me and him dating, but you wouldn't take my calls and refused to listen. You've acted like a child all the way through, in fact.' She reached for her bag. 'It's lucky at least one of us is capable of behaving like an adult. I think I should probably go.'

'Back to the flat where I used to live?' I said. 'By the way, does Tom know Paulo beat him to first go on you?'

The second the words were out of my mouth I regretted it. It was a disgusting thing to say.

She flushed a deep red. 'That was a really low shot. I was ill that night, as you well know. And by the way, you're very welcome.' She motioned around her.

'Believe me, I'm making every effort to get the hell out of your life.'

She said nothing, but turned and shoved her feet angrily back into her shoes and yanked on her gloves. She reached the door, paused, turned back and said, 'I'm not out to get you, Alice. And I don't feel like I owe you anything either, so don't go thinking this is me soothing my guilty conscience, because it isn't. It's simply that you were there for me when I needed you. So I'm here for you. That's what true friendship is, in case you'd forgotten.'

She looked at me and waited for me to say something, but I didn't.

Gretchen shook her head in disappointment, walked through the door and closed it quietly behind her.

Chapter Twenty-Six

I wasn't entirely surprised to have another visitor the following night. I'd barely been back from work long enough to make a cup of tea before the front doorbell rang. On answering it, I discovered Tom on the other side.

'Hi,' he said awkwardly. He looked more like the old him than the last time I'd seen him – he was wearing his glasses and his hair looked a little more dishevelled than styled. 'Someone was coming in downstairs and let me in, so I didn't buzz the intercom and just came straight up. I hope that's OK.'

'Of course it is!' I said quickly. Was this what we'd been reduced to? Polite explanations about intercoms?

'Can I come in? I'd like to talk to you.'

I opened the door wider. 'Would you like a tea?'

'Yes, please.' He stepped in and slipped his shoes off, then removed his coat, laying it carefully over the arm of the sofa. 'It's bloody nippy out there,' he shivered, padding over to the breakfast bar in his socks and settling on a stool.

'Good day at work?' I asked, reaching for a cup and

automatically putting in the spoonful of sugar I knew he took. It was the start to a conversation we'd had hundreds of times before, but never in such surreal circumstances.

'Could be worse,' he yawned, taking his glasses off and giving them a quick wipe before popping them back on. 'Everyone's working their arses off to get everything done in time for Christmas and they're just assuming I can pick up things where I left off six-odd months ago: "Come on, Tom, you know we keep those documents on the third floor at the back of the cupboard in what was Heather's office before she went on maternity leave, or try in Jonty's cabinet. He's sharing with Don now."' He shook his head. 'I don't know who any of these people are, and frankly it all makes me want to climb into the mythical Heather's cupboard and hope it leads to Narnia. Or back to New York. Either would be an improvement. Anyway, enough about me. How's your work going?'

'OK, thanks.' I decided not to mention the embarrassing episode I'd had earlier that morning. I'd been shooting some promo shots of a petulant ex popstar – who was desperately trying to reclaim the remainder of her fifteen minutes by doing any reality TV show going – when I'd unmistakably heard either her, or her agent, mutter something about Gretchen under their breath. My head had shot up immediately; Gretchen wasn't exactly a common name. They were gossiping about us? Could they possibly know she was now with my ex? Gretchen must have told them. What had she said?

I had felt myself begin to shake with adrenalin. Now I couldn't even come to work to escape her? 'If you've got something to say,' I said clearly, sounding far braver than I felt, 'please feel free to just say it. Perhaps I can clear up whatever misinformation you might have heard.'

The agent shot the sulky star a warning look and said smoothly, 'Sorry, Alice, all we were saying is how *great* it is for Gretchen that she's been off the scene for a few months and yet rumour has it she's up for a lead in a new Working Title project.' The surly girl huffed and then flounced off to the loo. 'Sorry about her,' the agent said uncomfortably. 'She's just jealous. I know Gretchen's your mate. No offence.'

'None taken,' I said faintly, bending over to fiddle with a light cable to hide my flaming face. I had to get a grip. Assuming clients were bitching about me, then having a go at them, was beyond unprofessional.

I plonked a tea in front of Tom and wondered what he'd *really* come to say.

'Thank you. So do you think you might break even this year?' Tom asked.

'With a bit of luck.' I tried a smile, but it fell rather flat.

'That's excellent! Well done you.' He took an appreciative sip of the tea and his glasses steamed up slightly.

We lapsed into silence and I said eventually, 'So, I take it this isn't just a social call?'

'No, it's not. I've come over to chat with you about this housing situation.'

I sat down and said, 'Has *she* sent you?'

He frowned and shook his head. 'No, no. She knows I'm here, but what I want to talk to you about is my idea. So . . . clearly you can't, and I imagine don't want to, continue living in what is, after all, her home – whatever she said last night.' He said it not unkindly, but with no sugar coating, but then I wouldn't have expected anything less from him.

'I don't—' I began, but he held up a hand and pushed his slipping glasses firmly on his nose with the other one. 'Please, just let me finish. I know this whole situation has been unbearably difficult for all of us, at some stage or another. But I'm actually proud of all of us. I'm proud that you and I are still able to be sat here talking, I'm proud that Gretchen didn't make a fuss about you still being here when we got back, and I think it says a great deal about all of us and the people we are. It's good and right that you support and help people you care about, even if sometimes it seems as if it's at a personal cost to yourself. We've all pulled it out of the bag when it's mattered, and that's been a real achievement.'

He still didn't get it. He still couldn't see her for what she was.

'But I'm *not* proud that I asked you to move out of our flat in the first place, because of what happened with Bailey. It was your home as much as mine. But I was hurt and . . . well anyway. That's water under the bridge. Gretchen needs to be able to move back in here and I wondered how you would feel about moving back into the flat?' He smiled but shifted rather uncomfortably in his seat. 'It seems a vacancy has come up.'

What? I stared at him. Had I just heard right? Live with him again? Was he mad?

'It's totally within your price range,' he continued. 'Two nice flatmates – well, Paulo is one of them, but you can't have everything – and you could move in as soon as you want. What do you say?' He looked at me earnestly.

The person who had replaced me was moving out? I looked at him incredulously. He was actually serious!

'Yeah, because Gretchen's going to *love* that,' I said sarcastically.

He looked puzzled. 'I can't see how it's any of her business.'

I raised an eyebrow in disbelief.

'Look, I know this is not where we imagined in a million years we would ever be, but here we are and you need somewhere to live, urgently.' He sat back. 'I should never have asked you to move out in the first place, Al – I feel really bad. If nothing else, just come back and use it as a temporary base, until you find an alternative. Whatever works for you.'

I opened my mouth to refuse, but then closed it again. I hadn't got any better options . . . suppose I did just stay there until the New Year when . . . No! What was I thinking?

'I can't,' I said firmly. 'This is insane!'

'I'll concede it's unusual,' he agreed. 'But it's not insane. In fact, it's what I want.' He hesitated and then said, 'Without wanting to rake things up, I regret that in the past I wasn't more spontaneous and less careful – always worrying about money and the sensible thing to do. If you see something you want, you have to make it happen. So . . .' He put his cup down firmly. 'What do you say?'

Whoa . . . what the hell was that supposed to mean? Was he talking about *us*?

'Tom,' I said quickly, 'I don't think—'

He held up a hand. 'Alice, there's absolutely no expectation of any kind of commitment. No expectation of anything at all, in fact. I think you should just take things day by day and see how you feel once you're back. If it's too weird, you just move out again.'

'But Gretchen—'

'Stop worrying about Gretchen! Leave that to me.' Then he motioned to a stack of my boxes next to the front door. 'It looks like you're already packed anyway.'

'I'm absolutely desperate to get out of here, Tom,' I said quietly. 'Like you wouldn't believe, but—'

'Then move back in! You could be back in your old

229

room by Sunday. I'd say Saturday, but we're having a sort of welcome home/early Christmas thing on Saturday night. It was the only date Paulo could do before he flies home for Christmas. Gretchen's coming.'

'Tom,' I said, 'you've just asked me to move back in and you're worried about a party?'

'Fair point, I guess.' He pulled a bit of a face. 'Leave it with me, I'll deal with it. Saturday it is then.' He raised his mug. 'To fresh starts,' he said.

I looked at him doubtfully. 'I haven't actually said yes.'

'I don't see,' he said, 'that you've got anything to lose.'

When I arrived at the flat on Saturday afternoon with my stuff, Paulo was the only one in.

'*Hola*, Alice!' he said with a big smile. 'Welcome home!' Which was nice of him. He even helped me carry my boxes up from the taxi, dumping them in my old office. It would be weird sleeping in there again. He looked at his watch and said, 'I have to go and buy drinks for tonight – I promise Tom. Do you want me to get you some?' I shook my head and he gave me a thumbs up before bounding downstairs shouting, 'See you later!'

The room had the air of someone unfamiliar having been in it, but was spotlessly clean. There were also nine boxes piled up in the sitting room, all taped up, which I assumed belonged to the person moving out. Perhaps they were halfway through a run and were on their way back to get the last ones. I went to take a sneaky peek, to see what Tom had done with our old bedroom, but oddly found it locked. Maybe that was sensible given someone was moving stuff out of the flat.

I walked out into the hallway, heard a key in the door, footsteps on the stairs and then came face to face with a smiling but totally unfamiliar dark-haired girl dressed casually in jeans and a parka. She was holding a couple of Sainsbury's bags. 'Hi!' she said, dropping them, kicking her shoes off and wrestling her arms out of the sleeves of her coat. 'You must be Alice. I'm Kitty.' She held out her hand and I shook it automatically. 'The others not back yet?' She glanced at her watch. 'Shit! I'm so late!'

She grabbed the shopping, walked straight into the kitchen, pulled the fridge door open and started shoving the contents of the bags in, wherever they would fit, in a very familiar way. I wondered if she was Paulo's girlfriend? 'It's so friggin cold out there!' she said chattily, reaching for the kettle, filling it up and shoving it on. 'Right! Best start getting ready! You all through in the bathroom?' she called over her shoulder as she marched out into the hall. Utterly confused I followed her and said, 'Er Kitty – sorry . . . are you . . . ?'

She was stood in front of Tom's door, fumbling with a set of keys. As she selected one and slid it into the lock, I heard the front door bang open and gasps of laughter followed by *Gretchen*'s voice. What the hell was she doing here? I thought he said he was going to deal with it?

'My fucking arms are going to fall off!' she cried.

'All right, potty mouth!' Tom laughed. 'Just the stairs, that's all! Biceps Bartholomew! Shit, we're late! The car'll be here to get the stuff in five. Come on!'

I turned to see them both staggering up, him carrying two boxes of beers he could hardly see over and her lugging several clinking carrier bags, puffing with the effort. They collapsed them down just as Kitty pushed Tom's door open and revealed a totally different interior than the one I was expecting to see. There were bursting bin bags everywhere, spewing girls' clothes out as if they'd popped like overripe

231

pieces of fruit. The bed was in a different position and the lampshade was an altogether more feminine affair, as were the curtains. There was a poster of the *Sex and the City* girls on the wall and it reeked of vanilla air freshener. It was just the kind of room I might have had when I'd just started flat sharing.

It plainly wasn't Tom's room any more.

'Oh, hi!' Tom said, genuine warmth in his voice as he saw me standing there. 'You're here! And you've met Kitty as well! Excellent!' He looked at his watch. 'Where's Paulo? This is his sodding party, too! OK, the car is arriving to get my boxes in about five—'

There was a honking downstairs.

'Make that the car is arriving *now*! OK, right. We'll load all my stuff up, whizz back over, unload and then we'll be back. No one is due before nine anyway. I feel bad that we're doing this party here, I really do. We should have done it at yours, Gretch.'

'Hi, Al,' Gretchen nodded a hello in my direction. 'We couldn't because we didn't know if Alice was going to want to move back, did we?' She shook her head in mock despair. 'Can I send him back if he gets too much?' she teased, glancing at Kitty then flicking a tiny ball of tissue from her coat pocket at Tom.

Kitty laughed. 'Nope. It's been very brief but memorable – how I like all of my men.'

Tom held up his hands in embarrassed good humour. 'OK, OK, ladies, I get the message. Are you all right, Alice?' he suddenly said. 'You look like you're about to throw up.'

'I'm fine.' I forced a smile. 'Tired . . . from moving earlier. I might go and have a quick lie-down.'

'Good idea,' he said. 'Got to be back on top form for the party later.'

232

He laughed a slightly too jolly laugh and looked at Gretchen, who immediately said, 'Oh, absolutely. It'll be good to have you there.'

I managed to hold it together and not start crying until I'd shut my bedroom door behind me.

Six hours later the flat was jammed with people I didn't know, bottles of booze on every surface and the buzz of conversation straining over the very loud stereo.

I was drunk and attempting to focus on Paulo's face, who was talking away animatedly, while I tried to wade through the waves of humiliation and misery that kept engulfing me every time I thought about Tom asking me to move back in.

How could I have been so fucking stupid? *They* were going to live together. He'd taken his stuff to *hers* already. Tom, Mr Slow But Steady, had moved in with someone after barely three months of dating? How was this happening?

'So it's not, you know, weird to be back?' Paulo ran his fingers through his hair. 'Tom helped Kitty move out of your old office: he thought it might be too strange for you to sleep in yours and his old room. It is all change!' He laughed and then looked rather surprised as I knocked my drink back in one. 'He seems happy with Gretchen, you think?'

We both glanced over at them. Tom had his hand in the small of Gretchen's back, which made me clutch my glass a little tighter. Gretchen was excitedly telling a story to a small audience who were hanging off her every word. She was all in black, but showing quite a lot of cleavage and leg. I actually thought she only just looked the right side of slutty, but was prepared to admit I might be very biased. 'I think he's very happy with her, yes,' I answered, my voice cracked and brittle. Tom must have felt us staring, because he looked over and smiled, raising a glass in our direction.

'That is bad for me,' Paulo said reflectively and then looked a little shifty. 'I find I still like her a bit, you know? Seeing her again after . . .' He trailed off, but I knew exactly what he was referring to. 'Maybe it's good for me that she is not going to be here any more. I will lose my heart somewhere else.'

Oh for fuck's sake. I stared at him in disbelief and found myself rather violently needing to be somewhere that a member of the Gretchen fan club wasn't. I put my empty glass down unsteadily and shoved through the throng to get to my room. Opening the door, I found two people I didn't know snogging on my bed, like teenagers. They'd actually gone to the trouble of lifting my boxes off it. 'Can you can go somewhere else, please?' I said. 'You're in my room.'

The girl sighed, as if I was doing it just to annoy them, and I wanted to hit her for it. She sat up, adjusted her top and gave me a filthy look as she got up and stalked out. The bloke just muttered 'Sorry' and pulled the door shut behind him. I sat down on the end of my bed and felt like I was falling apart from within. Drunken tears welled up and it was only because my door opened gently and I looked up, embarrassed to be caught crying, that they were prevented from spilling over.

Tom came in, clutching a beer can. He was wearing a fiercely fashionable top I didn't recognise and jeans over sneakers. He looked good in them, just not very comfortable. I suspected Gretchen had chosen them.

'You're crying,' he said and his face creased with a concerned frown. 'I knew this wasn't a good idea – I couldn't have done it if I had been you. I'm not trying to big myself up but . . . it's just too weird, isn't it?'

I nodded and a tear jumped out, weaving unsteadily down my cheek.

He sighed and pushed the door to. It drifted back open an inch as he came over and crouched down in front of me, setting the beer can carefully down on the carpet.

'Please don't cry, Al.'

But that just made it worse.

He awkwardly took my hand and said, 'I thought you were remarkably cool and calm about me saying I was moving in with her.'

And because I was drunk, I confessed, 'You didn't actually tell me you were. You just said you'd done a lot of thinking, knew what you wanted and then asked me to move back in here.'

He looked totally puzzled and then, as the realisation hit him, horrified. He exhaled and said, 'Oh Alice! Oh my God. You thought . . .'

I shook my head quickly. 'No, no. Please don't. It was me! I misunderstood.' But I found myself suddenly unable to let go of his hand.

His legs were clearly uncomfy, just crouching, so he knelt down instead, facing me.

'When you were saying all that stuff about what you wanted,' I said, the words rushing out because if I slowed down, I might actually realise the ramifications of what I was about to say and stop. 'About not holding back, living in the moment and all that crap. You were talking about her, weren't you? Not me?'

He nodded slowly and I smiled through my tears. 'How embarrassed am I?' I tried a laugh, but I wasn't fooling either of us.

He gazed at me and I couldn't fathom what he was thinking. He looked so sweet and earnest and just concerned about me that I felt my heart tighten painfully, which was followed by an impulsive, drunken and reckless desire to just kiss him. So I did.

I felt his lips, warm and dry, and for a second they instinctively moved against mine. We had, after all, been in similar positions many times before and I think, just for a moment, his body remembered a point in the past when his heart would have responded and his hands would have moved gratefully to me. But then . . . nothing happened. He didn't kiss back. It was like bumping into someone in a bus queue – an invasion of personal space that makes you step back and instinctively say sorry. I felt it and broke away. At first I looked at him in shock and dismay, then I glanced over his shoulder.

And saw Gretchen, visible only through the crack of the door, just staring at us, rigid with shock.

She and I held each other's gaze for what must have been no more than seconds, but it felt like eternity. I watched as her eyes dropped to the floor and she moved silently away. Just vanished.

'What are you doing?' Tom said to me in astonishment. Utterly bewildered he sat back, away from me. 'What was that?'

He stood up and raked his hands through his hair.

'I just wanted to,' I said.

His arms fell down by his side loosely. 'Oh please don't do this to me, Alice. Not now. It's not fair. I was happy . . . I *am* happy! All my stuff is there. I—'

'It doesn't have to be!' I said quickly. 'You could go and get it all tomorrow. Be back here by lunchtime and it could all go back to how it was!' But as I said the words and heard them on the loose in the air around us, I wasn't even sure I meant them.

236

Tom caught his breath and looked at me. 'Go back to how it was?' he said finally.

I hesitated and then nodded hastily. That was what I wanted – wasn't it?

'But how do I know there won't be another Bailey?'

'I promise there won't be! I love you, Tom!' I said passionately, and yet was utterly astonished to hear myself say it. 'I know you love me too.'

'I did, very much indeed,' he said quietly.

'Then surely you could again?' I pleaded.

'Alice, I worked so hard to fall out of love with you. It was the worst time of my life . . .' He trailed off. He looked like he was wrestling internally with something, a frown rushed across his face and he said, 'Tell me this, then. If Bailey walked in here now, said he wanted you back and you had to choose between us, who would win?'

I stared at him, thrown by imagining the scenario, picturing Bailey in the room. 'That would never happen,' I said.

'But if it did – who would you choose?'

My stomach knotted painfully and I didn't say automatically 'You', because my heart was racing at the thought of Bailey standing right there in front of me, wanting me again. 'You,' I managed eventually.

He looked at me and then closed his eyes briefly. 'You have no idea how much I imagined this happening,' he said, opening them and looking at the floor. 'But now it is . . .'

There was the longest silence in the world. All I had heard was the 'but' and, suspecting where it was leading, it only served to convince me completely that I wanted Tom more than anything.

He looked up at me and said, 'I'm sorry, Alice, but I think

it is too late. If I wasn't seeing her, then maybe I could try to trust you again . . . but I am. And I'm happy.'

'But you've only been going out for—' I began.

'I know, but she's fun. We have a good time. I know she's not without her faults, but I know how she feels about me and I think . . . I think I'd like to see where it could go.'

I closed my eyes as his words hit me. I'd offered him me – and he'd chosen her.

'I should go,' he said. 'I'm so, so sorry that you misunderstood the moving thing. I never meant to hurt you. Honestly.'

I nodded silently, doing my best to hold the tears back until he'd left the room. Seconds later I jumped as yet another pissed couple banged into the door and fell through it giggling, slopping some beer on the carpet before taking a look at me, then each other, and dissolving into more giggles, blurting an insincere 'Sorry!'

I didn't want to be around other people's happiness a minute longer. I jumped up, grabbed my keys and a cardigan and pushed through the crowd. I couldn't look at Tom, who was back in the sitting room, glancing around having been ambushed into conversation by an intense-looking short bloke. Presumably he was looking for Gretchen, but she was nowhere to be seen.

I squeezed past people on the stairs and stepped over a passed-out girl on a pile of coats, before opening the front door. I slipped round the side of the flat into the garden, a long, thin stretch of overgrown grass penned in by a rickety fence, gasping as the cold air sucked into my lungs. There was a gate at the back, leading on to an alley that ran behind the row of houses, little offshoots branching into other people's gardens.

I stood there in the dark and the cold, looking up towards

the house, and closed my swollen eyes, feeling the wind bite through the loose knit of my cardigan, making me shiver. So this was what rock bottom felt like. Then I jumped as a voice behind me said, 'Hello.'

I snapped my eyes open and turned around. Gretchen was standing there, wrapped in a coat, smoking a fag contemplatively and clutching a beer can with white fingers, her hair blowing across her face. The gate behind her was ajar and her make-up was a bit smudged; her lips in particular. She was staring very intently at me. She reached up and pulled the hair deftly away from her eyes. 'You'll catch your death out here like that, Al,' she said and sucked on her fag. The end glowed furiously for a moment, then dulled. 'Good party, isn't it?'

'You saw,' I said, suddenly feeling frightened.

'You know I fucking saw!' she burst. 'All these shitty silent moods I've put up with. After everything I've done for you!'

I gasped, starting to sober up. 'After everything you've done? You got that right! You didn't just meet him in New York and fall in love! You told him I'd cheated on him and then you sought him out and tracked him down! You might be able to fool everyone else – not me.'

'Oh, here we go. Alice's conspiracy theory,' she scoffed. 'Don't be such a twat – of course I didn't! Just how manipulative do you think I am? He was the one good thing I had, Alice. The *one* good thing, as well you know. I hope you'll be very happy together. Fuck you both. You deserve each other.' She dropped the fag and ground it into the long grass, the ripping sound as the blades gave way under her foot made me feel sick. 'I might have started seeing your ex, but you kissed my boyfriend – so don't you dare talk morals to me. I don't want to be your fucking friend any more.' She started to walk past me up to the house.

'He chose you anyway,' I said bitterly. She stopped and turned round. Her face had gone absolutely white with shock. 'What?' she said. 'But I saw you kissing!'

'You saw me kiss him.'

She swayed on the spot and her hand flew to her mouth. 'But he was holding your hand!'

'Because I was upset. When he asked me to move back in I didn't realise he was moving out to live with you. He told me that he's happy with you, that he wants to see where it goes,' I said dully.

'Shit.' She laughed in disbelief and bit her lip. 'Oh shit.' She looked up at the sky and then said slowly, 'You have no idea what you've done!' She shook her head. 'FUCK, Alice!' she shouted. Then she twisted her body and threw her beer can against the fence as she released a pent-up shriek. It jerked liquid everywhere on impact. 'You stupid bitch,' she whispered, her bottom lip beginning to tremble as her face creased and she let out a sob. She covered her mouth with a hand and ran back to the party.

I was utterly baffled by her reaction. She'd got him – everything she wanted. I just stood there motionless in the cold. But then I heard a movement behind me, like something shifting position and trying not to be heard. I spun round and looked at the gate, which Gretchen had left half open. Was there was someone in the alley? Had someone been there with her? What had they been doing back there?

'Hello?' I called, sounding braver than I felt. 'Who's there?' There was nothing. No response.

I took a step towards the gate. My heart started to thump. Someone was there, for sure. I reached out, put a shaking hand on the latch and pulled the gate wide open in a sudden, abrupt move, slamming it into the creaky fence that divided us from next door. It juddered back on rusty hinges. That and the sound of my breath was all I could hear.

I stepped into the alley and looked up the thin passage. It was lined with old metal bins, weeds, bits of glass and the odd empty crisp packet. Very tentatively, now holding my breath, I took two steps up and glanced left into one of the offshoots. There were two more bins in a dark, deep alcove, one with a decaying plastic lid hanging half off it and the other with a rubbish bag next to it that had been chewed by foxes or some other animal. I could see half a Weetabix packet sticking out of a corner, with a mouldy used teabag glued to the side that had gone crisp round the stained edges. But no sign of anything else.

I turned right and nearly screamed as something moved in the dark shadows, darting back behind a large sheet of corrugated roof that had been abandoned and propped against a wall. Was it a foot? Was someone hiding behind it? I froze, sick and silenced with fear, unable to bring myself to look but also too terrified to move. Then I nearly fainted as a cat shot out and darted through a gap in a fence, flattening its body down before disappearing into a garden. It must have been its movements among the rubbish that I had heard.

I gathered my cardigan round me and scurried back to the flat, but having plunged back into the relative safety of the party, I realised Gretchen and Tom were nowhere to be seen.

Chapter Twenty-Seven

I heard nothing from either of them after the party, but then, I didn't really expect to. What more was there to say? I thought about them constantly, though, and was eaten up by imagining them happily settling into Gretchen's flat as they got ready for their first Christmas together. Having lived there myself, I could picture the scene all too well.

My only diversion was Frances giving birth to a baby boy in the second week of December. I cried copiously, clutching my new nephew to me. I stroked his small, dark, furry head as he peered curiously up at me through scowling dark eyes. He was beautiful but, to my shame, I wasn't just crying with happiness.

'Fuck, Alice, get a grip,' Frances said, sitting up in her bed with an exaggerated gasp of pain, as her husband Adam placed a cup of tea at her bedside and anxiously adjusted the pillows behind her. 'It wasn't you that just almost needed stitches. Try not to hold him so tightly. He'll overheat.'

'Have you got a name for him yet?' I said, wiping my eyes,

expecting to hear something dreadful and festive like Noel.

'I like Bailey, actually.' Frances looked at the baby. 'You know, like that travel bloke you were seeing?' I felt my bottom lip start to give way again. 'But Adam says it's tacky and too modern. And I don't expect you really want to be reminded of that guy for ever, do you?' She patted my hand sympathetically and then eased back on the pillow slowly. 'Adam wants to call him after his father anyway, so Frederick it is. Alice, please . . . you're actually soaking him. Adam, can you take him from her and dry his head? He'll get cradle cap if he gets all damp.'

Over Christmas itself, Frances completely dominated all proceedings – it was like having Mary and the baby Jesus himself staying at the house. There were nappies, bottles and muslin cloths strewn everywhere, to my mum's tight-lipped irritation, but on the upside everyone was so busy catering to Frances' every whim and cooing over Freddie, no one got on my case about why I was so quiet and withdrawn. I was pretty much left to my own devices, except for the odd moment of humiliating agony. At Christmas lunch, Mum – apron straining and face the same colour as her wilting paper hat – looked confusedly at the table while, bored, we waited to be told where to sit.

'I've done something funny,' she said, looking round the place settings, perplexed. 'What's not right? Adam and Frances, Philip, me and John, Mum and Dad . . .' She counted through in her head. 'But this is *exactly* what I did last year and it all worked. One at each end, three down one side, four down the other . . . how am I one over?'

'Well Tom isn't here, is he?' said Frances, scowling at Mum as she gathered Freddie from Adam's arms. 'Tactful, Mum.' Everyone looked at me awkwardly and my gaze dropped to the floor. 'You had him next to Grandpa last year. It's bloody hot in here, you know. Freddie looks very uncomfortable.'

'That's because he's got a hat on, Frances,' said Mum. 'I'm not sure you're right actually; didn't Tom arrive after lunch? Oh no – that's it! I remember now, he brought that vast thing of champagne and we all had it as a lovely toast, didn't we? Anyway,' she said hurriedly, catching sight of my face as Phil visibly nudged her, 'never mind about last year. You come and sit next to me, Alice, so I can feed you up a bit. Let's all sit down.'

New Year's Eve wasn't much better. I sat dully in front of the TV, wedged in next to Granny on repeat loop in my ear, saying over and over again, 'The BBC does this sort of thing terribly well, doesn't it?' while they all sipped at their sherries and Grandpa said, 'Isn't that the nice girl from the M&S adverts? I didn't know she could play the piano too. What a talent she is.'

As the fireworks went off over Big Ben and it chimed in 2009, I wondered where in the world Bailey was, who he would be kissing . . . and what glamorous party Tom and Gretchen were at. I pictured them in black tie, laughing and clutching champagne stems, with a large group of witty friends.

'Now then, my little Alice, changing guards at Buckingham Palace,' said Grandpa kindly, cutting across my thoughts, 'don't be sad. You come and give *me* a kiss. You wait, my love, this will be your year.' He wrapped me in a hug, spilling his sherry all over the carpet as Mum suppressed a tut and quickly grabbed for a tea towel.

By ten past midnight I was in my old single bed, under the same duvet cover I'd had aged fifteen (ballet dancers in dresses of various colours, wistfully trailing ribbons behind them), wishing with all my heart I'd taken Vic up on her offer of New Year in Paris. On cue my phone buzzed with an answerphone message. I could hear cheering in the background and general merriment. 'Just remember this too will pass!' Vic shouted over the noise. It made me think of Gretchen's bloody tattoo. 'Happy New Year never seemed more appropriate! You are so brave and I'm proud of you! You'll get there – I know you will! Love you!'

Once the Christmas break was thankfully over, I went back to work. The familiarity of the studio was reassuring when I opened up and I was relieved to have something to focus my attention on. After a morning spent concentrating on a product shot that was technically very complicated, I realised that I hadn't thought about Bailey, Gretchen or Tom for at least three hours. It was quite a revelation.

But, it being January, things were a little slow in patches too. The studio owner cheerfully popped by to tell me he was putting his rates up; on the same day a celebrity hairdresser cancelled some head shots. In a moment of paranoia, I panicked that perhaps Gretchen might have had a few sly words in ears, she had contacts after all. But then I realised, of course, that would have suggested she cared enough to bother, when I knew she didn't. Even so, I felt better when the hairdresser rang back the following day with a date to reschedule.

But just as I was starting to put 2008 firmly behind me, Bailey surfaced again on Thursday January 15th at 5.04 p.m.

'Hello?' I answered my phone curiously; it had come up number withheld. I shut the lid to my laptop.

'Alice?' And even though we hadn't spoken since the evening he'd ended it all, I knew it was him straight away. Not only that, but the mere sound of his voice lit me up inside and I slithered back down a snake, dropping past the ladder of progress I'd painstakingly hauled myself up. How did he do that? Just by talking?

He didn't even bother with the niceties of 'How are you?' and 'Good Christmas?' but just cut to the chase. 'Ally, I know this is a bolt out of the blue and I'm the last person you probably want to speak to – which is why I withheld my number – but I need your help. I'm really worried about Gretchen.'

I nearly threw the fucking phone across the room. Why? Why did people only *ever* ask me about her? She had him, she had Tom. For God's sake, she apparently had the whole bloody *world* wrapped around her finger. Couldn't they just stop seeking me out and let me get on with my life? And since when had he ever called me *Ally*?

'I've fucked up massively. I'm supposed to be at Gretchen's – like now – but I missed my plane earlier. I'm in Spain, you see, and I'd call Tom but he's in Bath at some work thing and, well, he hates me. I phoned Gretchen and she sounds pissed. As in drunk. Incredibly drunk actually.'

'So?' I tucked the phone under my chin as I packed up my bag.

'It's five p.m.! I know she likes a drink but come on! Will you please go round and check on her? She just kept saying, "But you're supposed to be here," over and over and then she got really cross, told me I was a cunt and hung up.'

'Oh well, in that case, yes please, I'd love to go round,' I said sarcastically.

'Something's not right, Al. I can feel it,' he insisted. 'Something is going on.'

'OK, well the last person she's going to want to see is me. She's very far from my number one fan.'

'I know,' he said uncomfortably, and I wondered how

much she had told him, 'but I still need you to go round. Please. I'm worried.'

'Just call the police if you're that frightened,' I said, picking up my keys and turning the studio lights off. 'Or your parents.'

'They're doing a production of "Whoops There Go My Bloomers!" in Little Chalfont. No one's answering any phones. I can't phone the police just because she's drunk . . . Alice, *please*,' he begged. 'Please! Just check she's OK and then leave. I'm begging you. Please do this for me – please.' He played his trump card and waited. 'I'm counting on you. Don't let me down.'

Chapter Twenty-Eight

At twenty to seven I very grumpily and apprehensively arrived at Gretchen's flat. I'd already been home, vowing to myself that I *wasn't* going, before I'd finally given in and done an about-face. Someone was going into the block when I arrived and let me in with them, but I knocked and rang several times on her front door to no avail. Sighing, I eventually held open the letterbox and called in, 'It's me. I don't want to be here any more than you want me to be, but I promised Bailey. Please just open the door.'

I heard the scuffle of feet from across the room and watched through the very small gap as a half empty whisky bottle slid into sight and stopped spinning, the amber liquid still sloshing around, finally stilling. Then I saw a pair of bare legs weave quickly but unsteadily towards me, before stumbling out of view. There was a heavy thump, like the sound of someone falling over. Then silence.

'Gretchen,' I called worriedly, 'are you OK?' My irritation was instantly forgotten. 'Open up!' I hammered my hand on the door and, to my relief, heard her voice say, 'Coming, coming. I'm trying. Hang on.'

There was a heavy thud against the door, the sound of a lock being thrown back and then the door swung open to reveal her swaying slightly in a pink vest top and matching shorts, the sort that come in packs of three and blokes might picture sixteen-year-old girls wearing while having a pillow fight.

'You're late,' she said, looking agitated, and promptly sneezed as she walked back into the flat, leaving me to shut the door behind me. 'He said you'd be here ages ago. The timing is all buggered up, I had to stop and now I'm not sure where I'm at. It's a bit of a problem!' she said in a singsong voice. 'But, I think you should find me in the bathroom. Or maybe the sitting room. I don't know.' She looked anxious as she wrung her hands. 'I've never planned it before, just done it, and now it's gone all saggy tits up thanks to my stupid brother.'

My heart sank. She was manic. 'You're not making sense. Slow down. Have you come off your medication, Gretchen?' I asked, although the answer to that was obvious.

'I had to, you stupid cow!' she burst, eyes wild and wide as she rushed up to me and grabbed my coat front with both hands, getting so very suddenly up in my face I tensed with the shock and jerked away from her. Her breath stank of booze and there was a thin shining trail of snot running down from her bright red nose, before she wiped it away with the back of her hand and grabbed me again eagerly. 'There's something you don't know. I want to tell you a secret, because I need you to help me with my plan. I can only tell you if you say yes. Do you promise to help me?'

'Yes,' I agreed reluctantly, taking my coat off. I was going to somehow have to get her to sit quietly until Bailey

249

arrived because there was no doubt she was going to have to be admitted again – she was ramping up nicely to a major flip-out. I exhaled. I was going to see Bailey again. If I'd have only known I'd have worn some bloody make-up and wouldn't have come dressed in scuddy trainers and trackies.

She let go of me and stepped backwards, twisting her fingers and picking her nails frantically.

'I'm pregnant! No one knows – except you.'

I whooshed back to attention and my mouth fell open.

'I *had* to stop the lithium because it'd mess the baby up.' She started pacing in a small square. 'I said no way did I want one so that's partly why they put me on it. You shouldn't have lithium if you want one, they said that, they said that to me. So I stopped really fast, but of course there was the party night anyway . . . so I couldn't have had it, even if it was normal. Because he'd know. And that's why you've got to help me.' She raked a hand up through her hair. 'I *can't* do this alone.' Her eyes started shining with tears.

'Do what alone?'

She rushed up to me again, grabbed my hands and said rapidly, 'I've got a plan. I've thought about it and it's going to work. I just need your help. That's all. You're not going to have to do anything . . . except call the ambulance. That's all Bailey was going to have to do. Just find me and call. It won't be any different, you just have to *pretend* you found me and call for help.'

'An ambulance? What are you—'

'Shhh!' she said. 'I'll explain. Tom's away with work – that's why it's got to be tonight, he's back tomorrow. All we have to do . . . is actually do it.'

'Do *what*?'

'Get rid of the baby,' she said patiently, as if I was a bit slow on the uptake.

I pulled my hands away so sharply one of her nails scratched me. '*What?*' I said, thinking I'd misheard her.

'It's really simple,' she said, jiggling up and down like she was warming up for a run while explaining an easy-bake recipe to me. 'I've already had some whisky and if I have too much of my lithium, my co-proxamol and drink some more, I'll go into a coma – I learnt about how to do it on the psych unit. I'm sure that will be enough to get rid of it . . . I think I'm only about seven weeks. Everyone will just think I've tried to commit suicide again; they're all waiting for it to happen anyway. At home, over Christmas, I found a book under my mum's bed called *Living with Manic Depression* and she's folded the page down over this bit that says, "Research shows a high percentage of suicides within a year after a person has been discharged from hospital." You see? They all think I'm going to do it anyway and no one will even need to know about the baby! I need you to call the ambulance because I don't want to actually die. You'll have to call them when it looks like I'm going unconscious because if it goes too far I could have a heart attack.' She sneezed violently and wiped at her nose.

'Did you even hear what you just said?' My voice was trembling. 'Did you actually just say your poor mum is dreading and waiting for this to happen and that'll *fit with your plan*? And this is a BABY, Gretchen. Tom's baby. You can't do this! I won't let you! It's sick. It's more than that – it's evil.'

'It's not Tom's baby! Well, I suppose there is a chance it could be – but it doesn't *feel* like it is. You know what I did at the party in the garden. I saw you go and check in the alley. In fact,' her eyes blazed, 'this is all your fucking

251

fault anyway. If you hadn't have kissed Tom I wouldn't have thought you were getting back together and I'd never have let Paulo touch me again.'

'Paulo?' I said, horrified.

'Oh fuck off,' she said scornfully. 'Don't act like you didn't know, little miss I'm-so-good-and-innocent-but-you-can't-have-my-ex-boyfriend-because-I-don't-like-it!' She mimed a pout and stamped her foot. 'Do you know how sad I was, Alice? I cried and cried and Paulo found me and hugged me and then he was kissing me and . . . I'm not going to lose Tom, Alice. He's the one good thing I've got in my life.'

'But there are other ways. Other things you can—'

She shook her head vehemently. 'If he left you because of a kiss, he'll leave me for this. I've worked so hard – I didn't go all the way to America for nothing. I've had so much taken away from me, I'm not giving him up too.'

'You could . . . Hang on, what did you just say?' I suddenly realised what I'd just heard.

'I'm keeping him,' she said defiantly. 'And no one is going to stop me.'

'Before that,' I said, staring at her.

She looked confused. 'Before what? You have to stop talking, Alice.' She flapped her hands erratically. 'We need to just do this!'

'You followed him out to America?' My voice was higher than it had been a second ago. I felt a wave of anger rush through me.

'Yes! I mean no – I don't know. So what if I did?' She darted over to the sofa and snatched up a bottle of pills which I hadn't noticed and tipped out a handful. She ran over to the whisky, stumbling en route, dropped down next to it, unscrewed the cap with one hand, took a huge swig and then shoved the pills in. She swallowed, a look of pain flashing across her face as she forced them down. She took another gulp of drink and then gasped and coughed. She wiped her mouth on the back of her hand and said, 'See? You can't back out now.' She grinned manically, a flash of triumph in her eyes.

I was completely horrified by the surreal and totally terrifying thing I'd just seen her do. It was like watching a scene from a film.

She closed her eyes and took another slug of whisky so big she gagged and had to cover her mouth with her hand. 'Urgghh!' she said, lurching slightly. She paused and then smiled up at me through swimming eyes. 'I can't be sick.'

My instincts kicked in and I rushed over to the phone and started dialling 999. If I got her to A&E straight away she could probably have her stomach pumped and hopefully have done no more damage. I couldn't believe she was having a baby.

'No!' She rushed up and yanked it away from me. 'Not yet! It's too soon! It'll only take half an hour for me to go unconscious.' She poured another three or four pills into her hand and walked back over to the kitchen. 'I think that might be enough of them now,' she said, and I thought I detected a heavier slur in her voice, as if it were becoming more of an effort for her to talk.

'Have you already taken some?' I said and she nodded. 'When? Before I got here?'

'Um,' she looked confused, 'earlier I think, just before Bailey rang and said he wasn't coming over after all.'

Oh God. Then it might already be too late. *What had she done?*

I snatched up the phone and she went to grab it again. 'Don't!' I shouted and rounded on her with such a look of ferocity she backed off. I was about to dial when I glanced up at Gretchen and saw her sneak a small white something into her mouth. Another pill. 'Stop it!' I shouted desperately.

She paled suddenly. 'I'm going to be sick.' She got up and rushed to the bathroom. I heard an almighty crash, dropped the phone and dashed after her. She was hanging over the loo and heaving, a load of bottles that had been on the edge of the bath had been knocked off. I could see her muscles jerking and her face straining. 'No, no!' she said. 'If I'm sick it won't work!'

'Stick your fingers down your throat – *now*!' I grabbed her face, desperately trying to shove my fingers in her mouth, reminding myself she was ill, very ill, and this was a lunatic plan from a very unbalanced mind – this wasn't Gretchen. She needed help.

'Get . . . off . . . me!' She shoved at me and then *wham!* Her fist exploded into my face and caught the underside of my chin. I had never been hit before and the hot pain that seared into my cheekbone felt like someone had jabbed me with a branding iron. My hand rushed to my face with shock and I just stared at her and stated, very obviously, 'You hit me!'

She fell to her knees and then, pushing back on the bath, pulled herself up, tipped her head back, looked at the ceiling and her eyes rolled. 'I'm going back out there.' She staggered out into the living room, swiping the whisky bottle again as I followed her. Before she could even get the lid off she stumbled and crashed to the ground. It smashed everywhere and the sticky, burnt smell of spirits filled the room.

'Shit!' Her eyes filled with tears. 'I haven't got any more!' There was a big puddle of it on the rug and she leant forward and stuck her tongue out in desperation.

'No!' I yelled. 'There's glass everywhere!' I hauled her backwards and pushed her up against the wall. She leant against it and closed her eyes, scrunching her face up in pain, wrapping her arms round her middle. 'I want to be sick,' she whimpered. 'It hurts!'

'Just don't move!' I said, terrified. 'We're stopping this now!'

I got up, grabbed the phone and rushed back to her. But before I could dial she heaved and her head lolled forward. I dropped the phone, collapsed down next to her and grabbed her hair. 'Just be sick! It doesn't matter if it goes everywhere.' My legs were stuck out awkwardly in front of me as I cradled her.

Her movements were becoming sluggish. 'Nooooo,' she insisted, trying to push me off. I reached out for the phone again. 'I'll tell you more secrets. Listen, listen. Don't phone. Shhhh!' She put her fingers to her lips. 'I'll tell you about Bailey.'

I paused.

A small smile flickered over her face. She lifted a floppy hand up and rested it on my arm as she tried to raise her head and look at me. 'I told him not to see you any more. I said I didn't want him to be your boyfriend so he said "OK," and he dumped you. I didn't like you taking him away from me.'

'You're lying,' I whispered. 'You didn't do that. You were in America. With Tom.'

I picked up the phone. She frowned with annoyance and said with effort, 'I *did* tell Tom about you and Bailey deliberately. Tom was so sad about you, Alice. I had to love him better lots. So many times. In the bedroom, in the kitchen, in your flat.'

'Shut up!' I pushed her away from me with utter revulsion

and disgust. Her vile words felt like they'd burnt me and set fire to my insides.

Without me propping her up she slumped sideways to the floor. She fell silent and then her eyes shot open again. The phone was lying right in front of her face. I didn't move towards it this time and she smiled faintly with satisfaction.

'You want help, you phone them,' I said suddenly, my voice shaking and shivering. I stood up.

'Nooo!' she insisted. 'Got to be suicide. Don't leave me!'

She looked at the phone and, with a huge effort, brought an arm up and pushed it towards me. 'Now then,' she said, face half mashed into the carpet. 'Juss do it now then. You need to tell them Alice. Lots of pills.'

'What did I ever do to you?' I said in a whisper. 'You wreck everything – me, Tom, Paulo . . . I don't even know your poor mum and yet she's reading books and trying to help you – and now this. You told Bailey to finish with me? How could you? You just can't share, can you? It's all got to be yours. You're poison. Everything you touch turns bad. I trusted you!' I cried brokenly, heated tears streaming down my face. 'I thought you were my best friend! Tom thought I was mad when I told him I was suspicious . . . and you said you were just being nice to me, letting me live in your flat, but I *was* right! You just wanted me out of the way! And how can you do this to Tom? This will devastate him, he's so lovely – he's such a good man! Why can't you just leave us all alone – we'd all be so much better off without you! You're not ill – you're just sick!'

She had barely blinked and, as I ran out of energy and words, she pushed herself up with what was obviously the last of her strength until she was seated, but slumped.

256

She tried to kick the phone towards me with her foot, but missed. It was a tiny movement. It wouldn't have moved a feather.

She struggled to lift her head and looked at me through eyes that kept closing against her will.

'Please,' she said, in a breath of a whisper.

'This is just you! You're evil – you'll stop at nothing!' I had started to shake. 'I hate you. I hate you!'

'Help,' she said.

I didn't reach for the phone. I collapsed to the carpet and just sat there motionless, tears streaming down my face, hugging my knees to my chest.

We sat there and she looked at me through leaden eyes, unable to speak, but fully aware of what I was *not* doing.

Eventually, still staring at me, her eyes closed and her head slumped forward slightly.

I began to rock and moaned through my tears with distress and fear. Then I felt vomit rise in my gut and, getting up, I scrambled to the bathroom and was violently sick.

When I came back she hadn't moved.

I truthfully do not remember how long I sat there after that.

My teeth chattered, my whole body shook. But for how long? I don't know . . . I really don't know . . .

I remember the taste of vomit in my mouth was unbearable. I think I went back to the bathroom, rinsed, raised my head and caught my reflection in the mirror. Cold water droplets ran down and under my chin. I could still feel where she had hit me. I tilted my head, but there was no visible mark. I stared at myself, slightly open-mouthed, frozen. I could have been stood there for hours.

I went back to her though. I didn't leave her. And I *did* call. They came and found us.

257

She was right: everyone thinks it is a desperate suicide attempt by a manic depressive who has stopped her lithium again – just as she's done before. Everyone, that is, apart from that nurse who is convinced I helped her to do it, as part of some sort of mercy mission. I haven't told anybody about the pregnancy. I've kept that promise at least.

But if she wakes up, if she survives this 'secondary complication', she will tell them all what really happened. And if everyone thinks I deliberately didn't call when I had the chance, I will lose absolutely everything.

But then, if she never wakes up, if she dies . . . it will be all my fault.

Suppose she has died while I've been sitting here in this chapel? Then what will I do? Will I tell – or will I have to live with this secret for ever? Will Tom collapse on me with grief and will I nurse him through it? Will we become closer and closer as a result and end up back together as if Gretchen had never happened? Or will Bailey, devastated at his loss, cling to me as one of the few that ever understood his sister and decide we should try again?

Or will we all, torn apart by what has happened, be unable to be around each other as it is simply too painful, our grief too raw and too desperately sad to share? And if she dies, won't Tom find out she was going to have a baby anyway? They'd do a post-mortem, wouldn't they? Oh God – that would kill him, haunt him for the rest of his days. And it would still be all my fault.

Bailey is right, this chapel smells bad. Damp mixed in with dead air and dust, but I would still like to stay hidden away down in this room for ever. The night that lies ahead of me is, I know, going to be the longest one of my life. By the morning, according to that doctor, it will be apparent if Gretchen is going to pull through or not.

258

The only prayers I am sending now are ones of forgiveness for myself. I am very, very frightened.

I don't know how this can be happening to a normal girl like me who had a boyfriend, and a job, and a life.

Chapter Twenty-Nine

Although I can't see outside because the room has no windows, I know it must be light by now. Tom and Bailey are jubilantly shifting around in their seats with all the forced wide-eyed energy of two men who haven't slept a wink all night. It's like they've been on an overnight flight and have just arrived at their holiday destination, which has given them a renewed burst of life.

'I saw it again!' Bailey exclaims and points at Gretchen. 'Her eyes moved!'

The young nurse smiles and agrees, 'She's doing really well.' Bailey is looking at her like she might just be the most beautiful person he has ever seen and that the world is a truly, truly wonderful place. 'And tell me what her oxygen support is again?'

'Forty per cent!' the smiles nurse indulgently.

'Ha!' Bailey says delightedly, although this is the third time in an hour he's asked. Even Tom smiles, although he is more subdued with relief.

I am feeling so sick and panicky that I think if I move

too fast I will throw up everywhere. 'So when will she be able to write and speak?' I say.

The nurse shakes her head. 'She still has sedation on board. Tomorrow at the earliest.'

So I have just the rest of today . . . Oh dear God. What am I going to do? I'm going to have to leave – to just go. How can I possibly be here when she wakes up? As it is I'm afraid of even speaking to the nursing staff, for fear that they might have been told to watch me, watch for signs, an involuntary admission of guilt.

'Might it be OK then,' Bailey says, 'to go home and grab a shower, a change of clothes or something? Nothing will happen if we do that, will it?'

I *cannot* be here when she wakes up . . .

The nurse hesitates. 'Look, there are no guarantees but . . . like I say, she's doing really well.'

Bailey's face splits into a smile.

Tom looks more doubtful. 'I think I might stay.'

Bailey shakes his head firmly. 'Tom, she's out of danger. Do you really want to look like a stinking hobo when your girlfriend comes round tomorrow? All she's doing now is just lying here recovering. Tell you what, why don't we all meet back here after lunch. Go home, grab a bit of kip?'

'OK,' agrees Tom eventually. He looks totally shattered. 'I'll just change though and come straight back. I think I might have to get a cab, I'm not sure I'm safe to drive.'

Bailey stands. 'Today is a *great* day!' he laughs. 'See you later, sis!' He blows Gretchen a kiss. 'We'll share a taxi,' he decides. 'It can do one big loop. Drop you off, Tom, then Al, then me.'

Dr Miles Benedict gets out of his car. It's a crisp, bright January morning. It'll be February before long – which means Valentine's Day, he contemplates. He must remember to book a table somewhere or she'll cut his nuts off.

So, what shitstorm is he going to come into today? There's the motorbike accident boy – stupid kid came off at 50 mph wearing a T-shirt and jeans, the road literally cheese-grated his skin from his body. When they lifted him off the stretcher, his back stayed on it. Miles grimaces. Maybe he'll skip breakfast. He wonders idly if the overdose girl survived the night – very unlikely, she'd ingested enough shit to fell an elephant. Then he thinks perhaps he'll just grab a coffee before he goes up and maybe see if anyone's up for a round after shift. The green will be just perfect today.

Twenty minutes later he barges into ICU, now in a filthy mood, to do the morning handover. No one is free to play golf later, which really pisses him off, and some idiot in the café not only spilt hot coffee all over his hand but, worse still, gave him caffeinated not decaf. He only realised halfway down his takeout cup, and now he's already feeling twitchy and getting a headache. How hard is it to get a fucking *beverage* right when he saves lives?

He sweeps into room five and, to his surprise, finds the overdose girl is still in the land of the living; quite impressive determination and fight really. Mercifully there are no relatives to have to be polite to. Just the nurses. He looks at the charts in irritable silence and then snaps, 'She's on forty per cent – what's she still doing on sedation?'

The senior nurse accompanying him nudges the junior, who looks at the floor. The senior nurse says, 'I haven't been able to get there yet.'

Must he do *everything* himself? 'Well get the propofol off,' he says. 'Wake her up, let's get her extubated! She's a young girl, for Christ's sake. Come on! ASAP!' He looks crossly at the junior who can't meet his eye and is momentarily lifted by the fact she's got great tits. Shame about the face though, looks like she's been smacked by a shovel. Oh well.

'Right,' he says briskly. 'Lead on, Nurse. Next victim please.'

Down in the hospital car park all three of us wait for a taxi. We are *not* going to share one because despite the very odd bond we developed in that small hospital room, out here, back in the real world and waiting in the cold, it feels way too weird.

Hospital car parks are strange places. On the one hand there are new babies being placed in cars by proud, protective fathers, watched adoringly by the tired mothers. On the other hand there are confused, disorientated people pacing around making urgent calls on mobile phones relaying hideous news that will make someone, somewhere drop what they are doing and scramble to find their car keys and shoes.

Tom, who seems anxious to leave — probably wants to get there and back again as soon as he can — asks if he can take the first taxi, and as it pulls up plonks an absent kiss somewhere in the region of my left temple and says, 'See you later then,' before getting into it and disappearing up the road.

That leaves me and Bailey. Bailey watches Tom's taxi turn left and vanish out of view. 'He's such a funny bloke.' He shakes his head. 'So straight up and down. What you see is what you get.'

Another taxi arrives. 'Your turn,' he says and smiles happily, so clearly on top of a wave of overtiredness and relief it looks like he's king of the castle. 'You go, honestly. I'll see you back here in a bit.'

'What are you going to do now then?' I say, hand on the car door.

He yawns. 'Collapse, shower, sleep – that sort of thing.'

'Come back with me to mine,' I say suddenly, recklessly.

He looks confused at first and then smiles. 'Sweet of you, Al, but I'll be OK. Now she's back on the road to recovery I'll be all right on my own, promise. See you in a bit.' He blows me a kiss.

I force a smile and get into the taxi. It's got a gross, wrinkled, brown faux suede cover over the back seat and smells strongly of stale fags and the spinning Christmas tree air freshener dangling from the mirror. I blink back tears. That wasn't what I meant, Bailey.

'Where to, then?' the taxi driver asks, although I don't see his lips move, just his reflected eyes looking at me enquiringly. I give him the address and he silently turns the wheel, pulling us away from the hospital. I don't look back at Bailey, although out of the corner of my eye I see him wave.

I have just today left with him and Tom, that's all. Tomorrow she will be awake, able to write, maybe able to speak, certainly able to tell everyone that I deliberately didn't help her. Tom and Bailey will believe I wanted her to die. Today is all I have left.

All last night, as we sat there waiting and it became apparent that the worst was over, when they lowered her oxygen levels and everyone cheered when her eyes flickered, all I was thinking was: I've got no choice – I'll have to just leave. Just pack up and go. Tomorrow *will* arrive and she *will* wake up. I am sick with relief that she isn't going to die, but now I'm frightened for myself.

I feel stripped away, terrified that I can have done something so dreadful to someone whose hand I held –

while assuring her there was nothing she could do that would stop me being her friend. I have to go.

What is there to stay for anyway? I have a rented flat, a studio I hire on a job by job basis, no boyfriend, no ties. Fran now has her own little family, Mum and Dad are desperate to clear Phil out of the nest so the rest of their lives can begin, and it won't be long before Phil, bored with nothing to do, will decide that he wants to start building a more exciting life for himself anyway. I love them all very much, and I know they love me, but I'm not sure they really know me any more than I seem to know myself. Everyone has such hectic lives. We are the typical geographically fragmented and frantically busy, modern day family. Would it really make that much difference to them if I took some time out for me? I have been forced to face some very uncomfortable truths – maybe that's no bad thing. I could just take my camera and go. Make choices, stop letting things happen to me. I never wanted to hurt anyone, least of all people I love. I could start again? Build a new life . . . somewhere far away from Gretchen.

'Can we stop at a bank on the way?' I say to the taxi driver. 'I need to get some cash out.'

I'll leave a month's rent for Paulo. He can just throw away what stuff of mine I don't take. That's the least he can do. Maybe I'll do what I should have done in the first place and go to Vic's for a week and see what happens from there. She's been so amazing: listening, advising, comforting. But how can I tell her about this? For the first time ever, there is something she must never know. I can't tell anyone. I am now utterly alone.

What will I tell Tom and Bailey? That I'm going on holiday? That I've been offered a too-good-to-turn-down shoot? I think they'd buy it if I said I had to go to Pluto right now, especially now she's out of danger. All they are thinking about is her.

And as for her, if she wakes up and discovers that I'm not there, maybe she won't say anything at first – maybe she'll bide her time, waiting for me to return so her account of what *really* happened will carry maximum currency. But I just won't come back. The moment will pass and we will all just get on with our lives, as best we can.

The taxi goes over a speed bump and the suspension creaks. Then we turn right on to a busier main road and pull up to a set of traffic lights. To my left is a bus stop. A woman is standing there, hands in pockets, a carrier bag slung round her wrist. She's staring into space with a look of dead resignation that shows me she has waited by this bus stop every day for as long as she can remember. Behind her is a CREDIT PROBLEMS? WE CASH CHEQUES! shop front, next to a closed kebab shop called Big Joe's, which in turn is beside a launderette that announces DUVETS WASHED HERE! Where will I be when they are cashing their cheques, carving their greasy meat and cleaning their clothes next week and next month, even next year?

We drive past a closed flower shop, the window is already full of hearts in preparation for Valentine's Day. DON'T FORGET FEBRUARY THE 14TH! reads a banner that is being held up by a cut-out dove on either side.

Forget? How could I possibly do that?

Bailey's not so much the one that got away, because I can see now that he was never mine in the first place, much as I love him. But he is certainly the one that I could waste years of my life hoping and waiting for. He's the one that makes me behave recklessly – if he'd understood what I meant this morning, perhaps we'd be in this taxi now together heading back to my bed, and where would that have left me when *he* left? Because he would have done.

I'm not sure it's ever possible to get over someone like him. Perhaps you don't, perhaps you just have to not be around them, until your mind kindly allows you to forget how addictive they are and it hurts a little less and then a little less still. It's not been good for me, seeing him again at such close quarters when he is still so unobtainable, at least to me anyway. I know I lied when Tom asked me who I would choose – him or Bailey. It would be Bailey every time. I hope one day I'll experience a kiss again like the one we had in Leicester Square, but with someone that loves me too.

And as for Tom . . . There are men and then there is Tom. I hold him alone in my mind as an example of how good a human being ought to be. God loves a trier and, like me, I'm sure God loves Tom. He stands up to be counted, he squares his shoulders and always turns his face to the sun, but he is gentle, kind and true.

If my world was ending, I would want Tom there . . . and I do, so very much. I don't know in what way – I can see he will never be my happy ever after – but I think I would settle for anything; even him being with her, as long as I could somehow keep him in my life.

But of course she will not allow that and now it's almost time to say goodbye to them both.

I won't miss Gretchen. Just what I thought she was.

Chapter Thirty

Bailey has been on the phone to his mother for over an hour and a half, trying to persuade her to come to the hospital. She is by turns hysterical with relief and calm with anger. She can't come tonight, she insists, she's exhausted from appearing as the lead in 'Whoops There Go My Bloomers!' and anyway, Gretchen won't be awake until tomorrow.

Which is entirely the point, thinks Bailey wearily. Come and see her – do your crying and shouting while she can't hear you. But she stubbornly refuses and Bailey gives up the fight. When he gets off the phone, he checks his watch. Two p.m. He should go back to the hospital. He feels better for having slept, but to get rid of the last bit of stress and tension lurking in his shoulders, he decides to have a quick spliff and, on finding his gear in the tin on his chest of drawers, he decides to also call Annalisa, from whose bed he reluctantly dragged himself yesterday morning. Shit, was it only yesterday he woke up in Spain? Mental – absolutely mental. Thank you God, he thinks. I fucking owe you one.

★ ★ ★

Tom wakes up at 3.14 in the afternoon, face down on his and Gretchen's bed, completely disorientated. It takes him at least a minute of blinking and wondering before he can get his brain to work out that he closed his eyes for a minute over *four* hours ago. He swears and jumps to his feet. He was just so tired when he got back and discovered the flat stinking to high heaven of booze, shattered glass everywhere. By the time he'd carefully cleaned it all up, gathered the pieces of the whisky bottle and wrapped them in newspaper, then scrubbed the rug and collected the scattered pills, picked up the bottles in the bathroom and wiped up the remnants of vomit, he *had* to lie down, he had no choice in the matter.

Ten minutes later he has showered, changed and is ready to go. He gathers up his keys and then spies the rubbish bag, neatly tied up by the front door. He might as well take the rest of it out if he's taking that one down. He shoves his keys and wallet in his back pocket and marches into the kitchen.

He lifts the bag from the bin, only the bloody thing catches as he yanks it out, which slices it open as neatly as a surgeon's scalpel. The rubbish bulges out through the slit like an escaping intestine and Tom, by now wishing he hadn't bothered, nearly slides the bag back in and shuts the lid – but then grits his teeth, thinking, if a job's worth doing . . . and reaches for *another* bin bag, pulling open the drawer where they keep them. He holds the knackered one up and tries to lower it into the gaping second bag, without it touching his trousers or spilling anything. Unfortunately it spins mid-air and spits out an empty loo roll wedged either end with tissue, a soup can and – Tom nearly gags – some chicken bones and a polystyrene tray that once contained two fresh trout. It smells far from fresh now.

He grimaces and picks the bones up first. Then he turns to the loo roll and sees that the tissue has come out of one end as it landed and there is something white tucked in the tube.

At first he assumes it is a used tampon applicator – but it is too long and plastic for that. Then he realises that he is looking at a pregnancy test.

Stunned, he picks it up and inspects it carefully.

'Oh my God!' he says out loud. And then he runs for the door.

I get out of my second taxi of the day, back outside the hospital at just gone quarter past three. I've packed everything I plan to take with me tonight and it's all waiting back at the flat. I have called Vic, I've spoken to my dad, there is nothing left to do . . . except say my goodbyes to Bailey and Tom. I'm sure they will be here by now and will already be sitting watch over Gretchen's silent but rapidly recovering body.

I walk past the signs to the chapel, past the café, past X-ray, up round the flight of stairs and through the heavy double doors of the intensive care unit for the last time. There is no one at the nurses' station. The corridor looks just as it did this morning. I can see the door is open to Gretchen's room. I walk up, turn the corner into the room and jerk immediately to a stop, frozen with horror.

Gretchen is sitting up in bed. Conscious and looking right at me, like all of my nightmare imaginings – only this time it's real.

'Surprise,' she says, in a painful rasp. She is not smiling.

Chapter Thirty-One

I just stare at her. I am unable to speak. I can't feel my feet and my bag just slips from my shoulder and crashes to the ground. My fingers clumsily half move to stop it, but I am horrified and transfixed by her expressionless face looking back at me, her eyes roaming around my features as if she's reminding herself of me.

'How . . . why are you even here?' she says, forcing each word, and with that one sentence I know that she remembers everything.

Before I can say anything, a new nurse pops her head round the door and asks, 'All OK?' She smiles brightly, so she can't know anything. Gretchen nods heavily. 'Don't overdo it,' the nurse says. 'You're really tired. Try and keep it brief and make your friend do the talking.' She winks at me and disappears, pulling the door to gently.

'Good idea,' Gretchen whispers with effort, when she's gone.

But still I don't say anything. I can't. How can this be? They said tomorrow at the earliest . . .

'You left me,' Gretchen says eventually. 'You didn't call them.' She shifts position uncomfortably and then waits.

My heart starts to thump.

'I asked you to call me an ambulance and you didn't.'

'I did call them,' I insist. 'I was in the ambulance with you. I've been here ever since!'

She frowns, confused. 'I saw you deliberately,' she says the word carefully, '*not* calling them.' Her voice trails off completely at the end and she tries to sit up a little taller and reach for the glass of water next to her. Instinctively I take a step forward to help her and she gives me a look of 'You must be joking,' so I back off.

'How long did you wait?' She swallows painfully and flops back on to the pillow.

'I don't remember.'

'Doesn't really matter. Point is you waited at all. You did it on purpose.' She closes her eyes tiredly.

'I—' I begin.

'Go,' she says, opening her eyes, turning her head and looking straight at me. 'Just go. Don't come near me ever again. Stay away from me, from Tom and stay away from my brother.'

'I was going to anyway.' My eyes fill with tears. 'I'm leaving tonight.'

'Where?'

'Does it matter?' I shrug with a half-smile, throwing my arms out uselessly.

She considers that. 'Not really.'

'Gretchen—' I'm about to say how truly, truly sorry I am, but she cuts me off and says, with as much energy as she can muster, 'Just go, now.'

'I only want to say goodbye to Tom and Bailey,' I say. 'How can that hurt?'

272

She hauls herself back up determinedly and shakes her head. 'No. I want you to go.'

'But I'm going anyway. Can't you just—'

'If you try to stay,' she says hoarsely, 'I'll tell them what you did. You decide.'

I look at her sitting there, a small tube still embedded in her arm, her hair plastered greasily back, violent shadows under her eyes, still fragile as a spider's thread yet strong as steel, just like she was when she was telling me her lies about making Bailey dump me and confessing she had tracked Tom down to America.

'Did you lose the baby, Gretchen?'

'What baby?' she says.

'Your baby. The one you . . .' I exhale heavily. 'The one you wanted me to help you get rid of. You said it didn't feel like Tom's, you said I knew what you'd done in the alley with Paulo at the party.'

'What the hell are you are talking about?' She coughs painfully, grabbing her throat and then reaching for the water again.

I look at her in total disbelief. 'You remember me not calling an ambulance, but you don't remember what led to it in the first place? Bailey called me and said he'd been delayed in coming over to you and you seemed very worked up. I got to yours and you were drunk, had taken some pills and told me you were pregnant, wasn't sure whose baby it was and had a plan to get rid of it. You were going to make it look like a suicide attempt, you said that everyone would assume that was what it was. I just had to pretend to find you so it didn't go all the way, but far enough so you'd lose the baby. I tried to stop you – I begged you not to – and you punched me, then you told me you'd always wanted Tom, that you'd told him about Bailey on purpose

273

and that you'd made Bailey dump me . . .' I trail off and find that I'm shaking with adrenalin.

'I have,' she says and looks at me steadily, 'literally no idea what you are talking about. There's no *baby*, Alice. There's never been any baby! Ask the nurse who just helped me change my pad, if you don't believe me.'

I wince at such a graphic remark and feel overwhelmingly sad. 'So you lost it?' I say. 'Like you wanted.'

She doesn't flinch. 'There was nothing to lose! I have manic depression, I become delusionary. I'm ill! You know that.' She leans over and takes another sip of water. 'You can't believe anything I say when I'm manic – I'm beyond reason!'

'You didn't seem beyond reason yesterday! OK, you were clearly manic, but you seemed to have calculated exactly how far you needed to go!'

She leans back, closes her eyes again and says, 'It's very simple. I stopped taking my medication because I was happy, I didn't think I needed it. I obviously did. I'm sorry I hit you but I'm certainly not pregnant. I never was. And I'll tell you what I do remember: you, rational, sober and in your right mind, deliberately not helping me when I *needed* you to.' She forces the last words out with energy.

I sway slightly. 'I . . . I didn't want you to die, Gretchen,' I say eventually. 'I was just so appalled at what I thought you'd done. I didn't want Tom to have to keep going through this and I was very, very angry . . . You said some foul things to me.'

'So? You can't make this OK!' she croaks. 'I nearly died because of you!'

She's right, there is absolutely no excusing my part in this.

'I called them! I did – I didn't leave you!'

274

'Just GO!' she says fiercely. 'Go, or I'll call one of the nurses.'

I think of yesterday's nurse, already suspicious and armed with what I blurted out to her about not wanting Gretchen to wake up.

She reaches towards the emergency buzzer and my heart begins to race.

'Last chance,' she says. 'Go now and I won't tell anyone.'

'OK, OK!' I say. Tears have started to run down my face and I wildly grab my bag. 'But what are you going to say to Tom and Bailey?'

'I'll think of something.'

Chapter Thirty-Two

I'm running blindly down the corridor, unable to see for tears. At one point I bash into someone and they angrily shout 'Hey!' but I don't stop, I just sob 'I'm sorry!' and clatter round the corner – out into the car park and the cold January sun. I run desperately over to the taxi rank; thank God – there's one there. The driver sees me approaching, folds up his newspaper expectantly, shifts in his seat and undoes the window. I see him frown as I get closer.

'You all right, love?' he says – he's noticed I'm crying. I nod dumbly, tell him the address and he says kindly, 'Get in, we'll have you there in a jiffy.'

He swings out, rather too fast, and pulls on to the road. The traffic lights ahead are on amber, and at the last minute he decides not to go for it, slamming on the brakes and jolting me forward, making me look up in shock. 'Beg pardon!' he says, 'Lumpy petrol,' and looks sheepishly in his mirror.

But all I've seen is a taxi approaching from my left,

swinging round, with a man anxiously looking at his watch and then saying something to the driver and pointing out the hospital on his left.

'Tom!' I exclaim and grab the headrest to the passenger seat, shifting forward in my seat urgently. His taxi glides past us and I watch as he moves by me, totally unaware.

'Want to stop?' the taxi driver says, hand at the ready on the indicator. 'Someone you know?'

I open my mouth to say yes, because surely this is God's way of forgiving me just a little bit, offering me the chance to just say goodbye. But then she's right, I don't deserve it – she is ill, she needed me, and I withheld my help deliberately. What kind of person would do that to a perfect stranger, never mind someone who was their friend? Whatever I thought was the situation, whatever judgement call I made, whatever moment of madness, jealousy, anger – I should have picked up that phone. I should have called for help, no matter what she had done to me. I should have been the bigger person but I wasn't. I am bitterly ashamed and repulsed by what I have done.

'No,' I say. 'Keep going.'

I look desperately over my shoulder again. I can see him getting out, paying, becoming smaller and smaller and . . . I'm never going to see him again. At least not for a very, very long time. Just one goodbye! If I catch him before he goes in, she'll never know.

'Stop!' I shout. 'I need to go back, just—'

But the driver's already on it. He's hit the brakes and earned himself an angry honking from an oncoming BMW, which he completely ignores. He swings sharply round to the right and puts his foot down, roaring up behind Tom's taxi and screeching to a stop. But Tom has already paid up, and for some reason is legging it towards the hospital.

277

'Wait here!' I say breathlessly, hand already on the door, and jump out. 'Tom!' I shout.

He doesn't hear me.

'TOM!' I yell for all I'm worth.

This time the sound carries to him and he turns, looks astonished to see me, but then starts frantically beckoning me to him. I start to run, aware that a couple of people, shivering in dressing gowns and smoking, are staring curiously at us.

I reach him and, breathing heavily with the effort, can't get my words out.

'No, no! Don't stop running!' he says, grabbing my hand and dragging me towards the door.

I pull back. 'Tom! Stop!' I say desperately. 'What are you doing?'

'Al – she's pregnant! I didn't know! We have to tell them so they can do something. Before it's too late!'

At that I feel unbelievably sad and say, 'Oh Tom, she . . .' and just as I am about to say 'imagined it all' I suddenly realise that he can't even know she is conscious yet. He's just arrived. So how the hell does he know about the pregnancy, or rather, lack of it?

'What do you mean, she's pregnant?' I say carefully, as a bit of hair blows across my face and I draw it out of my eyes.

'I found a test!' he says. 'I wouldn't have, but the rubbish bag split and it fell out – she'd wrapped it right up. It was positive!'

'You're absolutely sure?' I say.

'Of course I am! I saw it with my own eyes! I have to get up there, and I have to say something, because they don't know! She must have come off the lithium because she knew it would harm the baby, but that made her manic

278

and confused. We have to do something! Quickly!' He looks at me urgently, with haunted eyes.

And it's then that I realise she has absolutely, totally, lied to me. There *was* a baby and there *was* a plan. She's done it again. This will be Gretchen for the rest of her life, doing whatever it takes to get whatever she wants, by whatever means necessary. Woe betide anyone who gets in the way, but . . .

She is undeniably ill. There is no question of that. Is it just cruel to expect her to be governed by the rules the rest of us live by when she is so very incapable of doing so? When does all this stop being devious manipulation on her part and become excusable – or at least explainable – because she is unwell? Where can a line ever be drawn with someone like her?

All I can be certain of is how *I* behaved; what *I* did.

'Alice, come on!' Tom shouts. 'Why are you just standing there?' He reaches out for my hand again, but I resist. I pull back and suddenly I know exactly what I have to do.

'Stop!' I say, wavering on the spot but taking a very deep breath. 'Tom, I have to tell you something.'

I lead him over to a bench, and even though it is freezing, we sit down and I begin to tell him everything. Absolutely everything, just as it happened. I leave nothing out.

He does not move as I speak. At various points he closes his eyes in shock and then anger – and at one point, when I start to cry but force myself to carry on, he reaches for me, but then I begin to say things that make him pull his hand away, and he looks at me in horrified disbelief.

But I say it anyway. I have to, because it is the truth, and I know that is all we have left now, and that it is the only thing that can set both of us— free.